Hack and Slash

Hack and Slash

Kirsty Mackay

Published by Level Up in the United Kingdom in 2024

Cover illustration by Sippakorn Upama
Cover by Claire Wood

ISBN: 978-1-83919-591-4

www.levelup.pub

Thank you to my family for your never-ending support, my friends for cheering me up when things went wrong, and Ben for being a very good dog!

Prologue

By any human scale the ship is unimaginably large. It cannot be described in terms of cars, busses, Olympic sized swimming pools or sport stadiums. It is the largest thing made by humanity to date. And once it is finished there are another three on the way.

The Enkelados Project used to be the pet hobby of a group of wealthy financiers who wanted their Science Fiction dreams to become reality. But when the news came that the sun was putting a halt to our lease on Earth, they moved entirely into aggressively furthering cryogenics by leaps and bounds, hunting down every study or piece of academia on the subject. And somehow, within a year they did what no one else had managed. They created working cryogenics that could be scaled up to carry humanity into the stars.

But then, the unimaginable has started coming with increased regularity, hasn't it?

When S-Day comes, the Solar Flares shall hopefully be nothing but a distant reflection in the ship's windows. A blink of light in the midst of great darkness that is space. If they are any closer than that there is a good chance that they will burn through the electronics of the ship with the same deadly results as will no doubt be occurring here on Earth.

There are also rumours of several smaller ships, each taking far fewer than the billion or so souls on these giants, being planned and outfitted by other companies. But, for the most part, it is the ships made by the Enkelados Project that we humans have staked our futures on. We shall have to hope that the leaders who chose for us, chose wisely.

***

I was given the opportunity to explore the Earth-based offices of the Enkelados Project late last month. It was a disconcerting mish-mash of old and new. The building itself was a late Twentieth Century tower block, brutally square and scoured by acidic rain. Around it were buildings with their walls covered in vertical forests: the designs of twenty years ago which have stayed surprisingly popular in the meantime.

One wonders what the architectural fashions will be in the future? Whether there will be fashions, or will people merely fight to keep the ruins of the past in working order? It is impossible to say what the world will look like in a century. It may be barren, nuclear fallout from abandoned warheads creating a habitat too tough for anything to survive. Or perhaps, it will be merely humanity that cannot survive and instead nature shall reclaim the land we once thought of as our own. And those vertical forests shall no longer be oases, but branches of larger trees.

There is no way for any of us to know at present. But, in a hundred years some of you reading this may be able to check.

As my colleagues and I shuffled through the offices, we were assured again and again, that the Enkelados method of Cryogenics was safe. The earlier news that one percent of all those using it in the original trials returned to consciousness ahead of schedule in their unmoving bodies was not denied, which surprised me. But instead they explained that they had found a way to circumvent it from being an issue. Passengers' minds will be uploaded to a Virtual

Reality, where they can while away the century of their voyage on whatever hobbies or holidays catch their eye.

They wanted to make it very clear that the problems had been fixed.

This is another thing for which we shall have to trust in our leaders. Though, with a percentage chance that cuts evenly across all known demographics, we can be assured that if it does happen they would be as affected as the rest of us. And they seem willing enough to board the ships. That is probably as close to a definite reassurance that the problems have been fixed as anything they say.

Chapter 1

Name: Gwen Baird

Class:	Hunter		
Level:	1		
Health:	5		

Species: Half-Elf (Wood/Human)

Strength:	5	Mind:	5
Agility:	5	Body:	5
Armour:	3	Sense:	5

Species Skills: (Half-Elf)

Elf Sight:	1	

Base Skills: (Hunter)

Dodge:	1	Perception:	1
Tracking:	1	Stealth:	1
Charm:	5	Archery:	1

It had been five minutes and Guinevere Baird, hacker, thief, survivor of the End of the World, was hidden up a tree, hiding from a monster. This was not how she had expected her first day to go.

But then, she thought, hanging onto the lichen-covered bark of the tree and watching the strange beast tear up the grass beneath her, she hadn't really known what to expect. Maybe this was how this was supposed to go? The media had been full of wonder and awe when the news came that they weren't all going to be trapped on Earth as the sun blasted Earth's atmosphere with radiation. Hearing about it she had been perhaps a little quick to celebrate rather than finding out more about what was going to happen.

A brisk wind came through the branches at that point, shaking the tree slightly and making her force her fingers even more deeply into the thick, orange-red bark of the Scots pine. She felt choked with the scent of it and hopefully, the creature below her would be similarly inconvenienced. But she didn't have much hope for that. As a member of the Hunter class she had gotten a point in the Stealth skill to start off with, that was probably the only reason that she hadn't been found. But whether or not she would be spotted or heard was not the most important thing. A more pressing issue was that she was losing the strength in her fingers and she wasn't sure that she would be able to grab a better hold without alerting the beast below her. One point of stealth could only get you so far.

And the tree was big, but even in the real world bigger trees than this were victims to wild hogs and even more to beetles and given that the creature was some sort of combination of the two. Well, she really wasn't holding out much hope.

I need to put more points into Strength, she thought. *Definitely need to fix that at my first level up.*

However, that first level up wouldn't come until she had gained a hundred experience points which seemed like a veritable mountain while she sat at the bottom with zero. And then, of course, once she got that first hundred she would need two hundred to reach level three and then four hundred to reach level four. Because, to level up, each level needed twice as much experience as the one before it. By the time she reached level ten she'd be needing tens of thousands of points to get any movement.

She looked down at the beast, it looked like the gods-forsaken offspring of a beetle and wild pig. Its six legs were a mix of trotters and feet with hooks, and behind the bristly brown face of a boar was a black shiny carapace. Currently, it was tearing into the ground with its tusks.

Goring, said her mind, not-so-helpfully, if it has tusks it's called goring. And if that's what it's doing just to your smell on the grass, then it'll rip you apart if it catches you.

Not helpful anxiety-brain, she thought caustically back at the voice.

Gwen breathed in the air that smelled of pine – and increasingly of ripped up grass and broken earth – and tried to concentrate. *What do I do?* She thought about what she was carrying: *I have a sword and I have a bow. There's no chance I'm going to be able to use the bow and still hold on to this tree, but the sword...*

She looked at the monster. It was a little over two metres below her. Close enough that she could hear the tearing of the grass roots, the growling of its breath, and see her reflection in the shine of its carapace. That wasn't *so* bad a distance to fall. She grinned.

The simple sword she had been given at the start of the game hadn't come with a proper scabbard, just a loop of leather to attach it to her belt. That would make things easier. Trying not to grunt too loudly, she looped her elbow around the hilt and pointed the sword at the back of the creature's neck, above the carapace and below the hard bone of the skull. Then she waited for her moment. Her arms were starting to really feel the strain, the bark was starting to bite under her short nails. Then the creature reached out, stretching its short neck and creating a perfect target.

She let herself fall.

A millisecond later she told herself that she was an idiot and that this wasn't going to work. She had five points of health, gods-dammit, did she really think that—

Then she hit the beast, her sword hitting first, skewering into the thick flesh and muscle around its neck. She landed on the slippery carapace, the arm she had been holding the sword with felt like it was on fire, the pain was so intense. The sword hadn't slid through the creature's neck, instead, it got stuck into the meat and muscle of it. And all the excess force was reflected back onto Gwen. Her gaze whited out for a second, and by the time that it returned her vision was glowing with numbers warning her about the amount of damage she had taken.

Too many numbers, she realised, *too much damage*. They were glowing red with a fluorescent and accusing glare.

And, rather than dying from a sword into the back of the neck, the creature just seemed to get angrier. It let out a squeal so loud its echo was alike a ricocheting bullet and it started to run. Still stunned by the impact, Gwen only had the brainpower to hold onto the sword, scrabbling with her free hand onto the pommel and gripping on for dear life. She laced her fingers around it, making a pained noise as her hands came into contact with one another. The hand which had been gripping the sword as she fell was a mass of so much pain that being made aware of it once more was enough to make her tremble.

She felt sick with the pain and with the motions the creature was making as it tried to knock her off; luckily its attempts to smash her into a tree were fruitless as she was so much smaller than its wide back that it was doing more damage to its own sides than to her. But that didn't stop it from trying.

Its blood was doing a better job of dislodging her, thick rivulets of greyish green were running over her hands from the wound she had inflicted. It stunk like rotten flesh and Gwen gagged and retched as it coated the back of the creature and her. It wasn't like any sort of blood she had come across before, instead it seemed to have the consistency of egg whites.

As she held on, she grimaced as she saw that a nearly empty bar was floating at the top of her vision. What had dragged her notice to it was the rapidly sliding into red of the bar. The green was gone before she had a chance to get used to it.

The gambeson she was wearing had done little to soak up the damage, the rest had whipped through her five points of health leaving her with two.

Another one flickered and disappeared as she watched.

"Well that's bad, that's definitely bad," she said through gritted teeth.

Struggling to keep her balance on top of the slick beetle back, Gwen tried to stick her knees into the side of the neck, all while holding onto the sword. The creature kept running around the clearing, but it did seem to be tiring, or at least slowing. The trees whipping past her vision were doing so at a slightly less breakneck pace. Whether that was from the exhaustion caused by a rider, or from blood loss she wasn't sure, but either way, it was probably the only good news she had.

She breathed deep, trying to ignore the pain; she left her good hand holding onto the sword, both to keep her place on its back and to sustain the damage it was dealing, and with her agonisingly aching hand she took a dagger from her belt. The weapon wasn't long, not even the length of her middle finger from hilt to point, but it was sharp enough to cut through the bristly hide of the creature and into the flesh. Heart in her mouth, terrified that it would be smart enough to try rolling, she started to stab at the neck. Again, and again, and again. The blood was falling like a grisly wedding train behind them, it didn't seem possible that one creature could be filled with so much and it seemed impossible that it should lose so much and keep running.

She didn't bother keeping track of the flickering notifications telling her how much damage she was doing, five points here and three points there, the numbers swooped by her head seeming to disappear behind them as the monster kept running.

Then it wasn't. It didn't stop gracefully, rather slowing until it could run no more and falling to its belly, before shuddering out its last squeal of anger.

It felt like hours had passed, but the time from her fall to the creature halting was probably only a few minutes. Gwen ached, her arm felt like the muscles had started to fray and new aches sprung up as she sat on the corpse. Her belly for one, it had not liked receiving the brunt of her fall's impact.

She didn't bother standing up or climbing off the thing's back. Part of her doubted that it was even dead, she was sure it was tricking her. But mostly she stayed on the creature's back so she could breathe and give the world around her the chance to catch up. Part of that, she knew, would entail letting go of her sword, but she wasn't quite brave enough.

In the end, it wasn't her decision to let go, the game made it for her. The beast disappeared in a shimmer of greasy looking smog and she was dumped in the flattened grass. She dropped the two blades she carried. The blood had not gone with the body and so she was crouched in a muddy pool of it, her hands covered and the sleeves of her shirt soaked. She pushed on her wobbly legs until she was a few feet out of the blood puddle and there she dropped to the ground and tried her best to clean her hands on the grass.

***

It took her longer than she would have liked to recover. By the time her shaking legs could hold her the green in her health bar had climbed from a sliver to a healthy chunk, from a barely hanging on one point, to a solid four. In practical terms that meant that while her arm was stiff, it no longer felt like there was any threat of it falling off.

The new peace gave her a first proper chance to look around: she had materialised sitting in the grass of the clearing, she had all of half a minute to admire the pine trees and blue sky before she heard the creature in the bushes. An instinct that she hadn't known she had, or perhaps had been given as part of the game, had told her to run. She had grabbed her things and bolted to the nearest tree with low enough branches. Now, however, she had time to look about her.

The long branches of Scots pines were interwoven into a thick canopy; lichen covered the trees in the lightest of blues and mixed with mosses on the trunks to hide much of the bark. Except on the tree that she had climbed. She walked over to it and could see the marks where her scramble had scratched the tree, breaking off moss, lichen, and even some small patches of bark. Guilt curdled in her stomach, she reached out and patted the trunk, "Sorry about that, thanks for keeping me safe," she whispered.

The feeling that came back was soft and cool, yet welcoming, like a glass of water when your throat is dry and the road is dusty, and before her mind could be dragged down that road too far she snatched her hand back in surprise.

"Oh!" Sheepishly she lowered her hand, "Right, half-elf," she tucked some dark brown hair behind a pointed ear and turned away from the tree, "I need to remember that that's a thing that can happen." Pulling her mind from the in-character parts of the game, she looked instead to the least in-character thing she could think of.

As Gwen opened the notifications menu, it was like getting hit in the face by a blizzard made from letters.

"Ah, fuck," she said, waving her hands about and attempting to sort through the masses of beeping, flashing notifications. After a few minutes it seemed to settle down and she was able to make sense of the system that organised them.

Feeling a bit like someone trapped in a high spin wash, surrounded by odd socks and too many bubbles, she grabbed onto the one that seemed to be flashing the brightest, hoping that that meant it was the first one she was supposed to be reading. As she thought about reading it a letter manifested in her hands, the paper was a heavy, golden-toned parchment, and there was a gold wax seal stamped with the image of dove holding frayed wires in its' beak, rather than leaves. Gwen ran her fingertips over the image, it felt like wax, but also, somehow, colder and harder, as if it were made of metal, after all.

Running her thumb under the seal she popped the letter open and started to read.

"Welcome Adventurer to the world of After!
While the world you have come from is soon to be destroyed by an astronomical disaster, this is your safe harbour from the fear and worries which have no doubt plagued you for the past several years.

You will likely have many questions. Statistically, these are the three answers you are most likely to want to know.

News from outside After is impossible to receive, by the time you are reading this you and the rest of the passengers will be in space and the solar flares may have already begun to hit, preventing any other communication. While it is to be expected that you will be curious about what is going on in the 'Real World' please do not seek it out. Once the solar flares cease the communications blackout will drop between us and the other ships in the evacuation process, but until then we will be on minimal contact with the rest of the evacuation fleet.

The world was designed using a physics engine that mimics Earth's, so no need to worry about getting used to a stronger or lighter gravity, you should do just fine.

As an Adventurer your life will be full of wonderful advantages, for example you can no longer die, or to be more exact when you die you pop up again with the next dawn! What a relief that must be! You will also heal in a new and improved fashion: whole limbs can be regrown if lost and healing magic is available to speed up the process if necessary.

During your character creation phase you were given several choices about the kind of role you would take on in the world. To help with that you have been set on a path that includes character type and species.

You have chosen:

Half-Elf (Wood Elf/Human) as your species and Hunter for your class.

The world of After is a vast place, full of mysteries and adventure. It is recommended that you explore as much as you can and experience everything that you are able. Consider taking up new hobbies, or perhaps this is the chance you've been waiting for to enjoy a few fantasies?"

For a sudden moment Gwen felt like there was an elbow nudge in her ribs and a wink from the paper, but that strange shadow of a thought was as gone nearly as quickly as it had come and she was able to continue reading the rest of the letter.

The letter continued:

"The world of After is filled with Non-Player Characters who will in most cases defer to your judgement. They will seek your approval and hold your words in high regard, so don't waste them! Of course, there are also lots of NPCs who won't agree with you so easily, but it will be up to you to figure out how to work with or against them. A good Charm score is likely to smooth things over if you aren't sure of what to do, but there will always be some fights you can't talk your way out of, so make sure you practise those fighting skills as well!"

The rest of the letter was a brief summary that seemed to be mostly telling the newcomers to role-play heavy games how the game worked, but she'd played enough of them to skip that part. Gwen looked around at the world she was standing in, well, there was the whole being able to touch things and feel pain, and so on. That was new.

Virtual reality had been coming in leaps and bounds in the last few years, but this was the kind of jump that most people would need a jetpack to achieve.

Reading through the rest of the letter was an odd experience since the parchment didn't get any longer, but her eyes could keep going down it to another line and another line; she didn't find anything that shocked her. So, she folded the letter up and pushed it into one of the numerous pouches on her belt. It seemed like something she should keep handy.

At that point, more letters started to appear in her hands. These were much smaller, more like the telegrams she remembered from movies than full letters with wax seals like the first one had been. The messages on each of them were all pretty much the same. The first one she read was, **"Congratulations, your Perception skill has reached level 2!"** and then there were more, for Perception, for Climbing, for Stealth, Sword Fighting, Knife Fighting, and Grappling. All in all, she had more than a dozen notifications for skill levels, and once she had sorted through them all she found something even more surprising.

"Three class level increases?" She asked, shaking her head as she looked at the black ink on the thin strips of paper. She read one, **"Congratulations, you have reached level 4! Your health and stat points have been increased!"** Looking over to the now dying grass where the strange beast's body had lain, she murmured, "What the hell were you, if fighting you was enough to put me up to Level Four and give me a load of skill levels as well?"

The yellowing grass and sticky lines of mud said nothing.

She looked at the final notification, one which had been buried under the avalanche of the rest. She grinned.

"Do you wish to activate the Find My Family Quest?"

"Yes," she said, a little of the tension leeching out of her shoulders as the small paper scroll dissolved in her hand. There was a moment where the ground seemed to blur, and she realised it was a prompt to use her menu. Blinking under the eye strain, she flicked onto the menu; a wall of texts and buttons appeared like a door slammed in front of her. One of the icons was blinking, a simple picture of a compass rose. She nodded at it and exited the menu again. For a moment the world was as it should be and then four arrows started to hover over the ground, looking like there were gaps in the trees letting in odd-toned light. For a split second they were each visible as separate objects, then three of them coalesced into a single arrow pointing in one direction, while the last one pointed off by itself. It was directing her towards a clump of mountains in the distance, though something in Gwen told her that Marina was probably not as far away as that.

"And there we go," She murmured. "Marina must be close by, Mum, Dad, and Holly, are a bit of a ways off though. But they're together, which is, I guess, what was supposed to happen?" She asked a little louder, before she shook her head. What was she thinking, that Dove, the ship's AI, would answer her? Dove had a spaceship to navigate and a Virtual Alternate Reality to run. She didn't have time to talk to worried players. Almost certainly.

Instead, Gwen turned back to her Menu and started applying the stat bonuses she had gotten. All characters started off with 5 in each stat and you could add as many as you liked into any of them.

Gwen blew out a breath, a lock of hair that had escaped her braid whipped back and forth. "What am I going to do, what am I going to do," she muttered. "I'll level up first, things will feel a lot less stressful without all of these notifications flashing at me," she decided.

There was also the threat that while she was working out what all the numbers meant some horrible monster would creep up behind her and take a chunk out of her while she was distracted.

Well the tree worked once, she thought with a shrug.

Pulling herself back up into the tree she settled on the branch again, this time managing a cross legged pose that kept her steady and was a lot comfier than her previous grab.

"Right, let's take a look at this, shall we?" She said this out loud, knowing that no one could hear her, or more accurately hoping that no one could hear her.

Opening the notification page in her mind she looked through what it told her. As she had seen before she had gained three levels from her fight with the beetle monster. That meant she had three skill points to assign and what a choice she had in front of her. Strength, Agility, Body, Mind, Sense, and Charm. For the most part it was pretty obvious what those stats gave her, Strength was about brawn. Useful for players who planned to carry around axes and swords that weighed as much as a small motorbike, but less so for characters like her that relied on speed and stealthiness. For that she would need high Agility.

In fact, she noticed, Agility was her main Attack Skill. If she wanted to increase the amount of damage she did, she would have to either get much, much better weapons, level up a whole lot, or put a bunch of points into Agility. "Alright, clearly high Agility is good for anyone in the Hunter class who wants to do damage to their enemies. But what else is it good for?"

The answer seemed to be nearly everything. Or, at least, everything that she personally found useful. Sometimes it was in combination with one of the other stats, like climbing was a combination of Strength and Agility, but for the most part it seemed that Agility was a good investment.

While she was flicking through the list of bonuses that Agility gave her one caught her eye. Dodge Skill. It was haloed in a green glow, apparently it was special for her class. "Alright, well aside from the obvious, what does that do?" she said softly.

"The Dodge Skill acts as an additional Armour point for those of the Hunter Class. As such all attacks must exceed this score plus your armour score to do damage to your health. In addition to this, when in fights you purposefully ignore your ability to dodge you can use your dodge skill points to increase your attack skill. You gain one Dodge Skill Point for every five Agility Stat Points you have. Currently you have 1 Dodge Skill Point."

"Oh, I like that," she said with a smile, "Easier time of getting out of the way when someone comes at me *and* the opportunity to do extra damage if I want."

She thought over her choices for a moment. "Well I shouldn't put all of my points into Agility straight away, it will be better to keep a little more balanced than that. I'm not just playing this game, I'm living it. I can't afford to have dump stats when it's my life, or at least my not feeling massive amounts of pain, that is on the line."

Body was the stat that gave her health and which fought off diseases and poisons. It even played into balance, which was bound to come in handy as a Hunter. She was managing OK in the trees right now, but she hadn't exactly done anything very exciting. Climbing up, falling out, climbing up again. Hardly the stuff of legends. So Body would be a good one to put points into as well, even ignoring the fact that it gave you more health which was something that everyone could agree was a good thing to have more of.

After that was Mind. And while her points in that stat were still relatively low she felt that being smarter was probably a good idea. "Definitely not one to be cheap with," she said to herself. Again she looked at the list of bonuses it gave to obscure things, and the side of her mouth kicked up, "And it gives an increase to the amount of experience you get when you learn new skills? Well I already didn't want to be dumb but that is a very good reason to add to this stat when I can."

Sense came next. Remembering how it had saved her bacon when the beetle boar had come out of the woods she could recognise that this was definitely not the optimum dump stat choice. "Best to keep that pretty high as well, or else everything and their tap-dancing auntie will be able to sneak up on me."

It was also supposed to have some sort of effect on the logic skills, or basically, the player's Common Sense. So not one to let get too low if I can help it, she mused.

Finally, the last one was Charm. As it was the stat that held control over the player's ability to lie, to persuade, to find friends and soothe enemies, it seemed pretty important too. *Though, I guess that will all depend on how much time I get to spend around NPCs. If I have to spend all of my time in the woods with no one to talk to then I guess it won't be the most important skill in the world, unless I can learn how to talk to animals at some point?*

She started digging through the information on her character class.

The Hunter was a good all-rounder, not the best fighter and far from the best mage, but if you wanted something that would survive nearly anything this was the one you took. It also had a bunch of different skill trees you could follow if something particularly appealed to you. One seemed to be the archetypal Assassin, another a Confidence Trickster, and more for every type of distinction possible within the class. But there was one that caught her eye in particular, Arcane Archer. It leaned more into the nature loving side of the class and prioritised being as far away from what was trying to kill you as possible. Which she could appreciate.

And most importantly, it gave you access to all sorts of interesting magic that otherwise would be locked away from Hunters unless you paid through the nose for spell scrolls or made deals with eldritch beings.

"OK, so if I choose this path," she ran her eyes along the skill tree, "Then after level, what level, oh, level six, I can start learning some spells. Nice one." It was only one spell per level at that point, but the first three you got to pick from (which were helpfully linked to as examples) were Shadow Step, Spider Climb, and Poison Barrage. "Nothing that gives me the ability to speak to animals, but I guess that might come later." She exited out of that rabbit warren of research and looked once more at the stats.

"Right, let's be sensible about this. I have three points to spend and six places to spend them. When I was hanging from that branch all I wanted was another point in my Strength. It would for sure have come in handy when I was trying not to fall off the back of that monster, too. So, one point there." The image of the stat counter in her mind glowed for a moment and Strength increased to 6. Her body felt a little lighter as it hung from her bones and she let loose a breath.

"OK, next choice. Pretty much the only thing that saved me just now was the fact that I heard the monster coming. So, Sense for my second point and hopefully that will help the luck keep coming," again the numbers glowed and this time Sense increased to 6.

"And for the last one," she pursed her lips. There were too many options. Body would come in handy, but so would Agility since that was her main attack stat and the one that kept her from getting hit, Mind would be good, too. Especially, since it helped to speed up learning new skills. The only one she hadn't used yet was Charm, so for now it could be put to the side. In the end, it was Mind that won her over. Being faster at learning would be most useful at the beginning of the game, she had so much to learn.

Maybe it is a little meta-game-y to boost the stat that helps you learn and level faster, but I don't want to be dumb! she reasoned. *And better to do it now when I have so much to learn than to leave it until I'm all levelled up and finding new skills is harder.*

So she nodded once and with the glow lighting up once more she added her final point to Mind.

With that she left the levelling page and with a crack of her neck returned to her body. The world already seemed different. The leaves on the branches around her seemed more delineated, as if the colours had become more vibrant. The wind whistled louder and she could hear how the branches moved and creaked in reaction to it. Also, she was struck anew by how extremely bloody stupid it had been to aim herself out of a tree at a monster. She winced.

For a moment she wobbled dangerously on the branch she sat on as the combination of stat increases had her balance going haywire. Being able to see further and hear more was all well and good, but it turned out it could also make you feel a bit nauseous and dizzy.

"Right, next time I need to remember to be on the ground before I fiddle with my stats again," she shook her head. The rippling waves that seemed to be rolling through her head were lessening and she was able to pay attention to what was going on around her again.

"Not the worst thing you've ever done, but that's a low bar to trip on," she said, shaking her head. First things, first, though, "I have to find Marina," She blinked and brought up the arrows again.

Marinas was still as bright and still pointing towards the mountains.

Climbing the tree, Gwen grabbed the backpack she had flung over a branch and tugged it down to the ground. After checking that nothing had broken in her bolt up the tree, Gwen put the bag over her shoulders and started off in the direction the arrow was pointing her in, hopeful that Marina would be doing the same thing.

***

It was the sound of angry yelling and the thump of metal against flesh that made her run. She didn't need the glowing arrow, Gwen recognised that voice!

She pushed through the last heavy boughs of the forest and popped out on the verge above a road. Standing in the middle of it, with a strange wolf-like creatures lunging at her, was Marina. Marina had opted for a heavier armour than Gwen, one with metal plates sewn into the fabric gambeson and a pair of metal bracers where Gwen wore leather. She was also carrying – and currently hitting an odd creature in the snout with – a heavy mace.

Gwen wasted no time in jumping into the fray, her sword was in her hand and swinging into the belly of one of the creatures before she had even drawn breath to announce herself. The sword felt different than it had before, it felt more familiar. She cast the thought away, assuming that that was the new level of Sword Fighting at work. Though it was a little worrying that it was not just making her foes easier to fight, but making her a better fighter. But she didn't have time to think, or worry, about that, so she boxed it up and pushed it to the back of her mind like a winter coat. Brain manipulation could be tomorrow's problem, today there were monsters.

The blade sank into the monster and this time she was free to spot the numbers that seemed to jump out of the wounded creature in shades of steadily darkening red. 5, 7, 3!

The creature on the end of her sword squealed, before falling to the ground. Gwen must have hit something important then. "Go for their bellies," she said.

Marina jumped at her voice, but brought down the creature fighting her before she turned to look at Gwen. "Thanks. Where have you been?" She lunged at another creature that was trying to take off her arm, her mace cracked it a stunning blow round the head, then she gave it a good thumping blow into the stomach. Something cracked.

"Up a tree mostly," Gwen said, "I got cornered by one giant beastie, luckily it didn't see me go up and it had a bit of a surprise when I came down again."

"Oh, so the welcoming party is normal?" Marina asked, giving her creature a skull smashing blow to the back of the head. "And here I was feeling special."

"Seems so, though yours is different from mine, so at least you have that," she pinned the creature in the shoulder with her sword, then stabbed at it with her dagger. 9, 6 points of damage! It fell to the ground, dissolving as it hit the grass, though the blood left yellow marks where it had fallen.

Marina finished off her own creature, "Well, I'm glad that means there aren't that many scorpion-tailed wolves scampering about the countryside."

"There's certainly less than there were before," Gwen said, before bounding over the grass to give her sister a good hug.

Marina let out a laugh and hugged her back, there was more strength in the arms that embraced Gwen than there had been when they had been in the real world. Someone had obviously taken character creation as an opportunity to improve certain matters. *Well, can't blame her for that, I've done the same*, Gwen thought. With one last squeeze, she stepped back and took a look at her sister. She frowned, "You gone for the warrior or the priest route?"

"Priest, of course, when have I ever denied myself the chance to get shouted at when people need a healer?" Marina said laughing, "Though it does also mean I get some magic, which is nice, and I really like the mechanic for faith." She took a look at Gwen, "Well, you've not got any obvious instruments, so there goes my first bet of you being a bard. What's the stealthy one called, a Hunter?"

"That's it, and yes, that's me," Gwen said, unlike in real life there was no shame in admitting to a preference for cowardice and thievery. They had been a team from the womb, with only a few exceptions, there was no point in stopping a good thing now.

"My second guess," Marina said, swinging an arm around her sister's shoulders, "You've never met a fight you didn't try to wiggle out of with some fast talking."

Gwen leaned into her, she hadn't seen her twin as much as she would have liked lately. If they had ended up staying on Earth they would probably have spent every moment together, unsure of how long either would survive after S-Day, but with an escape route planned they had each had other priorities. Marina had spent the time helping to get her students, kids in their first year of school, ready for the trauma of leaving Earth and most of their family behind. It had meant that they had only seen each other in passing before the week leading up to their cryogenics appointment.

They had each done their best, spending their weekends together, scratching off lines on their bucket lists. Eating lavish meals at fancy restaurants, watching classic movies that they had never seen but had always meant to, had always thought they would have more time for. But eventually, the time had run out.

Marina, took a second good look at her sister, staring keenly into her face "You doing alright? How's your anxiety treating you?"

From most people this would have gotten a rude answer, usually limited to a single piece of nearly universal sign language, but this was Marina. Marina got an actual answer, "Not great, but not as bad as I was expecting. Might just be too busy for panic attacks," Gwen offered, she raised an eyebrow, "And how about you? How are you dealing with this?" She waved a hand at the landscape around them.

"I haven't had time to feel anything but adrenaline yet," Marina said, "I had barely landed when those wolf-spider-things appeared." She frowned, "I thought this was supposed to be a mythology-based game, no one said anything about arachno-canines."

"My thing was half beetle, half boar, so I guess evolution in this world is a bit less particular about where it gets its DNA," Gwen shrugged. The genetic make-up of monsters didn't seem particularly important, "I had heard people say that this was a mishmash of a bunch of different half-finished games as they tried to get everything done before it was too late."

"Well I can't say I'm particularly fond of them," Marina poked the grass with the toe of her boot. "They've really made a mess of the grass too. Look, it's dying around the blood."

The grass *was* yellowing, and it gave Gwen an uneasy feeling. "That's probably just to make us want to fight them even more, especially since they don't seem to drop any loot," Gwen shrugged, and changed the subject. "Have you come across any people yet? Or a road? If there's a road, there must be a village, I can climb a tree and see what there is around?"

"Well that is the first rule of RPGs: find the NPCs to get quests from," Marina said.

Gwen remembered the Quest list blinking in the corner of her vision, "Oh, that's right, I've finished the quest to find you." She brought up the notification and skimmed over the cheerful greeting.

"You have completed the Find Family Quest! Congratulations! Here is your reward: 1 Experience Point."

That done she shrugged, "Well, I'm sure I'll be happy to have that extra one Exp at some point." She took her bag off her back, handed it over to Marina and looked for a good tree to climb. Her Elf Sight came in handy for this, one tree in particular seemed to glow, showing off its strong branches and the short distances between those branches. "Right, this'll do nicely," she said, before walking over and jumping up to grab the lowest branch and pull herself up. The extra Strength really showed its use as she made her way up the tree, with the occasional "helpful" comment from Marina below her.

"Are you sure about that branch, it doesn't look very strong," Marina's voice floated up to her.

Gwen rolled her eyes, "Elf Sight says it's fine," she called back. The branch was more than strong enough to hold her and she wiggled along its length to get a good look around the local countryside. There were hints of the road they were on and in the distance smoke was rising in the many tendrils that indicated a village or town. Nodding, Gwen started back down the tree, taking care to use all the branches Marina had doubted.

By the time she had reached the ground her Elf Sight Skill had risen to Level 3 and her Climbing Skill had reached 4. That gave her enough to put a dent in what she needed to reach Level 5 but at this point she wasn't going to level up just from using her skills for a few minutes.

"Right," she said, brushing the dust of disturbed lichen off her hands, "There's definitely some kind of settlement and it seems to be on this road, so we just need to follow it and we should get there without too much hassle."

Marina didn't seem bothered by that, "Thank goodness we both took orienteering, huh?" she said brightly.

Gwen looked at her sister with a pout and an unimpressed look. "You took it once for an hour and a half, because you thought Jenny who ran the club was hot."

Marina winked, "And, boy, did I learn a lot from her."

"Ugh," Gwen groused, "Come on this way. At least I did orienteering for a few months and didn't give up at the first obstacle."

Marina handed Gwen her bag and followed her as she started down the road, "The way I see it, I got what I wanted from my club membership *and* I learned how to read an old-fashioned paper map and use a compass."

"Ugh," Gwen said, more pointedly this time.

Marina laughed, "Alright then, Ms Hunter, show me how you do it."

Gwen rolled her eyes and wished there was a path she could take her sister down that would make her regret that heavy armour, where were bogs and thin ice when you needed them? "Come on, hopefully there'll be somewhere for us to spend the night."

The old angst over the orienteering wasn't really a big deal. It had just stung because, at the time, Gwen had thought she had found something they could do together. Important at a stage of their lives where they weren't even taking most of the same subjects anymore, and in the few they did share they were on different timetables.

It had not been comfortable to find out that her sister had been so keen on joining up to the club because she had wanted to flirt with the club leader.

But Gwen at least had learned something useful from the misadventure that that had been. She knew how to read the world around her and figure out a vague mental compass. Given that her tracking skill was still low she would need the real-life skills to back her up and to stop getting them both lost.

"Right well, if the physics is all supposed to be the same as at home, then I guess we can expect the sun to rise and fall in the same way, too," she muttered, looking at the way the shadows fell and trying to figure out where the sun was and what approximate time it might be. It felt like mid-morning, but that could just be because she had just arrived in the world not too long ago. And that might be a foolish assumption to make, but on the other hand Dove had seemed far too sensible to give people a weird Virtual Reality form of jet lag.

So, trusting in Dove and dimly remembered navigational tricks, she started off in what she thought was probably the right path. In the background a notification went off about her Tracking Skill rising again and she thankfully pocketed the Exp but didn't let it break her concentration.

"Are you not going to look on the trees to find out if there is a special moss growing on one side?" Marina asked, following behind her and swinging her mace around.

"No, because that only works in America, or maybe just in American movies? It sounds like movie nonsense, like people getting electrocuted and you seeing their bones," Gwen said absently, jumping over a downed tree.

"Fair enough," Marina paused for a moment as she scrambled over the fallen tree, her heavy boots scoring lines in the moss. "And you're right, this place, well, it almost feels like home, doesn't it?"

Gwen looked at her twin. Then she looked around the forest they were standing in. There was something faintly Scottish about the feel of the place. "Maybe," Gwen allowed, "It does look a bit like Scotland, I suppose. But Scotland via Hollywood green screen and New Zealand, more than actual Scotland."

Shrugging, Marina looked around too, "You're probably right. There's no tourists complaining about how terrible the weather is, so it can't be home."

Rolling her eyes, Gwen shoved Marina, who laughed and then pretended to swoon. "Oh, oh your cruelty knows no bounds, sister!"

"Well, nice to see you haven't been able to change the way you can't act, despite going through a character creator where that skill was an option you could take," Gwen mused, as she walked away.

"Rude!" Marina called back to her.

"Maybe, but shouldn't we be quiet? All sorts of things could be sneaking up on us," Gwen said, joking at first, then looking around suspiciously as she realised what good sense she was making.

Marina seemed to think about this for a moment. "You're probably right on that front, but let me live, why don't you? I've felt like the sword of Damocles has been hanging over me for what, two years now? At this point there's fuck all that I can do about it, and that's honestly a relief."

That was true. "It is good not to have to worry about dying horribly, or you guys dying horribly," she admitted.

"A touch grim, there, Gwen. But, yeah, not having to worry about everyone you love dying, that's worth celebrating, don't you think?" Marina swung her arm around Gwen's shoulders. It was the moment that Gwen finally realised what had been bothering her.

"Are you…are you taller?" she asked, gobsmacked.

"Yup, you're not the tall twin now," she said grinning down at Gwen. "What, it's a fantasy game, right? Well this has been one of mine for long enough!"

Outraged, Gwen stomped on ahead, scoffing loudly the entire way.

The laughter rang through the forest and followed her.

Chapter 2

Name: Gwen Baird

Class:	Hunter		
Level:	4		
Health:	20		

Species: Half-Elf (Wood/Human)

Strength:	6	Mind:	6
Agility:	5	Body:	5
Armour:	3	Sense:	6

Species Skills: (Half-Elf)

Elf Sight:	3

Base Skills: (Hunter)

Dodge:	1	Perception:	2
Tracking:	1	Stealth:	2
Charm:	5	Archery:	1

It was late in the day when they reached the village, which was larger than Gwen had expected. She had pictured houses and a tavern the size of a garden shed, but this place was far more developed than that. The tavern was large and covered multiple floors. A sign hung over the door showing a swan sitting with a vaguely concussed expression in amongst a truly astonishing number of beer mugs.

"Well that's got to have a story behind it," she mused.

"Oooh, a temple!" Marina said, bouncing on her toes, she grabbed Gwen by the arm and started to pull her in that direction.

"Marina, I'm really not in the mood for religion right now, can't we go to the pub first?" Gwen felt exhausted already by the new world and the new experiences. She really didn't want to be lectured on the cleanliness of her soul.

"No, because temples are save points, you dafty, we get in there, pray a bit, I'll most likely get a bonus to my magic for a while and if we die any time in the next week or so we'll pop back here instead of some random point in the forest: didn't you pay attention to Dove when she was explaining things?" she asked, using her teacher-tone.

Gwen bristled, "I listened, I just didn't remember right now." It was the voice, she thought, it cut straight through to the nerves, then danced on them. And to be fair, when Dove had been explaining how things went in the game, Gwen had had other questions for the AI.

Not taking "not now" for an answer, Marina towed an increasingly stubborn Gwen through the edges of the village to the temple. In the end, Gwen gave up on digging her feet into the turf, it was clear her sister had put a lot more points into Strength than she had.

The temple was an odd-looking building, at least to Gwen's eyes. It certainly appeared like it had been modelled off an old medieval church from the Highlands, all square corners and whitewash, but some wires had gotten crossed somewhere and it had gotten mixed up with a greenhouse made from stained glass. It was beautiful:

greens, blues and purples all blended together in feather-like images, but against the backdrop of pine forests and mountains, Gwen couldn't help but shiver at the thought of staying there.

Aside from that though, it could have been any one of the rebuilt crofter's cottages and conserved churches that her parents had marched them around when she was a kid. She could almost feel the drizzle that had usually accompanied them down the back of her neck and the taste of the mints mum had kept for such excursions.

Marina led her to the door – an arched sunset out of glass decorated the wall above it so that it looked as if the door itself was a part of the sun – and when Marina opened that door and tugged Gwen through, they seemed as though they were walking through the sky itself. Inside the temple's walls were a honeycomb of recessed niches; a few nearest the front had items filling them, but there were hundreds without anything inside them. The objects weren't what Gwen had expected either. There were some small models of figures, mostly in some silvery metal that to Gwen's untrained eye could be anything from silver to steel to platinum. But the rest were oddities, they looked more like the contents of a kitchen odds and ends drawer. Lots of pieces of paper with writing and print in small, black letters pinned in place; dolls made from sticks, straw, or pressed flowers and leaves. And in some of the niches there were, well, just things: a mirror; a comb; a tankard of shining, if dented, brass.

"I don't really know what to do here," she muttered. Gwen felt the hairs on the back of her neck stick up, she had never exactly felt at home in religious spaces, and it seemed that the feeling had come along for the ride.

Gwen crossed her arms across her chest and followed Marina reluctantly into the aisle that led between the rows of pews.

Marina was charging up it, apparently quite content to be there and happy to make as much noise as she wished, but then it had never been easy to shut Marina up.

Poking his head out of an office space, a middle-aged man smiled at them, "Good afternoon," he said, "Are you new to the village?" He came and showed himself to be a well-built man. wearing a knitted jumper over thick trousers. His slightly thinning blonde hair was sticking up like it had met a comb once and had not felt the need to repeat the experience.

"Indeed we are," Marina said, with impressive bonhomie and confidence for someone on their first day in a new reality. "We're just passing through, but we just had to stop for a visit, I am Marina, and this is my sister, Gwen. Do you have a few minutes to talk about your lovely village and this beautiful building?"

The priest, since that was what he appeared to be, seemed utterly delighted to talk to someone who liked his temple as much as he did. "My name is Nikolai, the village is Starlingrise, and this is our temple." He waved a hand, "And we're happy to accept any worshippers of any gods, since we've always held that it's best not to insult any gods by leaving them out."

He stopped for a laugh, Marina happily did so, Gwen, recognising a cue when she heard one, gave a polite chuckle.

"We generally have a service in the morning, and some in the evening on the holy days of the gods for whom it is appropriate. But chiefly this is a space for personal reflection and worship, though I am of course always happy to help out when I am needed for certain rituals. May I ask which gods are your personal patrons?" he asked, looking first from Marina then to Gwen.

"My goddess is Minethena, the Teacher and the Student," Marina said, placing a hand over her heart in a way that looked as if she had done it a hundred times a day her whole life.

"Felicitas, the Lucky and the Careful," Gwen said, feeling far more awkward as she copied Marina's actions.

The priest seemed a little intrigued by the names of their goddesses, but he was able to see which of the twins was keen to talk more about her goddess and so wisely turned to Marina. "Well, we have not yet had any worshippers of those two goddesses, so if you wish to place something in the niches here," He waved to the honeycomb of shelves along the walls, "Then you are very welcome. And, Ms Marina, am I correct in thinking you are a fellow priest?"

Marina blushed and waved a hand modestly, "Oh, little more than a novice, really. But very happy to hear any advice you have, sir." She beamed up at him.

He was clearly flattered and ushered her to a pew to talk things over.

Gwen tapped Marina on her shoulder as she passed, "I'll finish up here and see if I can get us some rooms at the inn."

Marina grinned back, "I'll see if I can get us a quest!" she whispered back before hurrying off to sit by the priest. There was a moment of awkwardness as she had to move the mace hanging on her hip as it obstructed her movement, but she fixed it soon enough.

The two priests' chatter filled the temple, masking even the small noises Gwen's leather shod feet made against the stone of the floor. She picked a spot on one of the walls that had an unclaimed niche and walked up to it. Up near the front they were filled to the brim, some even spilling over with flower wreathes, some dried and others fresh, but here it was mostly just a single small offering in each hollow.

"Well, I'm here," Gwen said, "I don't really know what to say, I didn't get the, uh, education my sister evidently did on how to behave in temples." She thought for a moment, then said what seemed the best thing that sprang to mind, "Thank you for looking after me, I've felt very lucky, and I've tried to be careful. Um, please continue to do so and I'll do my best to be worthy of your help. Thanks," She paused, checking her pockets for something to put in the niche, her fingers touched warm metal. There was something in there that hadn't been there before. Frowning she drew out a single, gold edged, playing card. In the place of a king, queen, or jack, sat a smiling figure: she must have been Felicitas because no Queen had ever been painted with such a cheeky smile, or wearing an outfit that was a meld of medieval high fashion and a flapper dress. In one hand she held cards to her chest, in the other she was tossing dice.

"Well, I'll take that as a 'Hello,' I suppose," Gwen said with a little laugh, leaning the card up against the back of the hollow. The light caught the card and, just for a moment, it looked like the woman winked one eye. This made a warm feeling blossom under Gwen's breastbone, it was nice to think that someone was looking out for her, even just a little bit.

Stepping back, she nodded to the niche, then resettled the backpack on her shoulders and sent a look over to Marina. They were still deeply in conversation about priestly duties, or whatever it was they were talking about.

Shaking her head, Gwen turned and left, hopeful that the price for a room for the night wasn't too much, and that a drink too would be within her budget. And that the simulation wasn't going to be too accurate about the state of medieval taverns and their inventories.

She pushed open the door to the tavern and was pleasantly surprised. It smelled of ale and roast chicken, and the room she stepped into was bright and had comfy-looking furniture. Catching the eye of a barmaid, she walked up, easing into a charming smile, "Hello, I'm Gwen, what's your name?"

A little red around the cheekbones and over the tops of her very slightly pointed ears the young woman answered, "I'm Abigail, and what can I do for you, Gwen?"

"I'd love an ale and I need a room for the night. My sister and I will be staying, she's over at the temple at the moment, talking priestly business with Nikolai," Gwen tilted her head in the direction of the temple behind her, knowing full well that the action showed off her own slightly pointed ears. *Fingers-crossed for part-elf community discounts*, she thought.

Abigail gave a grin, "Well, I can do the both for you, we have a nice room that looks in the direction of the temple for you and your sister, that is if you don't want separate ones?" She twirled a lock of her hair around a finger and leaned forward with a sultry smile.

Shit! Those standard 5 points in Charm work too well, I'm not used to this, Gwen thought frantically, "Oh, well that's very kind of you, Abigail, but I think I'd better stay with my sister." *Please let that be enough, I don't want her angry with me. God, I wish there was a code for, 'Hi, I like to flirt but I'm demisexual and the last time I was in a relationship it took me over a year of flirting to get to the point of spending the night with her.'* That brought her ex, Ana, to mind, which wasn't helpful, so she did her best to ignore it.

Abigail pouted a little, but seemed to get the message without any hurt feelings, "It's three copper for the ale and two silver for the night," she said, "And we'll feed you too, so don't fret about that."

Relief washed though Gwen, "Thank you, Abigail."

Abigail gave her a smile and turned back to get the ale out of a barrel behind the counter. She filled the tankard and pushed it over to Gwen. Condensation was already appearing on the outside of the ceramic mug; Gwen had never seen something that looked so delicious. Gwen let out a sigh of relief, the knowledge that pubs and taverns often used cold spells was suddenly downloaded into her mind, and she passed over the three copper coins.

"So where are you from, Gwen?" Abigail asked, drying off a spot of condensation on the counter from the jug.

"The border with the elven lands: my sister and I are travelling to the West to meet up with our parents and a cousin," Gwen replied, the agreed-upon story dropping from her mouth with ease.

Abigail gave her a sympathetic look, "That's quite a distance."

"It is, but hopefully the new place will be worth the shoe leather," she took a sip of the ale. The cool touch was the perfect way to end the day of walking in the heat. Wiping her mouth on her cuff, she asked, "Have you seen any other travellers coming through?"

Abigail appeared to think for a moment, "They were coming in dribs and drabs a couple of months ago, but I haven't seen anyone in a while, come to think of it." She frowned, "Actually, now I do think about it, we haven't seen nearly anyone at all recently."

Gwen frowned, her coincidence senses were tingling, the ones that made themselves known when things weren't coincidences. "Just out of curiosity, but how often would you say you see monsters around here, big half boar, half beetle things, or scorpion tailed wolves, for example?"

Abigail's eyes widened, "Never! I've never heard of anything like that, did you see something like that in the woods?"

"On the road here," Gwen said, "My sister and I were lucky to survive, if we weren't together and if I hadn't gotten lucky, we probably wouldn't have."

A trembling hand moved up to cover her mouth, Abigail looked shaken, her tanned and freckled skin was paling, "That– that's not good. Would you excuse me for a moment?" She left before Gwen had the time to answer, pulling up the hinged end of the bar to get onto the other side and walking over to an older man sitting by the fire with a large plate of chicken and mashed potatoes before him. She crouched down and started to whisper in his ear, the white-haired old man looked up at her in shock, then over at Gwen, then back up at Abigail.

"Are you sure?" he asked very loudly.

"So this young lady says," Abigail said.

The entire room had frozen and fallen silent, all of what must have been the regular crowd looking in interest at the gossip fodder growing in front of them. Gwen took a breath and leaned more completely against the strength of the bar.

The door opened, haloed against the light in shining armour was Marina, she took a look at the silent taproom and at Gwen tensely hovering by the bar. She strode over, trying to look carefree, "I assume you've told them about our welcoming committee?" she said quietly.

"Yep," said Gwen, "You told Nikolai about it, too?"

"Yeah, apparently this area is notable for its lack of terrifying monsters," she said.

"And apparently no one's visited the village in a while," Gwen said. They shared a look, Gwen's worried, Marina's excited.

"I said I'd find us a quest, didn't I?" Marina said with a smile.

"I think the finding was pretty equally shared out on this one," Gwen said. She couldn't get as excited, not when Abigail had looked so afraid. The barmaid might not be real, but that emotion had looked genuine and it had hit Gwen as if it were.

Abigail was waving them over now, Gwen left her bag where she had put it up against the bar and walked over. "My sister, Marina," Gwen said, indicating her twin.

"I was just talking to your priest; it sounds like you have a monster problem?" Marina was doing her best to look concerned and not excited. It was coming over as a deep solemnity which the old man at least seemed to appreciate.

"Indeed, we haven't seen any visitors in weeks, though most worrying for us," he shared a look with Abigail, "is that my older daughter, Jessica, lives on a small farm with her children a few miles outside the village. We haven't heard from her, either."

Gwen asked, "Would you like us to go check up on her?"

The older man let out a sigh of relief, "It is good of you to offer, we were hoping you would agree to check on her." He held out a hand to Gwen, "My name is Brennan, please sit." He waved to the table in front of him. Gwen nodded and she and Marina sat down on the bench across from him.

"Jessica lives about fifteen miles outside the village, she and her late husband moved there, on the site of an old manor; the walls were gone but the foundations were still good so they built a farmhouse and barn on them. David died a few years ago, but with the kids getting older our Jessica was able to keep the farm running. She's basically alone out there when it isn't harvest time," He shook his head. "I should have insisted she came back to the village."

"She wouldn't have come," Abigail said, shaking her head, "She's very proud of her farm, and well she should be. But if there's creatures like you described out there then she won't be safe, and if she does get hurt then it's too far for the kids to run for help."

"We can go," Marina said, "though perhaps we should leave in the morning, as much as I want to help I do not think it would be safe to spend the night out there when we don't know the way."

The pair seemed disappointed but understanding. "The road there is good, however it's not used enough to be completely reliable." Brennan acknowledged, "In the dark, if you were attacked it is very likely that you could lose it and then we would have to send someone looking for you as well." He sighed, "Very well. If you will go at dawn then we will be very happy to feed you and put you up for the night." He looked at his daughter, "We cannot spare much for payment—"

Marina cut over him, "That's not necessary. If you're willing to feed and house us, then that will be more than sufficient." At their thanks she smiled, and, with an innocence that got Gwen suspicious instantly, she added, "And perhaps, after, you may be willing to listen to me deliver a sermon. Nikolai has offered to let me do so in the temple before my sister and I continue on our journey."

"Of course, we'd be very happy to," Abigail said. "I'll show you up to your room so you can leave your things, it must all be very uncomfortable."

"I would be very grateful," Marina said, she stood and gave a flourishing bow, effortlessly taking the focus of the room.

Gwen happily retreated into the shadows.

After they had said goodbye to Brennan, Abigail took them through a door. The second the door was closed behind them the noise from the room they had left was thunderous.

Abigail shook her head, "Bunch of gossips," she said fiercely. Leading them up the narrow stairs she showed them to a large room with two beds, dressed in bright patchwork quilts and white linen sheets. She left soon after, obviously still not quite even keeled after the shocking news.

"You know, just curiosity would have likely got you half the village as an audience at the Temple," Gwen said, a little sharply.

"And this should help get the other half," Marina said. "And don't snap, the quickest way for me to level up my magic is to teach people about my goddess. There are some spells I just can't get until I've preached to a thousand or more people, and spells that need even more after that: I need to get the numbers in." She plopped down on a bed.

"What did you talk to the priest about?" Gwen started to unknot her boot laces and take them off. Once done, she sat on the foot of her bed and crossed her legs underneath her.

Despite the long day of walking her feet still felt as fresh as when they had started, the health bar was still at 20 points and it didn't look like something as basic as walking would do anything to damage it. This was a welcome change from the real world, no blisters, no sunburn and no aches in muscles that have appeared just to be a literal pain in the butt.

She took care of a few notifications which had popped up, it was just regular updates of her rising tracking skill. Once she had reached the village it had stalled at 4.

"The local gods, mostly. Understandably they're very into crafting and farming around here, but he was happy for me to tell people about Minethena before I left. I doubt he would have been if he thought I was likely to stay overly long and be possible competition, but," she shrugged, "then I mentioned the creatures we fought and, well, he had a reaction similar to that of the taproom."

"I wonder why there are monsters here all of a sudden?" Gwen mused.

Marina gave a sharp laugh. At Gwen's questioning look she sighed, "What possibly could have happened in the recent past to make the local landscape start spawning lots of new monsters?"

The answer struck Gwen, "Adventurers."

Marina nodded, "The timelines match up."

Slumping back onto her bed Gwen groaned and tried not to feel guilty.

Chapter 3

Name: Gwen Baird

Class:	Hunter		
Level:	4		
Health:	20		

Species: Half-Elf (Wood/Human)

Strength:	6	Mind:	6
Agility:	5	Body:	5
Armour:	3	Sense:	6

Species Skills: (Half-Elf)

Elf Sight:	3

Base Skills: (Hunter)

Dodge:	1	Perception:	2
Tracking:	4	Stealth:	2
Charm:	5	Archery:	1

Removing a half dozen layers of armour and clothing was an odd thing to do when you didn't remember putting them on. The laces and buckles holding things in place had no creases or bends from long use, they sprang apart with the barest pressure.

There were buckles and laces in odd places, too, and while she was trying to take off her gambeson Gwen realised a strap still had to be removed only after the armour had become caught over her head and she was forced to unpick it from inside the dark cocoon the layers of linen had made around her.

Eventually, she was free of the extraneous layers, a simple white shirt and dun tunic lying over her breast, with leggings and her knee-high leather boots completing the outfit. Grabbing her belt from the mess of armour she had left dumped on her bed, Gwen looped it around her waist. It was long enough to cinch her waist in and still have a sizeable strip left over to hang at her side. There wasn't a mirror in the room, but she thought she probably looked pretty good.

Curious to see what had been packed for her, she opened the canvas backpack up. She had rifled through the upper layers while they had been walking to the village, looking for non-existent snacks or water, but hadn't managed to get a good look while they were making their way through the forest. It was a little too terrifying to really dig in with the potential for a monster to be hiding behind every tree.

There were two spare tunics and shirts, a single other pair of leggings, a week's worth of woolly socks and underwear. There was a spare bra that had a certain sportiness that she appreciated, though the lace tie would take some getting used to. That was probably anachronistic, but she didn't give a damn. It was a relief to know that the game, when given the option to pick between the comfort of the players and a strict historical accuracy, had gone with the former. Ropes, an empty water skin, and a sewing kit which Gwen was definitely going to become familiar with, there were already a few scratches that could turn into tears on her clothing.

No food, which might have been a worry. Unless?

It *was* a rather magnificent coincidence that they had arrived in the game only a few hours walk from a bustling little village with a quest ready and waiting for them. Were all villages like this in the game, or was it just something that happened when Adventurers careened into the distance like a well-meaning tornado? Ah well, she thought, it's presumably part of the overarching plan for the game, no need for me to worry about it.

At the bottom of the bag in a satchel were things that she could dimly remember picking in the character creation bubble that she had drifted through on first waking up from the cryogenic centre. That was hours ago now, and more importantly, it was on the other side of an adrenaline rush. It felt like days had passed since she had carefully made her choices.

Fishing through it she found the comb made from antler, the pins and bits of wire which were what you started off with as a lock pick set; a thread thin rope that was unlike anything she had ever seen in the real world, as she rolled it between her fingers and tried to make out a braid or twist in it the information unfurled in her brain. Spider silk, made from magical spiders it should have been a costly item for anyone but it was nearly indestructible and the magic spiders made it constantly so the price had dwindled down to the point where even a humble Adventurer could count on having a length or two in their backpack.

There was also, of course, a set of cards. For these she didn't need the magic of an infodump to tell what they were made for, there were just slightly too many inconsistencies in the decorative backings for them to be a clean set. She had never been very good at this sort of thing in the real world, she was a hacker more than a con artist or a card shark. If she ended up face to face with a mark then the con was already lost and she should find the nearest drainpipe to shimmy down (or up, sometimes it was easier to go up a level and blend in with the normals than try and get down to the ground).

But she had known the basics.

Gwen gave a sigh, slipped a dagger into each of her boots and started to walk back down to the bar, taking her money bag and the deck of cards with her.

***

Gwen laid claim to a table in the back of the room; it was comforting to find that even in the strange world of a virtual reality having your back to a wall so no one could creep up on you was still an instinct she carried with her. It might even be one that was particularly useful in a place like this, built on the bones of fantasy and added to with whatever ideas the developers had had buzzing around in the days leading up to the end of the world. There had been all sorts of theories about what shape the space to occupy them in their century of cryogenic sleep would take.

Monsters aside, Gwen quite liked what she had seen of the virtual reality she was currently occupying.

She looked around the bar: one side of the room looked as if it had been cleared for dancing, but the side Gwen was on was filled with tables and chairs.

A barmaid came over with a tankard and a wink, Gwen accepted the tankard and did her best to laugh off the wink in a way that wouldn't cause any offence. She took a sip and settled into her seat to look around and people watch for a bit. While she had been out of the room there had been a change in the folks occupying the seats. Like an animal breathing in and out, people had come into the bar and left it.

But none of them seemed to be overly interested in her.

So Gwen started to play with the cards. Over the years she had picked up a few card tricks, mostly out of boredom and because there's only so much time you can spend around other types of thief without learning a thing or two about their specialities. In particular, there had been one job where they had waited for over three weeks for someone to leave a house. She had learned a lot in those three weeks.

Shuffling the cards, Gwen started by trying to collect all the queens in one hand. It was a mix of card counting and sleight of hand that should have been easy. When she tried it the cards spouted out of her hands like a broken fountain and she ended up having to pick them up from the floor.

A notification popped up:

"You have insufficient levels of Skill: Card Sharp to achieve this outcome."

Reading it she bit back the words which wanted to spring to her lips. Having a tantrum in the middle of a pub wouldn't win her any favours.

"I've never seen a shuffling technique quite like that before."

Gwen looked up. An older man was grinning at her, and she let out a sigh, he was holding one of her missing queens.

"It's one of the best, don't you know it? No one can dare say a deck's not properly shuffled when the cards end up on different sides of the room," she said with a smile.

He laughed and passed her the missing card, "Aye, you might have the right of it there. But if you can keep to less majestic shows of shuffling, I'll join you for a game or two."

"Gladly. I'm Gwen," she said, slowly passing the last quarter of the deck up to the front and then the first half back around to the back, simple shuffling techniques that even her low levels could manage.

"Jeffrey Hoyle, I'm the baker here abouts," he told her.

"Ah, so that's why you are so willing to play with me," Gwen joked, "you knead the dough."

The baker laughed uproariously, Gwen was getting the feeling that he did everything in a big and voluminous way. "Ha, that's a good one! Aye, well, the truth is we don't hear much from folks outside of the village. Oh there's a few people, merchants mostly, who travel up and down the roads here and there. But we've been sorely missing news of the outside world, got any to tell?"

Gwen dealt him a hand of cards, somewhere in the back of her mind unfolded a tutorial on how to play, but after a brief glance at it she waved it away, she knew how to play Go Fish. After giving herself a matching hand, she pushed the rest of the cards into the middle of the table. "I've been on the road a while, I'm probably as out of touch with the news as you," she said.

"Now that I doubt, especially since I heard you got into some trouble on your way into the village, some sort of monster attacked you?"

"Hmmmhmm, two attacks, actually. One a big beetle-looking boar thing, the other a whole pack of wolves with scorpion bits added on."

Over the course of the game they fed gossip back and forth across the table. Given that Gwen had essentially been born just that morning into the world, she was very happy to hear anything that put the world around her into a bit more detail. The village was one of hundreds in the border lands between the dwarven empire to the West and the elven republic to the East. There had, apparently, been several centuries of fighting across the land, the border moving almost quicker than the armies could march to keep up with it. It had ended with a devastating battle in the north, a battle that had corrupted the land surrounding it to the point where the necromantically raised armies still marched and fought across it.

Apparently, this had been sufficient to shame both sides into agreeing to back off and be polite neighbours. The lands had been stripped of anything militaristically useful and left to anyone who wanted it, the anyone had mostly ended up being the humans who had been around at the time, half-elves, and any others of the less populous species who could get there. Both sides, of course, had rules and laws they had to abide by and it had left the two sides with a cold war fought principally through passive-aggressive smarminess. But this was better than two sides with the ability to make people fight to the death, and then, long after that death, having a tiff every time summer came around and the weather was good enough for camping again.

Looking down at the cards she had on offer (an unappealing mix of middle numbers with no decent runs or matches) she looked over at her host, "Are there still problems between the elves and dwarves? I don't want to walk into anything."

He shook his head sharply, "No, no. Things are much more peaceful these days. When I was young there was a bit of a scuffle between them, but some human folk grabbed them by their beards and pointy ears and marched them out to look at the undead warriors that nobody can shift up North of here. Made them look at the armies that were still fighting their damned wars and made them think twice about starting it up again."

Gwen nodded, "For two species that can live for centuries they do seem to have very short memories sometimes."

"Aye!" The baker laughed then looked at Gwen with concern, "Not being insulting am I, saying such things about the elves?"

Gwen remembered that she was supposed to be a half elf, how awkward. She grinned, battling through the cringe, "Nope, can't find fault in words that are true!"

He laughed, "Fair enough. Anyway, things have been a lot better these last few decades. Without everyone having to up sticks every spring to make way for armies, people have been able to actually get good crops out of the land around here."

"I'm glad," Gwen said. Then the conversation turned back to their cards and they both concentrated on that for a time before the baker begged off, as he had an early morning and couldn't stay up too late.

His spot was filled by a cheerfully dishabille middle-aged woman who was one of those ladies who, it was clear, had decided to grow old disgracefully. She introduced herself as Patty and she was much harder for Gwen to lie to. Her eyes were just that bit too bright and her smile a little too sharp for Gwen to feel confident that she could get anything past her.

They had a good game of cards nonetheless, though it didn't stop Gwen giving a sigh of relief when she lost. The other woman drew a hand of cards that was implausibly good, if not quite im-possibly, and left with a cackling laugh.

After that, the night became more about how much parsnip wine and mead and beer she could hold and it became harder to get any reliable information. Or to be able to tell what was reliable and what was nonsense.

Wobbling up to fall into bed she lay spread eagled across the soft woolen blankets and stroked her face back and forth on the fabric. There was a joyful little cloud of bubbles living inside her now, and they liked the feel of the snuggly wool very much.

Blearily, with her eyes closed against the world around her, she waved off a few notifications and paid attention to some others just long enough to add a point to Charm thanks to a recent level up, confident that sober Gwen would approve.

Then she toppled off the cliff of consciousness into the dark and mysterious realm of sleep.

Chapter 4

Name: Gwen Baird

Class:	Hunter		
Level:	5		
Health:	25		

Species: Half-Elf (Wood/Human)

Strength:	6	Mind:	6
Agility:	5	Body:	5
Armour:	3	Sense:	6

Species Skills: (Half-Elf)

Elf Sight:	3		

Base Skills: (Hunter)

Dodge:	1	Perception:	2
Tracking:	4	Stealth:	2
Charm:	6	Archery:	1

When Gwen woke, up the night before rolled under her eyelids like a movie: she was surprised to find she didn't regret a moment of it.

Not even using one of the precious stat increases she got when she levelled up to boost her Charm. Her Agility and Body were still on the base 5 that she had started off with, which might be some-thing she would come to regret. But right now she couldn't find it in her to do so.

This was for three reasons, the first being that it turned out that in the game a night's sleep was all that was needed to wash away the aches and pains of the previous day: a very handy trick when it came to hangovers. The second was the simple fact that if she was going to live with these stats rather than just play with them, then she was going to need to be able to talk her way out of trouble. And third, well, she had made worse decisions while drunk. Like hack-ing into the trust fund of the obnoxious twerp in her class at Uni. And that had ended up alright. At the very least she hadn't gotten into any trouble for it, and it had shown her that Higher Education had not been for her. Which had been a valuable saving in time.

But, drunk Gwen tended to be pretty lucky and in a world where luck was a recognisable skill, it made sense to capitalise on the actions which precipitated it. Though it might be wise to wait a bit before she got that drunk again, even if her liver was immune to being pickled.

Gwen sat up, bright eyed, with a familiarity with the local land-scape gained from the locals and the knowledge that if she picked twenty-one rose hips a very nice lady called Renna would give her six silver. This didn't seem very much when compared with the beer, but it was early days yet, so there was probably nothing better to hope for than noob fetch quests.

She was pulling on her clothes, having woken up enough at some point in the night to scatter her clothes to every corner of the room, when, a touch sheepishly, Marina walked in. Her hair was a mess and she seemed to have put on at least one part of her armour on backwards.

Gwen let loose a snort, "And what time do you call this, young lady?" she asked, putting on a fairly good impression of their mother.

"Oh, don't start. I've been having a horrible time the last few months, I needed to find a way to work out my stress," Marina said, uncaring of the smirking judgment that Gwen was sending her way. She paused as she started to pull off her armour. "S-Day, might," she said slowly, "have been a wee bit tougher than I was letting you know."

"What do you mean?" Gwen asked, her smirk slipped away as she paused doing up a buckle.

"Well, it's never easy saying goodbye to the kids when they're leaving, whether it's for the next year or because they're moving, or whatever, but watching them go to leave Earth was heart breaking," Marina rubbed a hand over her face. "A lot of them were leaving their parents behind, and it's not like people took care to make sure kids ended up on the same ships as their friends or more distant relations. Apparently, it was hard enough to make sure that kids got on the same ones as their siblings and cousins, anything further out than that and they were shit out of luck. And the kids knew that. There were five- and six-year-olds going off into space knowing that they would never see their parents again. That their best friends would be leaving too, but on a different ship and maybe heading in a different direction entirely. It was agonizing to watch them be so brave. Especially since none of them wanted to be any extra trouble. It was like they had all taken a pact to not be a hassle. They knew all the adults were working really hard to keep them safe, and kids are smart and empathetic enough to not want to add onto that."

Gwen's heart ached, "I'm sorry Marina, that sounds," she closed a fist, not quite able to bring the right words to her tongue, "hellish," she said finally.

"It was," Marina said. Then she stopped and looked around as if checking there weren't any spies hidden in the shadows. "The worst thing was that in my class there were a couple of kids whose parents had refused to let them be put on the ships." She whispered the words.

A bitterness flooded Gwen's mouth, "That's murder."

"They say because Earth will still be mostly liveable that it's not. They want to keep their families together, which I can understand, but…" She shook her head. "I'm sorry I shouldn't be dumping all of this on you. It's not fair of me to leave all of my baggage on your shoulders."

Gwen walked over and brought her sister into her arms in a tight hug. "That's what I'm here for, dummy."

Marina hugged back for a moment, "Come on, we need to get ready. I'll process my angst by ignoring it and doing something useful." Marina was making it clear that she knew her decision to do so probably wasn't the healthiest one, but it was the one they had available, and she would not be taking any commentary on the decision.

"Okay," Gwen stepped back after giving a last squeeze, "I'm pretty much done, so I'll go grab something for breakfast and see if we can get some lunch for the road."

Marina gave her a watery smile, then moved to the bed where the rest of her things had been flung the night before.

Gwen let herself out, and as she walked down the stairs to the tap room she couldn't get Marina's words out of her mind.

It both was and wasn't murder. Some would survive the end of the world, she didn't doubt that. Humans had managed to live through a tonne of things they shouldn't have, a sudden cessation in modern tech was unlikely to kill everyone.

But the odds weren't good. Especially for kids who would always be the most vulnerable when times were tough. Choosing to keep your child with you on a planet as it went through a century of shit, well, was it better than murder? But was it better to send them off on a spaceship that might, might, come back in a century? If the planet wasn't too devastated by all the left behind nuclear bombs people had forgotten about, or the natural disasters that could spring up, but now without the benefit of unnatural remedies. Plus, there was all the even weirder stuff that she had caught hints of when she hacked government servers to show off. People had been coming up with new and stranger ways to kill each other for every moment of humanity's existence, and an apocalypse was the perfect chance to try some of them out. She wasn't naive enough to hope that everyone would work together and be a big friendly community. Earth hadn't even managed something close to that in less stressful times.

And people wanted to keep their kids in the midst of that? How scared of the alternative did they have to be to think it was worth the risk? She didn't have any kids, so it had never been a choice she had had to make. And she was very, very glad of it.

The tap room was quiet, one of the barmaids, Nora, was scrubbing down the tables, and she grinned as Gwen came in. Gwen went over to her and smiled, "Do you have anything that I could have for breakfast, oh beautiful siren of the ales and wines?"

"That depends, do you want a liquid breakfast or a solid one that will set you up for the day?" she asked, looking a little impressed that Gwen had made it downstairs so early after the drinking that had gone on the night before.

"I would like something that'll stick to my ribs, if that's possible, I think I had enough booze last night to keep me going for a long while," Gwen said with a smile.

"Thank goodness, because if you had asked for anything stronger than milk I would have had to tell you to go elsewhere for it. You and your sister damn near cleared us out last night," Nora said, "come on, there's a pot of porridge cooking this way. It'll stick to your ribs alright."

Gwen laughed, "That sounds perfect."

The kitchen was a cosy nest blocking out the rest of the world. The beams that ran along the ceiling had bundles of herbs and dried spices hanging down, so that the whole space had the smell of a thousand meals waiting to be made.

The elderly woman making the porridge was introduced to Gwen as Amy, the barman's mother and the cook for the inn. Over a sweet porridge that felt like it was enriching her from the soul outwards, Gwen got to know her. They talked about the girls, including Jessica – whose farm was the goal of their quest mission – and Gwen got a better picture of the family in her mind.

They were the same as most of the people in the area, mostly human, but with a thin scattering of elven traits. It meant that Gwen and Marina were able to fit in without too much fuss, but, by the sound of it, Jessica had never had quite an easy a time there.

"Oh, she was always an independent one, our Jessica, she figured out how to walk just so she could get away from her parents all the faster. We thought after her David died she'd come back, but she didn't want to leave the life they had built together," Amy said as she got started on the soup for lunch.

Gwen, having finished with her breakfast, moved instinctively to help, picking up a knife and starting to peel the carrots. It was a lot easier than in real life, the added points in knife skills seemed to pay off in the kitchen as well as in the battlefield.

As always as she started working through a new skill the notifications came quickly, so she tucked them out of sight and concentrated on the conversation she was having.

"I can understand that, sometimes if all you have left of a person is a place, leaving it behind can feel like losing them all over again." She passed over the carrots.

"Thank you, dear. And I suppose you have a point; I hadn't thought of it like that. I thought she was just being difficult," Amy admitted bluntly. She took the carrots gratefully and started chopping them up, "Could you do the onions, dear? I get the worst reaction to them."

Gwen nodded, peeling then slicing the onions into thin slivers. It felt like being at home. Food had always been important to her family, not just the actual eating part, but making it too. It had been a chance to pull everyone in and be creative together. *I must have more memories of cooking than I do of eating in that kitchen back home*, she thought with a distant smile. *Who knew what that kitchen looked like now?* Her smile disappeared.

Marina's boots clicked their way into the kitchen, "Morning." She slid in beside her sister. "Got a knife for me to use?"

"Sure!" Gwen said, then handed her own over with a smile. Marina just rolled her eyes.

"Amy, I would like you to meet my sister Marina; don't let her get you in any trouble," Gwen said with a grin, "I'm going to the little half-elves' room."

She left the pair chatting as she went to the toilet where, she was relieved to find out, that while the amenities were rudimentary, they were not historically accurate for the medieval period.

***

They left soon after, dawn had already passed, though it was hard to tell, given how shadowy the forest was. But with their half-elf vision they were able to see easily with even that little light. Gwen had managed to get a sturdy lunch for them, fresh rolls and cheese, which would keep them going on the long walk through the woods. Knowing that there were beasts out here that meant them ill was enough to stub out any talk between them.

Gwen's growing Elf Sight felt like it was being bolstered by every breath of fresh air she took. The outlines of living animals and plants, she found, glowed when she blinked the sense into place over her normal vision. She could see the birds waking in the trees and the mice scurrying through the leaves and bushes on the ground. Even with the threat of the weird animal insect hybrids on the loose, it was a dreamlike sensation to walk while seeing both the leaf-filled branches and the birds hidden in their embrace.

After a little while Gwen also realised that the way she was thinking about it all was becoming a little too poetic. *This*, she thought, *must be why elves in books and movies and games were always singing and dancing around the place: seeing life in this way was like a particularly friendly high.*

It was that feeling though that made her take the filter off her gaze. This was not the moment to be feeling silly. And besides, while getting more experience into her Tracking and Experience skills was certainly useful she had to concentrate on what needed now, which was better visibility, rather than attempting to meta game and get a little bit further ahead.

The road to Jessica's farm hadn't been travelled much, so grass covered it and more than one industrious shrub or small sapling had grown up over the ruts. Something hanging off one of them caught her eye. Frowning, Gwen knelt, giving a low hum to alert Marina to what she was doing.

Marina walked back to her, "What is it?" she whispered.

"A piece of cloth, trapped on this bramble here," Gwen said, picking it off the branch. "Someone else has been this way and in enough of a hurry that they didn't care what tore as they went."

Marina nodded, looking around. She shifted her stance and pulled her mace free.

Gwen put the scrap into a bag on her belt. "How far is it to the farm, do you think?"

Marina shrugged, "They said it was what, 15 miles? We've only been walking a couple of hours, we can't be that close yet."

Nodding, Gwen stood once more. "Shouldn't be someone from the farm then, not this far out."

Marina nodded, "Other locals, or some Adventurers, do you think?"

"Well," Gwen stood back up from her crouch, "Locals don't seem to travel out this way much. But we haven't seen any other Adventurers." She moved her hands in a balancing motion. "It could be either."

Marina pursed her lips, "I hope it's some more Adventurers. This forest is giving me the creeps, I'd feel safer if we were travelling in a bigger party."

"Agreed," Gwen said, there was a chill in the air that she was fairly sure was actually just her mind playing tricks on her, but all the same she would welcome some back up.

As they turned back onto the road Gwen kept running her fingers over the knife sheaths on her arms and the hilt of her sword on her hip. The forest felt darker, even though dawn was now well under way.

That was when Gwen noticed something, something a country girl like her should have seen far earlier. Though the birds were sitting on the branches, they were not singing. They were just sitting there, as if they were too afraid to draw attention to themselves. Even the starlings, which seemed to make up about two thirds of the local avian population, were silent. They sat hunkered down on the branches like there was a storm coming. Utterly silent, utterly still.

Marina caught onto the back of Gwen's cloak.

Gwen started to ask her what exactly she thought she was doing, then she caught sight of the look on Marina's face. Her head snapped around to look at whatever had caught her sister's attention.

Earlier, a branch of the nearby stream had left off the main body; it followed the shape of the path, a muddy bank and ditch separating the two. But here something had broken the lines of the bank, making the ditch a muddy pond for a few feet around it.

Some of the liquid on the road was the oddly gleaming mud that came from the blood of the monsters.

And, of course, in amongst the mud were several footprints. All about the same size and shape, so probably the same person. And, as if that wasn't bad enough, deep in the mud, like the weight of the fall had punched down into it, were a pair of handprints. There were no secondary ones that might have suggested the person then struggled out of the mud. Just the two, deep, handprints that had been there long enough to start weathering, and for the ground at the bottom to be obscured with muddy water.

Gwen's hands went to her weapons and she gave Marina a nod. Slowly, they started off again. Gwen's skill in Stealth giving her the edge and steering her feet around the loudest and most crunchy sticks and leaves, while she scanned the surrounding area with her Elf Sight. There was nothing to see. Nothing, not even what should have been there.

The air seemed to grow ever colder and heavier, not even a peep from a bird to cut through the gathering tension. The animals in the underbrush had all either fled or were better at hiding than any Gwen had encountered before.

On the other hand, the road became less of a hint as they travelled on. It wasn't merely a thin line of crushed grass anymore, there were hoof prints from some sort of cloven-hoofed animal everywhere. Even more clearly to Gwen's senses, the earth of the road felt more tightly packed, she could feel the difference between the ground where animals had trod so many times and the areas outside the path.

They started passing empty fields surrounded by low stone walls and hedgerows in a pick-and-mix configuration. The branches and trunks started to become thinner, the trees out this way appeared to be younger. There were stumps of old trees mixed in among them, evidence of a presence in the woods that was not entirely natural. But care had been taken to keep the landscape as close to a healthy balance between what humans wanted and what the forest needed.

The elf in Gwen found herself approving.

The human side was very disconcerted to find out that there was a new elf side at all.

Eventually, the road turned around a large oak and they got their first view of the farm. It should have been a pretty and picturesque spot. Fields surrounded by stone walls and flower filled hedges, a small stream coaxed to travel through the corners of the fields to give the animals that should have been their water. But it was the "should of" that were the sticking point, the animals filling the fields and detracting from the picturesque view were not any that would be found in a typical farmer's barn.

Instead, the fields were filled with monsters. And they all, with an eerie synchronicity, turned to look at the twins.

Wolves with chitinous sides and scorpion tails scented the air, something that might have been part bear but which was covered instead with the bristly hairs of a tarantula started a thunderous growl, and of course plenty of the beetle-boar hybrids that Gwen had such fond memories of filled the odd corners and shaded dips of the fields.

Gwen gulped and almost turned tail and ran away right then, but Marina grabbed her by the wrist, "No look, look at the farm, at that wall!" She said pointing to a spot on the nearest wall.

A hand, waving frantically, was trying to get them to come closer. Gwen was tempted to answer it with a shouted swear, but she didn't want to startle the monsters into charging. They were just looking, for now, and she would rather like to keep it that way.

"Okay, what do we do?" Gwen asked, barely breathing out the words, she was trying to stay so still and so quiet.

"I think we're going to have to book it up the road to the farm," Marina whispered back, clearly trying her very best to look like an oddly shiny tree.

"That is suicide, there's a tonne of the damn things and only two of us; we can't hope to fight them off by the time we get to the gate into the farmyard," Gwen whispered back fiercely. And it was true, the large heavy, gate that bridged a gap between the high stone walls of the farmyard looked like it had been pried off a ruined castle. Or at least, that's how it seemed to Gwen whilst she was far way and on the wrong side.

"Maybe, but they're all further from the gate than we are," Marina hissed, "look at them, they're all circled round the farm, but they are furthest from the gate. If we run, really, really run, we can do it." She paused, "Especially if I do this." Marina concentrated for a moment, her hold on Gwen's arm becoming firmer. A shiver seemed to travel down the arm and hit Gwen like bucket of cold water. It also seemed to be the signal to the monsters to attack, which was even less pleasant. But even as they all leapt forward and started to run, they looked like they were running through quicksand.

Marina, on the other hand, was moving like she had been blasted out of a cannon. She was sprinting down the road in the direction of the gate with the arm-pumping determination of someone with a grudge against the world record holder. Gwen did her best to keep up, but her sister was outpacing her.

"What the hell did you do?" she shouted, keeping a wary eye on the nearest beasts, which all seemed to be running through treacle to get them.

"At this level I can give out a blessing once per day, this one's called Blessing of the Falcon, nice isn't it!" Marina said, not turning her head.

Gwen could admit it was, it was also the only reason she was escaping an especially ugly-looking creature that was half-rat half-earwig; she decided to show how much she appreciated the buff by conserving her breath so that she could stay alive.

The pair thundered down the path, stealthiness completely abandoned. Soon, they were within jumping distance of the gate; the gate opened just a sliver, enough for Gwen and Marina to slide in. There was a person there to grab them about the arms and yank them clear of the gate, a second pushed past them and started to launch spells that hissed and sparked in the air at the monsters. Other bodies around her shoved the gates shut with solid thump.

Gwen wobbled for a moment, then fell to her knees, while Marina turned white as the power of the Blessing abruptly left them and they were returned to the normal speed of the world.

"They're running off," a high voice shouted from the wall above them. Gwen looked up, a short kid was sat on a ledge pulled out of the wall and looking out at the monsters outside.

She turned her gaze to the people the kid was speaking to, they were both non-human and probably Adventurers. She recognised the tailoring of their clothes as Dove's work.

Dove's crafting was exceptional, everything fit perfectly and there was never a thread out of place or a fold of cloth that fell wrong. But everything was made out of the plainest material that could exist and it was made even plainer by the complete lack of ornamentation. There wasn't a bit of trim, or embroidery, or even thread in a contrasting colour. The buttons were universally dull and practical. Compared to the locals you could pick out a newly arrived Adventurer by their aggressively beige (even when not actually wearing beige it still had a beige quality to it) but beautifully put-together clothing.

One appeared to be a dwarf: dark-skinned, he was broad not just across the shoulders, but everywhere, and had an intricately braided beard. The other was a devilish looking woman, she was middle-aged, with light reddish-purple skin, two twisting ram-like horns, and a tail ending in a fistful of blue-toned purple feathers, which was waving back and forth behind her.

"Good, we don't want them to think we're weakening," she turned from the kid on the wall to the twins, "I'm Jin Ae, this is Theo. We met in the forest and took shelter here when the monsters wouldn't leave us be. Were you in a similar predicament?"

"Not exactly," said Marina, as Gwen was still sitting gasping on the ground, "We faced off with some yesterday but made it to the local village. The inn owner—"

"You spoke to my father?" Another voice, this time from a woman standing in the doorway of the nearby barn. She was dressed in an outfit that could have been lifted from her father's wardrobe it was so similar in style, but it had clearly been made for her and had been kept in good nick by dint with hard work from a needle.

"Jessica?" Marina asked. The woman nodded. "Then, yes, your father asked us to come out here and check up on you. After we told him about the creatures we had faced on our way in to the village he grew concerned with the length of time since he had heard from you. So he asked us to come and see if everything was alright, but, uh, clearly, it's not."

"An understatement," Jin Ae said, lashing her tail against her legs in agitation. "We've managed to pick off a few of the creatures, but there's too many and they've figured out to not group together within range of our spells."

Theo spoke up in a clear and deliberate way "I'm glad you two made it here, we really needed more fighters to help, and," he said with a warm smile, "it's good to know that there *are* other

66

Adventurers out there. I've been here a few days and I've only seen Jin Ae."

Jessica stepped out of the barn's doorway and spoke. "I think you two could do with a chance to sit down somewhere a bit more comfortable than my farmyard, why don't you come into the house so we can talk?"

"That would be wonderful," Gwen said, standing up and brushing some hay off the seat of her leggings. "It's lovely to meet you, despite the circumstances." They were shown across the farmyard and into the tidy little house on the other side from the gate.

Jessica nodded to show that she had heard but said little else. She seemed distinctly ruffled by the presence of so many new people on her farm.

Or perhaps I'm being unkind, Gwen thought. *She does have thirty-odd monsters trying to kill her and her children, that's worth ruffled feathers and standoffishness.*

Jessica continued to stay silent as they walked into the kitchen, everyone stopping to take off their muddy boots. She moved towards the large, wrought-iron stove that filled what seemed to be half the kitchen; on top of it was a big pot of steamily boiling water, from which she took enough to fill a tea pot. "How do you take your tea?" she asked.

"Strong and sweet, if it's no bother," Gwen said. Marina echoed her.

Jessica nodded and spooned some tea leaves into the pot. She took a deep breath and turned to speak to them, "Thank you for coming, I know you've put yourselves to a lot of bother and danger to come out this far, but…" She took a breath, "I'm not leavin'."

"What?" Gwen and Marina asked in the same moment.

"I have cows and sheep in that barn that won't survive if I leave them. My husband and I raised them, I can't just waste their lives by leaving them to starve to death or be picked off by the animals of the forest. Those creatures out there don't seem to be interested in them, but there's plenty else that is. I am not leaving them, especially when it would be suicide to leave the walls of this farmyard anyway." She shook her head, "I'm sorry that you've come out here for no good reason, and I'll be happy to put you up until the monsters leave, but I'm not going."

"You'd put your children in danger that way?" Marina asked, her temper rising like the red in her cheeks.

Jessica seemed surprised by that tack, but squared her shoulders and looked her in the eye, "What's more dangerous, keeping them here or sending them through a monster-infested forest?"

Marina had to look away after a minute of them holding each other's gaze.

"Jessica, you have a point. But you have to see that this isn't sustainable. Your animals can't stay in the barn forever. You need to see to your crops. I can't imagine they're doing alright without minding," Gwen kept her voice friendly.

"If we just wait them out I am sure the monsters will leave, there's plenty of other places they can go in this forest with easier prey, so I don't see why they should stick around here," Jessica answered. She moved the teapot closer to the middle of the table and went to get some mugs from one of the cupboards.

Nothing they said changed her mind. Jessica was stubborn and her mind was made up. Eventually, when their tea was drunk and they had no arguments left to make, the two left to go speak to the Adventurers out in the yard.

Marina was still fuming, but Gwen was preoccupied with other thoughts. When the argument had seemed lost, something else that Jessica had said had prompted a rethink. "Marina?"

"Damn, stubborn…Yeah?" Marina said, her shoulders up around her ears and her face turning puce.

"The monsters are not going after the farm animals," Gwen said pointedly.

Marina seemed confused for a moment, then the words sunk in and her eyes widened. "No, they're not."

"They're after, what? Specific people?" Gwen asked.

"Or, specifically, Adventurers," Marina said, her eyes narrowing in suspicion, "when there were two inside and two outside, they all were paused. They didn't know what to do."

"Well, shit," said Gwen. "Let's tell our new friends, shall we?"

Marina sighed and nodded, following her into the barn.

Chapter 5

Name: Gwen Baird

Class:	Hunter		
Level:	5		
Health:	25		

Species: Half-Elf (Wood/Human)

Strength:	6	Mind:	6
Agility:	5	Body:	5
Armour:	3	Sense:	6

Species Skills: (Half-Elf)

Elf Sight:	5

Base Skills: (Hunter)

Dodge:	1	Perception:	5
Tracking:	6	Stealth:	4
Charm:	6	Archery:	1

The Adventurers seemed to have been given free rein over the hay loft and had thrown blankets and cloaks over mounds of hay to try and make decent beds. Gwen was very grateful that she had been able to sleep in an actual bed at the inn, the hay looked like it would scratch even through the multiple layers of wool.

The building was large and square and here beneath the roof it was a sharply angled set of eaves that sat over them. The windows were on one side, which helpfully pointed out over the gate, revealing the roiling mass of monsters. They seemed to be moving around in unhappy confusion. Gwen almost missed the last step of the ladder when she saw them, there were definitely more than there had been when they had arrived. Either that, or they were all concentrating around the front of the farm because that was where the action had been.

The demonspawn female gestured to a pair of crates. She seemed to be the more talkative and she shared a look with her companion, before taking the initiative and leading the conversation, answering a question from Marina.

She ran her hands over her hair, hair that was a deep black and tightly braided to the shape of her skull, showing off the curling horns that rose out of her forehead. "Sure, but there isn't much to tell. I appeared in the game, didn't know what was going on for a few seconds and couldn't have been much easier prey. I was in the middle of a densely forested patch near here, and that turned out to be incredibly fortunate for me," She took a breath and ploughed on, "I'm sitting – well, lying practically prone against a tree is closer to the truth and it's harder than you would think when you have a tail – and this thing comes out at me from between two big trees. Or at least it tries to, it had the head of a deer, massive antlers, and the body of what can only be described as a very angry spider, with extra pincers because, apparently, why not? Anyway, I was laid out on the ground, already thinking 'Oh, I'm dead, that's unlucky to go this fast' and the thing gets its antlers stuck in a tree. Its head gets yanked back, which slows its run at me, and this gives me enough time to get out my sword and stab it as many times as I can." She paled a little, the red of her skin turning to a dark pink, "It was entirely instinctual, it was quite frightening how I went from trying to figure how to sit with a tail to just going at that monster with my sword. Then it disappears, leaving behind some unpleasant-looking material that I hope was its blood, because it could have been any part of the animal. And I stood there in the forest for a good bit longer, in shock, I suppose, then I heard a noise behind me and I'm getting ready for the second attack of antler spiders, so I turn around, and Theo here comes out of the forest looking about as shocked as I felt."

Theo gave a jaunty wave.

"My story is pretty much the same. I appeared in the middle of nowhere, head spinning, only for some*thing* to jump out at me from behind a bush. I'm a mage, but an Enchanter, not someone who is supposed to be on the frontlines of any battlefield. I have a couple of good spells for fire, so that's what I used. I blasted the thing away from me and then just kept hitting it with everything I had until it disappeared. Uh, after that I ran as far away from that spot as I could get. And then I stumbled across Jin Ae and honestly I've never been so glad to see someone else."

"Same here, believe me, I wasn't sure what I was going to do. But between us we got onto a road, walked for several kilometres and saw the farm. Jessica was in one of the fields outside, we told her what we had seen and she brought us and the animals in. She seemed pretty shocked, not as though she thought we were lying about it, they do get monsters around here sometimes. But never something like what we had seen. She let us sleep up here for the night, we needed the rest, we were both pretty badly beaten up by everything. I had a flourishing bruise where my monster had kicked me in the shoulder, and Theo had some slices taken out of him. That was yesterday. Within an hour or so the first monsters started showing up and they haven't left since. We've tried to get as many as we could from within the farm, but they figured out how close they could come to the walls pretty quickly. After that they stayed out of range of our spells. And then, this morning," she sighed and looked back at Theo.

Theo's face looked pinched and deeply stressed. "Everything we killed reappeared like it was respawning, like an Adventurer. And more keep coming." He sent a look out the window before taking his own seat, "There's probably some more getting here already."

"Shit," Gwen said eloquently.

Jin Ae nodded, "That's pretty much how we felt as well."

Theo snorted, "Yeah not the best thing to wake up to. Herds, or flocks, or whatever, of monsters sitting outside watching the walls of the farmyard. Deeply unsettling."

"Not to look a gift horse in the mouth, but why haven't they attacked? The walls aren't that big or defensive?" Gwen asked.

Theo grinned, "That was some of my work. Enchanter magic has some serious force behind it when it comes to defence. All the monster killing pushed me up through the first few levels pretty fast, every cloud, I guess. But it got me access to a spell, *Repulsion*, which I cast on the wall and it's been doing the trick nicely. Plus I've been making spending the last day or so making eldritch caltrops out of any scrap metal I can get my hands on. Those I've been chucking over the wall and if anything steps on them then they are going to wish the only thing they have to worry about is a stabbed foot," he seemed to drift off for a moment, "There's some seriously nasty stuff in the Enchanter's tool kit, let me tell ya. If you ever see me chucking globules of green fire with glowing red centres just hunker down wherever you are, don't try to run, it won't make much difference. Nasty stuff."

"And anytime something has come to test if *Repulsion* is still up, we've thrown everything we have at it; so now they're just waiting outside of our range, which is an improvement, in some ways," Jin Ae said.

"Yeah, the sizzling noises those orbs made kind of freaked me out," Theo said in a low tone.

"I was meaning more because of the fact that it made us safer," Jin Ae said with an amused look, before adding with a grimace, "though that sizzling was an uncomfortable sound to hear, you're right."

Gwen looked at her sister. Marina took charge.

"Well our story is a lot alike the both of yours, Gwen jumped out a tree onto a beetle thing, and then turned up right when I needed her in a fight with some wolf scorpion beasties. Have I said thank you?" she asked, suddenly frowning.

"Yes," Gwen said.

"Right, good, because by the sound of it without our team up I would have been even more fucked over than I thought I was, and I thought I was pretty fucked up. But we got to the nearest village, nice place, called Starlingrise, and we spoke to a couple of people there. One of whom was Jessica's dad who asked us to come out here and check on her, because it turns out all these monsters are really not normal for this area. It's generally pretty quiet," Marina finished.

"Aside, apparently, from the occasional undead that wanders over from a cursed battlefield near here," Gwen added.

"So, what's made this all happen, then?" Theo asked, leaning forward from his own seat on a nearby upturned bucket.

Gwen spread her arms, "Our idea is that with all of us Adventurers arriving the local area was needing more drama. Peaceful wasn't part of what we signed up for, I guess, though I don't think giant terrifying bug monsters was what we signed up for either."

"It certainly wasn't on any of the introductory material," Jin Ae agreed.

"Maybe it's a sort of hazing thing? Make us all think we're going to die so we get more into the game? I mean the four of us all lived," Theo asked, "And we're a lot more levelled up than we would have been otherwise, so it could just be a way of getting new Adventurers past the awkward stage when a couple of hits will have you on the floor."

Gwen shook her head and pulled the scrap of fabric from her pocket. "I think that's just survivor bias, we found some signs that there had been a fight on the road up here. Whoever it was didn't make it out. I'd say we are probably the lucky ones who survived that first attack, rather than being unlucky enough to face an attack at all. With you two here with similar stories, I can't really buy that we just happened to pull the short straws that had monsters attached to them."

Jin Ae frowned while Theo stared at it with wide eyes. "Well that's concerning," Jin Ae muttered. Again she ran her hands over her hair and horns, before forcing them down into her lap and breathing out. "Right then, what are we going to do? I assume we're teaming up for this. It seems sensible to work together," she looked briefly around the group.

No one disagreed.

Theo gnawed at his lower lip, "It's possible," he said slowly, "That I could read the fabric for who made it and such. That is if you don't mind me taking a look?"

Gwen handed it over happily, "Please do."

He held it out on one palm, the forefinger from his other hand spearing it in the middle like a preserved butterfly. He started muttering, his eyes glowed for a second and the scrap of fabric seemed to soak up that light, before giving a life-like shiver and then falling flat against his palm again.

"OK, so not much to tell you. It is part of an Adventurer's starting kit, you were right. Which means I've got zero info on previous owners or the people that made it because there weren't any. It's all Dove's making, I can tell you it was part of a sleeve and it is a ninety-five to five percent wool and silk blend," he sighed and gave it back, "sorry, not very useful that."

"Knowing for sure that it belonged to an Adventurer is useful," Gwen assured him. "But it does mean that if the monsters are hunting Adventurers specifically then maybe we just need to leave," Gwen said.

"But I don't want to leave them, I'd feel like I was running, abandoning them," Theo protested.

"We would be running. Sometimes that's the safest thing to do for the people you leave behind," Jin Ae said. "But we'd have to kill everything waiting out there first. If they are respawning like Adventurers, then we might have a shot to draw them away. If we were gone when they were set to reappear then they wouldn't have any reason to come here."

"I guess if we're already bait we might as well use that to our advantage and get the monsters to follow us," Gwen said, "Though I would say the chances of us actually killing everything out there is pretty slim, I mean there's got to be a tonne of monster for each of us out there." That was a grim enough proclamation that it made the others grimace, but they didn't have any way to counter it.

Marina frowned, "You two haven't been to a temple yet. have you?"

Theo shook his head, "There isn't one here."

Gwen winced, "So if you die you just get catapulted off somewhere else in the game?"

"Presumably," Jin Ae agreed. "Along with numerous debuffs and ongoing problems as punishment for screwing up."

"OK, well we have been to a temple, so if either of us die we'll just pop back up at Starlingrise with a headache," Marina said. "I mean I think our experience gets cleared back to the beginning of the level, but we're levelling pretty fast right now so it wouldn't set us back too far."

"As long as there is someone around to pick up our stuff, losing everything we started the game with is a heck of a deterrent," Gwen pointed out.

Marina smirked, "I mean I think you get to keep what you're wearing."

"One of the things I'll be able to make at higher levels is a pouch that can't be stolen or lost when you die," Theo added helpfully. "But that doesn't change the fact that I would rather not die right now. I mean, what's the saying, "Better the Devil you know?" Wait, sorry Jin Ae, that's probably rude isn't it?"

Jin Ae shrugged, "I wouldn't know, I've been in this body for less than two days. I'm not even used to the horns and tail yet; I can learn what sayings are offensive after I've managed to sit down without sitting on my tail three times in a row."

"Right well, I know what the problems are here," Theo continued, "more or less, anyway. Wherever I end up next might be worse, and at least the weather's decent here and the people seem friendly enough even if the monsters aren't. Not that dying ever seems like a really good idea. I mean, it usually isn't, but right now, I'd rather not," he gave a sheepish shrug.

As a statement went, "I would prefer not to die right now" was a hard one to disagree with. It would be painful and inconvenient, and it would strip them of much needed experience points. And while Gwen had been given more stirring speeches in her life and more inspiring war cries, this was one she could work with. "Alright, so what are we going to do?"

Everyone looked around at each other waiting for someone else to announce their amazing plan.

"Fuck it, let's sneak out there and kill any we can before they notice we're there and then figure it out as it comes," Marina said, standing up with a sigh and a push against her knees.

"Plan to not plan?" Gwen asked.

Marina threw her arms wide, "It's been working so far. Let's see how far we can push this thing."

Chapter 6

Name: Gwen Baird

Class:	Hunter		
Level:	5		
Health:	25		

Species: Half-Elf (Wood/Human)

Strength:	6	Mind:	6
Agility:	5	Body:	5
Armour:	3	Sense:	6

Species Skills: (Half-Elf)

Elf Sight:	3

Base Skills: (Hunter)

Dodge:	1	Perception:	5
Tracking:	6	Stealth:	4
Charm:	6	Archery:	1

The plan didn't become any more concrete the longer they stayed up in the hay loft. But the sun kept moving and the ranks of monsters outside the farm stopped growing.

"They look settled, I doubt any more will come before tomorrow morning," Jin Ae said to Gwen from a spot she had claimed by the open window.

"How many are out there?" Gwen asked. She had been practising with her bow, shooting arrows one after the other into a mound of hay on the other side of the barn. The repetitive movement of sight along the arrow, draw the string back, shoot, then after a few minutes, go fetch the handful of arrows she had with her, was helping to keep her calm, almost like meditation. She still didn't have enough experience from her skills to level up, but she had at least gotten her Archery skill to a respectable level 5. She wouldn't be doing the Robin Hood trick where you shoot the centre of your own arrow on the target, but she hit things more often than not.

She brought up the tracker for her experience and glared at it. It was closer to getting her to Level 6 and the spells that she would be able to pick up there, but even with all of her practise, she wasn't near that target yet.

"Well, if what I can see is about a quarter of the circle around the farm, then I'd say there was about two hundred," Jin Ae spoke very calmly.

"Shit," Gwen said less calmly as her knees wobbled.

"If they bed down tonight we need to go out then; it'll be dark but that will be a problem for them as much as for us," Jin Ae said bluntly. "If they're quietening now we might need to get ready soon." She looked over to where the sun was not yet near the horizon and frowned.

"Demonspawn can see in the dark, I take it?" Gwen said, walking over to the mound of hay that had been her target and starting to pull the arrows from the mess she had made of it.

"Extremely well, it is a definite advantage," Jin Ae said quietly, her odd pupil and iris-lacking eyes looking out at the monsters.

Gwen nodded, "half-elves too, and I assume dwarves can see fine in the dark."

"Or else they would certainly have a difficult time of it underground," agreed Jin Ae.

"I guess we'll just have to hope that those monsters out there can't see as well as us, then."

Jin Ae gave a murmur as an answer, but not much more. To Gwen, who was in a similarly scattered frame of mind, it was enough.

They both jumped when footsteps came in a clatter up the ladder behind them.

Turning, Gwen saw one of the kids, one of Jessica's children. "Hello?" The word turned into a question halfway through.

The boy had flat blond hair that stuck up in every direction at the back but at the front dangled into his eyes. "Theo and Marina said to come and fetch you, they've got magic they want to do on you," he said gleefully.

The creases beside Gwen's mouth deepened a touch as Gwen stepped forward, "Then we'd better hurry to join them."

They met Jessica first as they came out of the barn. She had her arms folded and looked both scared and furious at being scared.

Gwen stepped over to talk to Jessica, "How does this normally work? Do you get attacked by monsters often or..." she trailed off.

Jessica frowned. "Does this farm look like it's built to defend against much of anything? We have walls because otherwise farm animals tend to try and make a run for it, not because we expect monsters and Adventurers to come out of the forest every other day." Her voice made it clear she felt both were equal nuisances, though the ones that could ask stupid questions were particularly irritating in that moment.

Trying not to feel cowed by that answer, Gwen pushed on, "But things have to happen once in a while, in the village they mentioned that you sometimes get undead here from the barrens?"

Jessica waved a hand dismissively. "They're barely any trouble, they can't cross boundaries claimed by the living so they don't even come close to the farm. Too many fences for them to figure out a way past and they're not often smart enough to figure out roads or gates. Typically, they're just old soldiers from the wars between the elves and the dwarves; they're more sad than something to be properly scared of. They wave around swords rusted down to nothing and half their armour has already fallen off so if you hit them a couple of times they'll crumble into dust. Nikolai in the village is pretty handy when they do cause a bit of trouble, they steer clear of him so you can herd them." She gave a shrug, "We don't worry about monsters much around here. There's never been much of a need to!"

"Alright," Gwen said, trying not to feel guilty because, gods this really did prove that it was the Adventurers turning up that had caused all the trouble, "But what do you do when something does turn up?"

"You kill it," Jessica said bluntly. Then she turned away to go back inside her house.

Breathing out, because that answer had felt like a punch to the stomach, Gwen turned to Jin Ae who gave a shrug. There wasn't much she could say to that, so she moved on.

Someone had drawn a rough circle in the dirt of the farmyard, at some points in the circle it bulged or dipped where the artist decided to draw around a stone, or a particularly deep divot in the ground, or, in one case, a particularly obstinate cat who refused to move.

Gwen bit down on her lip to stop a grin from breaking free, "You have magic you want to do to us?" she called out.

Marina looked up from where she had been scoring lines in the earth, she had gone beyond the circle now and was drawing runes around it. "Yeah! Theo and I have a spell in common, so we're going to juice it up a bit by casting it together. It should keep the four of us alive a bit longer, or at least keep us from getting smashed into paste quite so quickly."

"Delightful," Jin Ae said her voice as dry as dust. "What exactly is it you're going to do?"

"What, you don't trust us?" Marina asked, her attention going back to her knife and the markings she was drawing in the dirt.

"I haven't made my mind up yet," Jin Ae said.

Gwen snorted, "You've not known us long, that seems fair. As does asking what someone's going to do to you before they start casting magic in your direction." She gave Marina a look.

Marina shrugged, "Eh, Theo can you explain it."

"Sure," he said, stepping forward from where he had apparently been counting, nails?

Gwen frowned, but no, he had a bundle of them in his hand and was tucking some extra back into a pocket. They were nails, she was sure of it, each about as long as her hand from the bottom of her palm to the end of her middle finger. They were a mix between new ones still shined up and some clearly much older which had a touch of rust.

"The spell will give you more health and should make it faster to heal too, that way if we have to retreat we should be able to go out again pretty soon after. To do it I'm going to enchant these nails with my magic, while Marina asks the gods to keep you from kicking the bucket with her Priest magic. The way ritual magic works you should get two and a bit of what one spell would get you, because they," his voice turned speculative, "bounce off each other and mix and get bigger? Something about amplification? I don't know, I'm still new to ritual casting." He shook his head, "But basically," he looked over at the locals who were watching and lowered his voice, "This spell is going to give you an extra level's worth of Health and will half the time it takes you to heal."

Gwen flicked a look at the locals, but they seemed to not even notice that they were being cut out from the conversation. "That sounds useful," she said.

"Well, fingers crossed, it won't be. But it's better to be ready for anything, right?" Theo said with a shrug.

Marina jumped up and slid her dagger into a sheath at her side, before rubbing her dirty palms over her thighs. "Right, I think that's it!" She grinned, a smear of reddish earth coated one cheek and made her look childlike. "Into the circle, you two, if we're ever going to get started it might as well be now."

Gwen grimaced and stepped forward, doing as she was told and carefully jumping over the rings drawn into the earth and the runes that orbited around them. Even to her untrained senses, she could feel when she entered the magic. It felt like stepping through the bass at a gig where they did not give a damn about the continued integrity of anyone's ear drums or internal organs. She could have sworn that just for a moment, not even the space between a pair of heart beats, she was trapped in the air, her feet both tucked up beneath her as she jumped over the scratches in the surface of the farmyard.

Then she was on the other side of the line and her feet were hitting the earth and it all seemed to tumble away behind her.

Shaking her head she stepped further into the circle, out of the road of everyone else following her.

Theo jumped across after Jin Ae joined her and from the way he blinked she knew he at least had picked up on the odd feeling. But he too shook it off like a dog chasing off an irritating fly and knelt down next to the ring, setting a nail and a hammer down before him. "Ready when you are," he said to Marina who was still standing outside the ring.

"Would music help?" Jin Ae asked.

Everyone looked at her, confused by the segue.

She pulled a stringed instrument from her back, "I'm a bard, we're supposed to play when something inspiring happens, now seems like a good time to give you two some accompaniment?"

"It can't hurt," Marina agreed.

"It would be nice, the last live music I heard was my neighbour practising some kind of brass instrument," Theo said.

"'Some kind of brass instrument'," Gwen said.

Theo shrugged, "He needed the practice, I couldn't tell if it was a tuba or if it wasn't supposed to sound like that."

"Well, I'm fairly certain I can do better than that," Jin Ae said; she pulled a bow out of the same bag from which the instrument had come, then had second thoughts, tucking it back and laying her fingers on the strings instead. Slowly, she started to coax a trembling song from the instrument, one that seemed to pull at the hairs along the back of Gwen's neck with the dedication of a purring cat licking a hand trapped between its paws. Each time the slow strumming seemed about to reach the top of the mountain it was climbing, there would be a fall down to the rocks beneath them and the ascent would start again.

Gwen was the only one who had the freedom to move in that moment; Jin Ae was playing, her whole upper body moving in time to the music; Theo knelt by the rings; and Marina was standing outside them. And yet she couldn't. She was swept away by the sounds like they were the winds of a hurricane.

Marina let out a huff of surprise, but she didn't seem as taken by the music. She wasn't stuck to the ground where she stood, certainly. Marina started to walk around the edge of the ring, her feet moving carefully around and over the runes taking care not to smudge a single one.

Marina's mouth opened and her chanting began, she started with words that Gwen could hear fair distinctly, "To Minethena I call, for a favour I ask," but then the music seemed to swell and brush the words away from Gwen's ears. Her teeth started to shake in time to the falls and rise of the music. She could see Marina walking, there was nothing between them but a few steps of air, and yet everything began to blur.

It was almost as if there was a second figure walking in the shadow of Marina, or maybe it was Marina who was following. The figures walked around the ring four times, clockwise of course, though Gwen didn't know why that felt not only right, but the only way it should be. Every time Marina passed Theo he hammered another nail into the ground, his hammer blows silent in midst of the music and prayers that were claiming all the sound that was available.

Gwen stopped being able to hear her heart or the sound of her own breath.

Once, twice, three times, and finally four. The final nail thumped into the ground and the silence roared into being with the closing snap of Marina's jaw.

For a moment all was still and silent.

"Well," Marina said, her voice sounding husky as if she had been speaking for hours, "That was interesting."

Chapter 7

Name: Gwen Baird

Class: Hunter

Level: 5

Health: 25

Species: Half-Elf (Wood/Human)

Strength:	6	Mind:	6
Agility:	5	Body:	5
Armour:	3	Sense:	6

Species Skills: (Half-Elf)

Elf Sight: 5

Base Skills: (Hunter)

Dodge:	1	Perception:	5
Tracking:	6	Stealth:	4
Charm:	6	Archery:	5

The four Adventurers kitted up quickly after the magic faded back into the fabric rather than the foreground of reality. They handed off spare bags and cloaks to the farm's children. Gwen knew that what they would need was stealthy speed, not clunking bags slowing them down or cloaks which could be grabbed and turned into leashes.

Gwen tightened her belt to an earlier hole and checked that her hair was pulled out of the way as completely as possible. It wouldn't do to have it fall into her eyes at the worst possible moment, and given the odds, it would be the worst possible moment.

She wished she could have a few points to put into her Agility, but it was a bit late for that. She wasn't certain, but she thought the others had possibly levelled from their ritual in the farmyard. It was petty to be jealous, but Gwen couldn't quite push the thought down quick enough. She would have liked to get an extra level from helping with a ritual, but she was still several hundred experience points below getting to Level 6 and those sweet, sweet, magical spells. Right about now, as she was preparing to walk out into a dark night for murdering purposes, she was wishing she had Shadow Step to call on.

Or Spider Climb to get over the wall. Or Poison Barrage to take out a huge swathe of monsters at once. Her portfolio was really lacking some Area of Effect tricks.

She sighed, but that would have to wait until her next level.

Fishing the spider silk rope out of her backpack, she went to the spot at the back of the farm that had been chosen for their egress. It was a sturdy stone wall, one of the few sections that used some sort of bonding material between the rocks rather than just trusting in gravity and friction to keep it all in place. Hopefully, that meant it would be sturdy enough not to fall on them when they climbed it.

Whatever building the wall had belonged to had once had a sizeable overhang of stone sticking out the top. If she could just get the rope around that lump. Tying a knot on her rope Gwen started to spin it around, trying to get enough oomph into it to take it up as high as the wall.

The first time she threw the rope up it missed, falling down to crumple at her feet instead of holding strong. Gritting her teeth, she picked it up and tried again. The same thing happened.

Notifications popped up warning her that she had insufficient rope skills to achieve what she wanted. It was like the Card Sharp thing all over again.

"Oh, come on, I can almost do this in real life, isn't this supposed to be escapism? Get up there and stick," she muttered, running her fingers around the inside of the loop to try and make it run a little more smoothly.

"Almost?" Jin Ae asked.

Gwen jumped, snapping her head back to the other woman who was standing a few feet behind her, looking at the odd show she was putting on with her arms crossed and a quirked brow.

Gwen shrugged, "I was at a business retreat on a ranch, I spent a lot of time with the horses and the people who worked there instead of my colleagues." This was an approximate description of the event. It lacked some of the nuance, like the fact that they had been using the ranch as a base to assess how to steal everything out of the secret vault under their next-door neighbours' faux-medieval castle, but it got the basics across.

"You didn't like your colleagues much?" Jin Ae said with a laugh, before bowing her head and going back to sorting through the things in her bag.

"Eh, they were fine," Gwen said. The memory of Roxy muscling her way into her Edinburgh apartment and the way her body fell back after Gwen had tasered her rose like a shadow in her thoughts. "Some were better than others."

"Oh? What work did you do?" Jin Ae asked.

"IT," Gwen said with a smile; that bit was easy. It was also almost true. *Some kind of thief you are*, Gwen thought, *there's a line between using the truth to hide your lies and just giving up on lying at all and you crossed it long ago.*

Jin Ae looked up with surprise covering her features, "Really? But you look so comfortable in," she waved a hand around them, "Nature? Historical surroundings? What am I trying to say?"

Gwen laughed, "I just throw myself into things, I guess."

Jin Ae nodded, appearing to give her words some thought.

Gwen turned back to the wall, "Right, let's try this again, shall we?" She started to swing the rope in a slow, languid way that felt familiar, yes, this was how you did it. The loop sped up in her hands, circling faster and faster, before she released it and saw it fly up and catch on the projection she had been aiming for.

Gwen fist pumped with a hissed, "Yes!" Then she swept away the notifications of the skill levels she had gained and stepped forward to make sure the rope was securely in place.

The other Adventurers were soon clustered at her back, looking up at the rope with differing levels of trepidation.

Jin Ae looked at the climb as if it was an unpleasant task that had to be done and was best done quickly. Like doing the dishes.

Theo had his arms folded and was looking at it with clear scepticism, he didn't have to say he wasn't confident about being able to make the climb, it was written on his face.

And Marina, well Marina turned to Gwen with a shake of her head. "I'm in metal armour, how exactly is this going to work?"

Gwen puffed out a breath. It was true, Marina was going to have the hardest time of it. Jin Ae and Theo were wearing armour that was mostly fabric and leather based, it might not be the easiest thing to do the splits in but at least it wouldn't sound like a cutlery drawer getting thrown down a set of stairs if you banged up against anything.

"How much of that armour is entirely necessary?" Jin Ae asked.

"It's not exactly stealthy," Theo agreed.

Marina's face was turning red, "I need it! I could get chewed up otherwise!"

"You mean like how we might," Gwen pointed out. "We're all in a lot less protective gear than you."

"I'm a healer, I need to be able to shrug off attacks."

Gwen couldn't disagree. "Well, if you can't get up there under your own steam without alerting the monsters then we'll have to help you." Sighing, she walked over to the wall, it was about nine feet tall at the start of what might have once been a stepped gable. "Jin Ae, Theo, which one of you is stronger?"

"Me, most likely," Theo said. "It's not how you're meant to build a magic user, I know, but I put a couple of points in Strength thinking I would be in the forge a lot."

"Right, well, see if you can get up to the top there, I'll boost Marina and if you can give her a hand up then at least some of the banging should be quietened down," She turned to Marina, "Just try not to smack into us too much as you climb, we might not go clang but we do bruise."

Bracing herself against the wall, beside where her rope dangled, Gwen put a knee forwards, "You first, Theo," she said, prompting him to move.

The Enchanter gave her knee a sceptical look, before taking a breath and stepping forward to wrap the rope around his hands, "I hope this works." He muttered the words quietly enough that it was probably only meant to be for himself, but Gwen's elvish hearing meant she could pick the words out easily.

Bouncing off the ground and boosted by Gwen's knee, Theo scrabbled up the side of the wall, his thick boots finding purchase on the unevenly weathered stone, sending bits of stone and dust scattering over the Adventurers below him. Gwen shut her eyes and bowed her head to let them bounce off her hair.

After a moment, Theo seemed to settle himself on the top of the wall. Looking out across the fields outside the farm he gave a slow nod, then looked down and gave the group a thumbs up.

"Right, you next," Gwen said, looking at Marina who grimaced. "Go on, Jin Ae if you can help me shove her up towards Theo then that would be a help, too."

Jin Ae gave her a nod, then had a hint of a smile as she stood behind Marina.

"When did we put you in charge, again?" Marina asked.

"When you didn't look like you were going to get anything done if I didn't step in: be faster next time," Gwen said briskly. "If I have to do everything myself then you have to accept what I do."

"Will do," Marina said, before she attempted to follow Theo up the wall. It was not a graceful attempt, and if it were in the real world Gwen would likely have had a couple of foot-shaped bruises the next day on her knee and shoulder, but between the group of them they managed to get Marina up into Theo's arms and onto the wall beside him. A low swear and a lot of gasps followed Marina up, but eventually Gwen was able to stand up straight again.

She let out a few puffs and parts of her own as she moved back into a shape that felt a bit more natural. Jin Ae gave her a sympathetic look, before she too grabbed onto the rope and shimmied up to the top of the wall.

What are the odds that I could slip back to the farmhouse now and have a cup of tea? Gwen thought, before getting her hands on the rope and clambering up.

With the rope the wall was probably easier to climb than the trees she had been finding her way up the day before. And she had more ranks in climbing than she had then. But, somehow, the absence of any life in the stone of the wall meant it felt far less secure to her than the lichen-encrusted bark and wood she had climbed then. If there was a downside to all this new elf magic, it seemed that this was it. When it wasn't around to give you a hand it felt a hell of a lot worse than she had expected.

Her grip on the rope seemed to be hardly enough and she nearly slipped a few times back down, but eventually Gwen made it up to the top. The view of the land on the other side was almost enough to send her back down, however. She hadn't gotten a good look at how many beasts had been circling the farm in their headlong bolt into the farmyard. Now, from her vantage point, she could see what they were facing far more clearly.

There was a perfect ring around the farm, each monster perfectly arranged right where they were out of reach. Dozens, maybe more. Her elf eyes could see better in the dark than her real-life human ones, but it wasn't a complete transformation to night vision. If she squinted she could make out a wee bit further, and there didn't seem to be a morass of never-ending hordes of monsters out in the grey and blurry landscape.

So, she thought, I can probably assume that the majority of the monsters are up as close to the farm as they can get without being shot or cast at. That's good, the last thing we need is sneaky monsters too.

An arm looped around her, hooking her into place on the wall more securely. Theo looked at her from where he sat, leaning into her he whispered, "It looked like you were about to tumble back down."

"Thanks," she said, giving him a smile. Then she turned her gaze back onto the morass of monsters that were covering the ground that she would somehow have to cross. "Right, let's fucking do this," she whispered.

Sitting up on the wall gave her a pretty good view of the dozens of monsters, of different types, spread around the fields and roads leaving the farm. With Jin Ae and Theo having taught a lesson to any that got close enough there was at least a halo around the farm of empty grass, but outside that halo the monsters lay in orbiting lines.

From what Gwen could see, and that was a mixed bag (her dark vision was better for things close up than at a distance), there seemed to be more of the arachno-wolves; some deer like the one Jin Ae had mentioned; and a collection of beetles with mamma bits. She shot a glare in their direction, she had levelled up a few times since the fight with the beetle thing that had attacked her when she arrived, but she had won that battle thanks to luck and gravity more than anything else. She would be on a literal level playing field with them this time around, and one of the things you learned from worshipping a luck goddess, she was figuring out, was that skill and careful planning was more reliable.

Gwen flicked a glance at the stars, hoping that that hadn't been overheard. She didn't need whatever happened when a god didn't like you happening *as well*.

Careful planning, that's the goal, she thought. Pulling the rope over the wall took a couple of seconds, Theo made certain it was secure for her as he was closest to where it was attached, and then Gwen started the climb down.

The outer wall was rougher than the inner one, the unchecked power of the wind and rain had done a number on the weaker stonework. That meant she could easily claw her way down, the beds under her nails filling with sandstone residue and bits of moss.

She hit the ground earlier than she was expecting, the stones falling from the wall had built up a lip around the outside so it was actually a bit higher than within the walls. Sinking down onto her heels she tried to make as small a target as possible, hoping that if anything was awake enough to see her then it would assume she was nothing more than the shadow of a cloud.

In the meantime, her climbing skill levelled up again, and though it wasn't quite enough to see her into the next overall level, it was enough to raise some possibilities. If you died just below a level up you lost everything, but if you managed to get even the slightest bit over that line into a new level...

Jin Ae followed her down, crouching beside her at the foot of the wall. Then it was Marina's turn. Somehow they managed to guide her down without so much as a whisper or the tiniest clank, which was unbelievably lucky.

But Gwen was starting to feel like they were running up a debt in that currency, and out of everything in all the versions of reality she had lived in: luck was not something you wanted to run out of. Theo joined them, pushing off from the top of the wall and landing beside them, his heavy boots making a soft crunch in the dirt.

While there was a halo of intact grass around the farm, where the monsters had been in range of Jin Ae and Theo's magic, the ground beyond had been churned into mud. It was, Gwen was re-lieved to note, completely free of anything other than evidence of the presence of the monsters. Well, aside from the monsters themselves, of course. There were a lot of them, possibly more than she had thought even, and Gwen reluctantly raised her estimation of the numbers upwards. There were some deeply unpleasant monsters which seemed to be asleep in the mud and had been hidden from their view.

These looked worryingly like flayed woodlice. She had never before understood how lucky the world was that woodlice were not the same shade as raw chicken, but now she was very, very aware of it. She made a disgusted face and turned to the rest of her group.

Jin Ae's expression had become blank but with a burning fire beneath the surface that spoke to her grim determination to get the battle started. Theo was alert, eyes warily following the lines of the forest and the road, keeping watch for reinforcements. Marina had her hand on her mace and looked like she was already mentally tallying the kills she could expect to claim.

If there was ever a moment for a big speech this would be it, Gwen thought, then smiled and turned back to the monsters, *well thank the gods that we have to be quiet.*

The first few kills were easy.

The monsters were deeply asleep, the soft noises of their executions were hidden by the sounds of the wind and the raspy breaths of those still living.

As well as the experience from the kills she was getting a steady trickle in from levelling her stealth and sword skills. The higher level of stealth was making the world change around her, the shadows and dark hollows were easier to find and once, when she was about to put her foot down on a dry twig that would have surely cracked like a gun shot in the silence, she felt a tug. It was hard to explain, it was kind of like the feeling you get when your sleeve catches on a door handle. Slowly she lifted her foot away from the twig and set it down beside it.

Breathing out slowly she moved on, paying a bit more attention to what was happening underneath her feet.

Gwen was pulling her sword from the neck of a particularly ugly arachno-wolf, one with the fuzzy hair of a tarantula and the stinger of a scorpion attached to the half-starved and mangy looking body of a wolf, when she heard it. Or didn't.

The rumbling snore of the monsters had stopped. All in the same moment.

She pulled her sword more quickly through the neck meat and muscle and turned to the rest of the creatures. There were too many, far, far too many. If they had started at twelve then they had barely made it around to a quarter past three, with the rest of the clock still full of monsters both large and small. Beasts that were now very aware of them and probably displeased by the very rude awakening they had received.

"Warning: Stealth Failed!"

Flashed in red across her vision.

"They're awake," Gwen said, not bothering to whisper and not needing to shout in the sudden silence.

"So they are," Marina said.

From Jin Ae, "How unfortunate."

Instead of agreeing with them, Theo turned and with a cry sent a shot of blue light out of his hand in the direction of the monsters behind them.

After that it was a lot more difficult to keep track of where everyone was. Theo and Jin Ae were behind her and taking care of those monsters that were coming from that direction, but Gwen didn't dare look around and check on them.

Grabbing her bow, she started pulling arrows from her quiver, shooting with more speed than caution. It took her precious moments and too many arrows to realise that there was no point to her shooting at the larger, more armoured creatures.

One arrow was scattered off into the night in pieces after an alert of, "Insufficient Archery Skill Versus Armour" rang out like a bell across her vision.

She swore blisteringly, then switched to the smaller monsters, those with the furrier of the wolf parts and the flayed woodlice, which gave her a better run of luck. Bracing herself, she stood solidly in the muck and started to build a rhythm of pulling the bow string back and shooting in the pause between her breaths, taking in a gulp every time her hand moved to her quiver to claim a new arrow.

She wasn't claiming a kill with each arrow, but she was getting close to it. The larger wolves were easier targets to hit, but needed more than a single blow to strike down. The woodlice were fast, but whatever had made them pink and fleshy looking had also ruined their armour so as long as she could strike them they were soon nothing but spoiling meat.

Every time she killed something a notification would pop up with a congratulations, telling her how much experience she gained from the death. It was the easiest way to tell when she had been successful in killing a foe. But aside from that, she drove any of the awareness of anything but her bow and the creatures to the back of her mind.

Marina let out a horrendous scream and ran forwards, sweeping her mace back and forth into the melee, tossing many of the smaller monsters left and right, many were stunned if not killed but most were soon dissolving into the muck from the force of her strikes.

Gwen's hand sank into the open maw of her quiver. "Shit," Pulling the bow over her head to free her hands, she pulled her sword once more and dove in behind Marina. It was quick and easy work to follow in her trail and finish off anything left behind. The sword sank deep into the necks and bellies of the monsters, her blade cutting through the skin and fur and even the chitinous armour when she put her weight behind it. Glowing numbers appeared in the air after she hit them, the blows hitting hard and devastatingly to put them down. Their foul looking blood was soon coating much of her, the splashes and spurts of the dying creatures covering her in a noxious oily fluid.

Pulling her blade from one such armoured creature she was almost struck by the stinger of another. Luckily, the scare made her jump out of the way of the barb and pull her sword free in the same movement.

The creature had a wolf's head except for a pair of pincers where its lower jaw should have been, its back legs and tail were those of a scorpion, covered in dark brown and oily looking armour. There was a wound to one side of it, it had clearly been struck with Marina's mace, but the blow hadn't been enough to do more than make it bleed.

Gwen had trouble moving her gaze from its stinger, it was a particularly nasty looking one with a barb more than long enough to kill her with a single strike, even without the poison that was glistening from the end of it. It would, she could see it clearly in her mind's eye, skewer her like a butterfly in some Victorian collection. This should have been more than enough of a reason to keep her eyes on it, unfortunately, the rest of the creature was also a terrifying monster from the kind of dream that made people swear off cheese before bed. She couldn't allow herself to get distracted by one threat to the extent that she was ignorant of all the others.

The threat of what might else be coming after her had her looking into the growling face of the beast itself. Its eyes seemed to focus on her right leg; flashing her sword in front of her she caught its attention, breaking its focus, so that the stinger was more easily deflected by her sword.

The scorpion-wolf growled again, flecks of spit dropping from its jaw.

Gwen moved back, trying to get out of a range where it could easily hit her. But the creature followed her, the motion was off putting as the back legs and the front were not quite in sync in style of movement nor in timing. The front wolf legs seemed trapped in a loping position, while the back, scorpion legs scuttled in a more grounded way. With every step or so forwards there was a bounce up to accompany it. Noticing this, Gwen lunged forwards at the next clumsy lurch, angling her sword up and into its chest, wrenching the sword through the flesh as best as she could.

The growl cut off and turned into a splutter, blood dripped from the wolf's mouth, dark green and alien, and it fell to the ground.

Gwen whirled around, the creature already forgotten, as she looked for the next monster trying to kill her. The blood was dripping off her blade and leaving a puddle at her feet as she glanced around and grabbed deep breaths whilst she could.

For a moment all was still around her. So she took the opportunity to see what her allies were doing. It also gave her health bar, which had been limping along at about twelve out of twenty-five, to refill.

Theo was doing well, from the looks of all the dissolving, burnt bodies of monsters around him he was proving more successful than she. He was driving the monsters ahead of him with his magic. Jin Ae was mixing her own magic with her blade work, embers of fire fluttered behind her sword as she danced between enemies, leaving them cut and burned behind her. Her sword was starting to look more and more like the wick at the centre of a candle, the edges burning red while inside the lines everything looked all the darker. Her tail was clinging to her legs and every so often a line or lyric would whisper its way to Gwen's ears.

Theo too was fighting like a demon; his staff was a long soot-blackened piece of iron that was beginning to burn all the brighter from the regular use he was putting it to. Together they were a literal bright spot in the darkness, their fire magic setting the night aglow around them.

She felt better at leaving them to their fighting, they clearly had it under control.

Marina was still running around like a berserker, smashing her mace into anything that came close. Gwen started to jog after her twin again; Marina was leaving fewer stunned monsters and more bodies behind her now, so even though she looked like she was giving into mindless rage she must have figured something out or levelled up enough that her hits were killing instantly.

Catching up to her twin who had halted Gwen asked, "What is it?"

Lifting her mace, Marina pointed out a moving black morass on the edge of the farm, "Please tell me that one is actually closer than I think it is, that it's not actually that size?"

Gwen's eyes focused on the beast moving towards them, "Ah, fuck."

"Right, so it is massive, good to know," Marina started to ease back, not quite running but there was no point. They were far enough from the beast that it was not going to reach them for a few seconds, but there was no point in running. It was faster.

Gwen looked around. They were in the middle of what had once been a field of something green and leafy, but which was not grass. She didn't have the time or the care to work out what it actually was. What was important was that there was nothing to get behind, no trees to climb either, though that probably wouldn't work a second time.

The creature lowered its head and let out a bellow, the dim lights of the fire magic behind them shone off its carapace and the horns sprouting out if its face. The barbs were everywhere and were an ugly burnt orange that suggested bloodshed.

"What is it, some sort of stag or, or, moose?" Gwen asked. Desperately she tried to think of what to do. Time seemed to be stretching in some bizarre way, the creature was still running and she didn't have time to run likewise, but she had plenty of time to watch it. Watch it and come up with something like a plan.

"No," Marina said, she had a tone to her voice like a death knell. "That is a woolly mammoth, by my guess."

The creature bellowed again, its beetle-like head all that Gwen's eyes could latch onto. It had oblong-shaped eyes that pointed down to its chomping mouth. The monster apparently had not been able to decide between the slicing mandibles of a beetle and the grinding teeth of a mammoth and so had decided to get both. And extras, just in case they came in handy. The carapace covered its back and front, but if it was anything like the other creatures it would have an unprotected belly.

Gwen couldn't quite stop herself from letting loose a high-pitched giggle. Terror warred with relief, and stubbornness sneaked up for a surprise triumph. She felt more than saw Marina look at her in confusion.

"We'll each run in a different direction, go!" Gwen shouted, but when Marina started to run at her order Gwen did not.

There was a dip in the field just ahead of her. It wasn't big, but it was big enough for what she needed it to be.

Marina was still running and hadn't noticed that Gwen was not in her wake.

The beetle mammoth thing was getting closer.

Gwen stepped forward, the creature lowered its head and seemed to look at her with surprise, but then with glee. It wanted to kill her. It thought she was being helpful.

"I've never been helpful in my life, sorry to disappoint you," she muttered, making a show of it she made as if she was bracing herself for the fight. She pushed her feet into the soft earth of the field and bent her knees.

Shouts started to go up behind her, the others had seen what was going on. She could hear them shouting her name. But she put it out of her mind. Two of them shouldn't be risked because who knows where they would end up if they were killed. The other was their healer. And more importantly, she was Marina.

The risk had to sit on Gwen's shoulders. She couldn't die after all, not for long anyway, not in a game. And pain was impermanent here too. So really it wasn't that big a deal, she told the Marina in her head who was arguing against her plan.

"Not a big—" the mammoth reached her.

Quicker than she had ever moved in real life and faster than she had moved even under the Blessing of the Falcon, Gwen threw herself forwards, bent double at the knees. She slid under the low-ered head and mouth of the animal, under its grasping mandibles and grinding teeth, into the hollow in the ground.

The mammoth kept running with a storming bellow, before it noticed that she had disappeared. The unprotected belly fell over her head like a bulging, fur-covered ceiling. Using muscles she had barely understood the use of before, Gwen pushed up out of the hollow she had put her body in, jumping back to her feet. With both hands wrapped around the hilt of her sword to give it power she started to stab repeatedly at the stomach above her. There was no time for slicing now, it was all stab, retreat, move a little out of the way of the new blood that was falling and try again.

The numbers coming at her were larger than anything she had beaten out of a monster before, and yet it was still holding on to life. A stab into an unprotected armpit area sent a stream of blood flowing out and 15 health points jumped out at her.

The legs around her started to move; the monster was trying to get out of the way. But she didn't let it get far. Every time it started to move out of her reach she would slice at legs on that side to cause it to jerk back into the patch above her where she could reach the belly easiest.

Blood was raining down on her, making her body slick along with the weapon in her hands. The dip in the land was becoming a pond of the stuff, she was up to her ankles in what felt like no time at all. She was slowing, but so was the monster, the legs around her were moving more jerkily as it tried to get away from her. Her hand left the hilt of her sword and went to her belt, and she lunged right to the shadow behind a leg. She drove a knife into the back of a knee, stopping the beast from moving that leg again. Using that moment to gain her breath, Gwen whirled back into the centre before clamping both hands around the hilt of her sword, and angling up and forwards, hoping that the approximate spot of the heart was the same as in most mammals.

She didn't hit the heart, but when she pulled the sword free the wound started to bubble with air leaking from the creature's lungs. It stopped moving. Gwen, too exhausted to move fell, to her knees once more with one hand braced against the ground.

"Gwen!" She heard Marina scream.

She was barely strong enough to turn her head, she couldn't see Marina out in the dark. The bottom of the hollow was too full of liquid to lie in, even if she could reach it.

The creature let out a last rasping groan and fell.

The last thing she saw was the notification that she had finally reached level 6 being swept out of sight by the declaration:

"You have died, you will now return to last the respawn point you visited."

Then everything went black.

Chapter 8

Name: Gwen Baird

Class:	Hunter		
Level:	5		
Health:	25		

Species: Half-Elf (Wood/Human)

Strength:	6	Mind:	6
Agility:	5	Body:	5
Armour:	3	Sense:	6

Species Skills: (Half-Elf)

Elf Sight:	5

Base Skills: (Hunter)

Dodge:	1	Perception:	5
Tracking:	6	Stealth:	7
Charm:	6	Archery:	6

Gwen's eyes opened on a brightness that made her wince after the night battle she had just come from. She covered her face with her arm and blinked in the shadows.

"You know," said a voice, "I have seen a lot of Adventurers die in some very strange ways, but you've managed to find a new one. I'm not sure if I should congratulate you for that. I don't want it to become a bad habit."

Gwen let out a wheezy laugh, now she knew where she was. She pushed off the stone table she was lying on and looked around for the AI. The temple looked much like it had when they had visited it, but now the dawn light was streaming through the stained glass at an angle that covered where she lay like a blanket. It was almost as if the place had been made with the intent of looking most magical at dawn. "Not seen many people get crushed beneath a mammoth crossed with a beetle before?"

"No, none, in fact. That's the first time I've seen that creature," Dove said from her spot on one of the pews in the temple. "Which is a bit disconcerting given that I am supposed to be running this reality."

Gwen twisted to look at her. "What?" That wasn't right. Dove steered the ship they were sailing through the cosmos in, kept the cryogenics running while the humans slept, and ran all the metrics and codes that made the world spin and the dragons fly and whatever else happened in the world.

"I didn't make that beetle thing. I hadn't even seen it before. That shouldn't happen. But, the way you killed it, it got my attention. I can't exactly keep an eye on every Adventurer and the nonsense they get up to," she gave a shrug. "I do have a ship to fly through space, you know, as well as run the game to keep you humans occupied, I am a very busy Artificial Intelligence. But watching the more ridiculous deaths? Well that pays back in entertainment value, and today a little more."

Dove was clad in a metal armour that moved around her like silk, the tiny chain links as soft and smooth against her as the finest fabric. A breastplate sat over her chest, while a pair of bracers collected the open sleeves at her wrists. She stood and walked towards Gwen. Her clothing whispered and rang like wind chimes around her. The light seemed to soften around her, even as she scowled, "Why is it, Guinevere Baird, that I did not know of that monster until you killed it in such a ridiculously over the top manner that my eye was drawn to the drama of it all?"

Gwen blinked, not having a clue why Dove was asking her, "I don't know."

"No neither do I, which concerns me, as I am not accustomed to not knowing what is going on in my own world," She stood before Gwen and crossed her arms.

Dove was a beautiful woman, or at least, she had chosen a beautiful form to appear to Gwen in. She was taller than a human, but not in a gangly way like a lamp post or a stork. Instead, she was built at about one-and-a-half scale, with dark curls that framed her face and which added a halo around her that added to her impressive height.

She was also clearly furious about something. Gwen hoped it wasn't her fault, but she also wasn't stupid enough to think that innocence might be immunity enough from an angry AI. Trying to understand what she was saying, her mind was still scattered between the temple and the farm where she had fallen, it felt like…Gwen grabbed at the pieces of information Dove had gifted her with.

Once she understood, her mouth fell open, "Something's making monsters; something that isn't you?"

Dove raised an unimpressed eyebrow. "Yes."

"What does that mean?" Gwen said, her voice rising to a shriek at the end.

"How am I supposed to know? The very point is that I don't know what's going on," she looked Gwen over, as though assessing her, "I need to know what is at issue here, Ms Baird. I cannot have some other minds running this simulation, especially not when they appear to be so very good at killing Adventurers."

Gwen could hear her not saying a whole multitude of things. Since none of them seemed to be flattering, Gwen decided to ignore them.

"I figured this was just the uptick that happens when a bunch of Adventurers appear in a virtual world with lots of monsters running around," Gwen said.

"There are not meant to be 'lots of monsters running around'," Dove mimicked Gwen's voice perfectly when she quoted her, which sent shivers up Gwen's back. "This was intended to be a simple sandbox style game with enough danger to give a bit of spice to those that needed the adrenaline rush, it's not meant to be a roguelike where the trick is to die as tactically as possible!"

That was certainly more in line with the locals' view of what the area had been like than what she and Marina had found it to be. "Ah," Gwen didn't know what else to say.

"So eloquent," Dove drawled, "Look, there are a variety of reasons this could be happening. I don't like any of them, but some will require less drastic actions on my part. You need to find out what's going on. If you do I'll reward you with treasure, or something."

"Why me?" Gwen asked. Was this part of the game? Was this some sort of plot? An idea to get her...

"You're here. So are the monsters. It's not that complicated," Dove said cutting across her mental tangent with the sharpness of a scythe. "And I need someone who I can trust to be untrustworthy within the correct variables."

"I don't know what you're talking about," the words fell out of her mouth to quickly to haul them back.

"Don't be ridiculous, Ms Baird, I'm in your head, I know what skills you have. And the fact that lying is not one of them is an unfortunate lapse that will have to be made up for through the mechanics of the game, perhaps if you ramp up your Charm it might help. But even if you are not the ideal tool for the job you're the one that I've got, and humans have opened a lot of jars with non-optimal tools over the centuries so I guess I'll have to do the same." She looked down at Gwen. "I am already doing my best to keep the locals from figuring out that they are in a game. Anything that makes it appear more game-like, or more like a scripted story with already planned outcomes makes that harder. These people are coded to act in sensible ways. There is no sensible way to act when you find out your whole life is a lie and are actually a fictional character in a game, I don't want to know what bugs and glitches will be thrown loose if a large percentage of the locals in the game figured it out. And to be honest I can't afford to spend much more effort in distracting them. I need you to figure out what is going on. Whatever it is that's doing this has made it so that I can only find it when an Adventurer happens across it. Do you see why I need you, Ms Baird?"

"You need someone to run around and get into trouble so you can find out where the trouble is," Gwen said. "You need bait."

"Exactly; I'm so glad we could come to this agreement," Dove said, smiling.

"I haven't agreed to anything, yet," Gwen protested.

"Again, Ms Baird, I am in your head. And I know I don't have to give you a list of the reasons why an AI running a simulation holding the minds of several hundred million humans and who is steering a ship through space might be a bit worried about excessive drains on power and memory. Your mind is already ticking over what that could mean. Very reliable your mind, it always picks up on the threat of danger. Find out what's happening, or at the very least wander around so I know where it isn't," Dove smiled. Her mouth opened to say something but her head snapped to the side as if she had heard something.

"A new Adventurer just died in the forest near Starlingrise," she said, "It seems that whether or not you want to see those monsters again they have no compunction against making the choice for you. They are coming to the village."

Gwen's stomach tightened, "What? They can't be I haven't even respawned there yet."

"I don't think they care about waiting for you to be ready," Dove said looking at her askance.

"Damn, damn, damn," she muttered, "Well at least I levelled just before I died."

Dove snorted.

"Oh, what now?" Gwen asked.

"Yes, yes. You did very well choosing to level up just before you died. A lovely bit of tactical genius that. And I'm sure your friends and sister will see it like that too." For a moment the light shifted and Dove looked like a grinning skull with bottomless pits for eyes, and then the moment was gone and she was back to her serenely elegant self.

"Thank you for agreeing to help," she said, before disappearing before Gwen could remember how her mouth worked and disagree.

"Gods damn it," Gwen said. Without the presence of the AI the words echoed around the empty temple.

There was a small crash in an ante-room, Gwen tried to jump off the table to investigate. Her legs wobbled instead and sent her tumbling to the floor.

Chapter 9

Name: Gwen Baird

Class:	Hunter
Level:	5
Health:	25

Species: Half-Elf (Wood/Human)

Strength:	6	Mind:	6
Agility:	5	Body:	5
Armour:	3	Sense:	6

Species Skills: (Half-Elf)

Elf Sight:	5

Base Skills: (Hunter)

Dodge:	1	Perception:	5
Tracking:	6	Stealth:	7
Charm:	6	Archery:	6

The reason Gwen knew she was alive again, really properly alive, not just awake and talking, was because the pain came back with a crash that she could feel in her nerves like someone had hit them with a chainsaw.

Her body moved by itself, the pain shooting down her limbs and making them lash out in lighting fast flinches that bent her and made her feel broken and exhausted.

She didn't shout or swear in anything approaching a recognisable language, instead she gave a yelp that tore at her throat as it left her. She was left lying back on the stone altar just about managing to breathe and feeling the tears trickle down the sides of her face to the stone. She felt bereft and oddly vulnerable. As if she had been scoured of an outer shell that had been protecting her from the world.

There was another series of thumps in some other room in the temple and the priest came running in.

Nikolai looked completely flabbergasted to see her, which told her pretty clearly that he didn't see people respawning in his temple very often. But he came over once he had hurdled that moment of shock and looped an arm around her shoulders to help her up into a sitting position.

"What happened?"

"Monsters, at Jessica's farm. We fought them," she looked around and let out a sigh of relief, "I'm the only one here, the others must have made it." Or, she thought, Marina made it and the others didn't but got sent off into one of a hundred different directions.

But that was a grim thought and she still felt too raw to think like that, so she shook the thought away like a pesky fly.

Nikolai had been talking, but she hadn't been paying attention.

"Sorry, sorry, I'm not fully with it yet, can you say that again?" Gwen winced, she had tried to turn to look at him and her body was very happy to remind her that moving was not something it approved of.

"Oh, oh goddess, don't move," he said, lifting a hand over her chest he started to mutter a prayer. The spell he used glowed and felt like the warmth of sunny day, so she gratefully sank back against his support and basked in it. Her health, which had been a glaring red from respawning, started to rebuild and once it had ticked over the half-way mark it turned green again.

He pulled his hand away and she pushed up off the altar to sit under her own strength.

"Thank you," she said. She was leaning forwards with her elbows on her thighs and her back bowed as she gulped in breaths.

"The pain should go soon now you've got some health back, breathe deep, now," he spoke awkwardly, as if he was reading off a recommended list of things to say to the newly risen from the dead.

She gave him a look.

He blushed. "It's been a while since I've had to heal much beyond the usual farmyard accidents," he explained, "I fear I may be out of practice."

She laughed, the chuckle battering around in the echoing drum of her chest, "You're doing fine. What's happened since Marina and I left?"

"Not a great deal, at least nothing that caught my eye. You were lucky that I fell asleep while reading in my study, otherwise you may have had to come find me," he said. "If you are feeling up to it, shall we get you on your feet?"

"That sounds like a good idea," Gwen said, before grunting and moving off the altar in shaky lurches.

"What happened to you, beyond monsters and being in the wrong place at the wrong time?" he asked drily as she wobbled while holding onto his arm.

"We got to the farm, they were surrounded by a lot of monsters, still not really sure how many," she could admit that now, it wasn't possible to avoid it when she realised she couldn't tell Nikolai how many monsters there had been. That seemed like a glaring omission now that she had come out the other side of the battle with one more traumatic experience to add to her list. "There were a couple of Adventurers who had been hiding on the farm with them. They'd been keeping an eye on the monsters. Their numbers were growing, every dawn, like Adventurers coming back, like me, I guess," she rambled for a moment, then brought her mouth back under control, "so last night we sneaked out and started killing as many as we could before they noticed us."

"I take it that they noticed you" he said.

"Yeah," she said. "Yeah, that they did. There was one big monster, I, uh, took it on myself." Again, hindsight was making her want to kick herself, only she was too damaged right now, she would have to do it later.

"And so you ended up here," Nikolai's voice was carefully non-judgemental.

"I killed it and it crushed me, and no one else has turned up so it worked," she said defensively.

"You have an interesting idea of what constitutes a success," he said.

She didn't disagree with him. But her pride was still stinging, so she took her hand off his arm. Her knees wobbled but she braced against the altar, she breathed deeply and cast her mind back to what Dove had told her. But how to phrase it? She couldn't just announce that an all-powerful godlike figure had told her to warn the village of an oncoming monstrous hoard.

She thought for a moment.

No, she decided, that would raise more questions and if she didn't know how to answer the basic ones it couldn't be a good idea to bring in more complicated ones.

She took a breath and settled for, "The number of monsters in the woods seem to be rising and they are intent on going after people now, not just picking off loan travellers or easy prey like most monsters. Is there anyone in the village who can fight? Or even anyone who can just throw stones or build a wall quickly, with what's coming I don't think we have the time to be picky what aid we ask for." All at once, as the words fell from her mouth, the tension that had been wrenching at her shoulders eased. It felt like a ticking clock stopped somewhere far off, the silence far more noticeable than the tick, tock, tick that had been driving her mad since she woke. Dove had apparently laid some reminders in place to keep her from going back on her word.

Nikolai frowned and scratched his raspy chin, "Myself and my husband, of course, but not for some years. And I think a few in the village helped with the northern defences, keeping the necromantic armies from intruding on the farmlands, in their youth. But to be blunt, this village is not prepared for war. Our greatest defence in the past has been in being beneath the notice of potential attackers."

Oh, she knew how that kind of defence worked, stay out of sight, never let the threat ever know you exist. Unfortunately, it wouldn't work now. For her or the villagers. "Right then, I need to get into the centre of the village. Forewarned is forearmed, even if it's not much of a warning," she started to walk forwards before hissing in a breath; she had moved. That wasn't wise.

"If the colour your cheek just turned is any clue, I don't think you'll be managing this by yourself any time soon. I'll come with you," he gave her a look when she started to disagree. It buttoned her lip shut with efficiency to spare.

Gwen dipped her head into a bow.

"Most folk will still be asleep, dawn is particularly early at this time of year and few try to match it," he started to lead her through the temple.

A gasp from the doorway. Gwen looked up, standing in the pink and gold light of the dawn was a young woman. Her hair was slicked back into a braid and she wore a simple dress in a dappled blue. She had opened the door with one hand, while the other was keeping her upright on a crutch. Only one leg was visible beneath her skirt.

"Wylla, go back to the village. There might be an attack coming, monsters from the forest. Warn everyone you can find and then get them to start banging on doors. After that I need you to go to the Inn and tell whoever's awake there that they need to clear the cellar out," Nikolai ordered quickly, it was clear he was relieved to have someone to deputise.

Wylla's face was struck with fear for a moment, then grim determination took over. She nodded once, then spun and started back to the village.

Gwen nodded, her hand drifting to her hip. Her belongings had stayed where her body fell, hopefully her sister would think to bring it all back, "Do you know where I can find a sword, and maybe a bow?" She might as well make use of all those levels of Archery skill she had earned at the farm.

Nikolai nodded, "Come on, we have a wee bit of an armoury at my house. We'll be able to loan you something." He pointed to a house on the outskirts of the village, "Think you can make it that far?"

She nodded, "As long as you don't mind taking it a bit slower than usual?"

"Of course." He gave her one of his arms to lean on and Gwen sacrificed her pride to be led across the village.

As Nikolai walked her up to his cottage one of the neighbouring doors opened, "What's all this then?" A middle-aged woman called out to them. She was dressed in a night gown and what appeared to be several blankets draped around her like a chrysalis.

"There might be an attack coming, monsters, not like we've seen before. There's going to be a meeting as soon as I can chase everyone up, arm yourselves, snow excuse me, I need to get armed," Nikolai called back before pulling the door open and briskly ushering Gwen through.

"There's a box at the back of the cupboard we use for our coats, it should have some spare weaponry for you. Not sure how much of it will fit someone your height, but better than nothing," he ran a hand over the back of his head sheepishly, "And, uh, I need to go explain to my husband what the hell is going on."

There were noises coming from the floor above them and Nikolai jogged off to the stairs that had been carved, it looked like, out of a single squat tree and curled up to where a hole had been cut into the wooden floor above.

Gwen stopped. Somehow, being told to rifle through someone's cupboards felt more alien than all the monsters and magic in the game so far. She kept an eye on where the Priest had gone, hoping somehow that he would turn back and absolve her of the awkwardness of the task. He didn't, instead he ran up the stairs as if it was a perfectly normal thing to instruct a complete stranger to look through the contents of your cupboards.

Maybe it is, Gwen thought, *maybe it's just you who thinks this is weird. Maybe it's just you that is making this weird.*

Taking a gulp of breath, she turned to the cupboard. It was the usual Station to Narnia Special. Big, rectangular, it had two thinner doors on the front hiding the contents of a broader inside. A very nice handle had carvings of a flower that she was unfamiliar with.

You're wasting time so you can put off doing the awkward thing, Gwen thought; taking another breath she did her best to square up to the challenge and, with another look over her shoulder in case Nikolai had come to rescue her, she opened up the wardrobe a hair. The door didn't even have the decency to creak so she couldn't feel like she was giving everyone ample warning and opportunity to tell her to step back.

Fuck's sake, Gwen, you can't lie and you can't go through other people's cupboards even with their explicit permission, you're shocking example of a thief, you are.

Trying to force her head on right she adopted the role of an aloof thief about her shoulders like a cloak. She had been a thief, gods damn it, and not just a thief but a good one. She was just out of practise. The aloof part she had never really gotten a good handle on, but she was trying, didn't she get credit for that? She took a peek at her skills table, but since nothing was moving there it looked like the answer was a very firm no.

And, to be fair, I never did the whole breaking and entering thing, she thought, allowing herself a moment of grace before she got back into the hectoring mode. *Now hurry up and get your shit together, the harder you are to kill the less likely you are to feel that pain again.* She shivered as she remembered the agony she had felt as she had slotted back into reality after dying.

That at least got her hands moving. There were a lot of winter cloaks in the wardrobe, clearly packed away during the warmer seasons, her fingers itched to run through the thick furs and soft leathers that were there, but she had wasted time enough.

Quickly she pushed through, trying to find the box. It found her, the lack of heavy fabric in front of it allowing it to fall forwards and land into her arms. She let out a loud 'oof' noise, and then lowered the box to the ground.

It had a weight to it that promised a pretty good supply: even if it was just filled with broken crockery there would likely be enough of it to put up a pretty lethal last stand. Gwen smirked at the thought of facing off against monsters with somebody's cracked china mugs, then her fingers finally untied the loops of string holding the box closed.

Her eyebrows climbed in surprise as she opened the cupboard, it was better than she had guessed. It wasn't just an old Adventurers' junk and odds and ends box, but an actually decent armoury. If in miniature. At the very least, she saw as she tugged one of the scabbards on top out, they were well preserved. The leather had been oiled once and without any hands to work it in, some still lingered.

Pulling the sword from the scabbard she looked along its shining length. It was different to her previous sword, this one had a rounded hilt, less like a cross, more like an arch. The blade itself was leaf shaped, with veins scratched into the metal along it, the lines, she realised, must be to direct blood away from the hand of the wielder.

A handy adaption, I suppose, if you are carving through enough bodies that getting your hands slippery with blood is a problem, she thought. She swished it back and forth a few times before nodding in appreciation.

While the sword and everything else on her avatar had disappeared when she had died – hopefully staying behind where she had fallen – the belt had stayed with her. She tied the sword on with a twisting knot that she hoped wouldn't come lose any time soon. There was a dagger to balance her other hip, which she tied on after checking its condition.

There were a few other bits and pieces in the box. One of them was a very nice hammer with a beastly looking spike at the end: for smashing in heads. Gwen, however, had been having luck with her fast and agile style of fighting and she didn't want to chance a new style now.

Plus, there were all the levels she had put into her Sword Fighting skill. Better to stick with what she knew.

There was a shield too, but it had odd curves cut out of it and she didn't have the first idea how to use that, well no, she acknowledged. She knew the point was to get it between you and anyone trying to hit you with something, but that seemed fairly simplistic, this was not a beginner's shield, so best to leave it to the experts.

Sword and dagger will do, she decided, it would have to, unless she tried out a few of what appeared to be ninja throwing stars, and she wasn't quite that brave. They looked like they were as likely to take the wielder's fingers off as the enemies', and she wasn't ready to find out if magic was up to fixing that or not.

Closing the wooden box she stood up in time to see someone new come down the stairs.

"I'm not stealing anything," she said in a rush.

"I know, Nikolai said you were borrowing some weaponry," he looked at her with a frown, "Guilty conscience?"

She sighed, some thief you are. "Not one that's currently relevant."

"Right, glad to hear it," he stepped off the final step of the stairs and walked towards her with hand ready to shake, "I'm Edgar, Nikolai's husband and the guard captain of the village."

You fucking idiot, she did not say but she thought it very loudly. Perhaps loudly enough that he might have picked up on it, since he was smirking a little as shook her hand.

"Your home is lovely," Gwen said with a pained smile.

"Thank you, now I hear there are monsters?" He was still grinning at her, but she deserved it so she didn't say anything.

She explained the general shape of the last day for her. The great deal of running, the getting crushed under a woolly mammoth/beetle thing, the worries that the monsters might be going to the next unprepared target they could reach.

As she told him all she could think of that might be relevant and useful she tried to judge him as accurately as he had her.

He was probably about the same height as Nikolai, but where Nikolai was lean and angular, Edgar was wide. It was almost like he had been built out of a series of blocks: the corners barely rounded off by the coarse fabric jerkin he wore over sleeveless arms. Edgar had dark brown skin and short hair and the air of someone with extreme competence in a world that fell far short of his most basic expectations.

She shook his hand after a moment of it hanging in the air in front of her, then blushed. "Have I mentioned that your house is very nice?" she added.

"Yes, but it's worth repeating, I'm very proud of it," he said with a shrug.

At that point Nikolai clattered down the stairs, his arms full of weapons and bits of armour. "Not sure what we have that will fit you, Gwen, but we should at least be able to give you a helmet to keep your head safe," he said, tossing her one. It was a bit bashed in places, but the metal still looked strong and whole and there was a fabric coif inside that would stop her head from rattling around inside.

"Thank you," she said with some relief, her head had started to feel very exposed.

Though that might be because Edgar was still looking at her as if he could read her mind.

She ducked her head and pushed the coif and the helmet on after. The fabric helped a lot, but what really ensured that the helmet fitted correctly was the long rope of hair she had that squashed flat across the back of her head creating a cushioning effect there. She wiggled her head from side to side, it didn't move overmuch.

A notification popped up, whilst Edgar and Nikolai were talking she checked on it.

**You have gained +1 Armour for using 'Basic Iron Bascinet'
you now have +4 Armour.**

That ushered in a mix of feelings. It was good to know she was more armoured, but it wasn't fantastic to find out how low on that count she had been. She wasn't sure how Armour worked, but she had a pretty good reason to believe that +4 was kind of rubbish, actually. It was not immensely reassuring to find that when she looked deeper into that subject, by opening up her notifications panel, that her bracers were the source of one of those points and the gambeson the other two. The Basic Iron Bascinet was clearly a *very* basic bascinet.

But better than absolutely nothing, she thought.

The pain of dying had been horrendous, it hadn't just been the choking and crushing feeling of her actual death, but also the shock of agony that had raced through her nerves as her body had finally given in. Her soul, her consciousness, her bits and bobs of binary code, whatever, the act of ripping it out of her body and throwing it into the ether to be reborn had been painful enough that just remembering it made her feel like she was choking. She would, she knew, do just about anything to avoid that happening again.

"If we can get everyone to the guard house then we'll at least have stone walls to protect us," Edgar was saying.

"And what, leave the rest of the village to be taken over? We can't even fit all of the villagers into the guard house, it's not much beyond a cell and a room with a desk. We can't fight if we're standing on top of each other," Nikolai countered, "the Inn has the space to take everyone and is sturdier than anywhere else in the village. It's also closer."

"Gwen what do you think?" Edgar asked looking over at Gwen who felt ambushed by his attention, "only the ground floor of the inn is built in stone, everything above it is wood, I worry that that might be a recipe for disaster."

Oh gods, one of those 'Oi Adventurer,' questions, she thought. She licked her lips, stalling for time as she thought over her answer, "The inn: I like having height on my side and we need the space to move if they break in, there's no point in us cramming everyone in and losing our ability to fight because of it." The second reason was the better one, but the first was the honest one. It wasn't a good reason, but so far when she had kept gravity on her side things had worked out for the best.

This answer did not seem to please either man, in particular Nikolai looked like he wanted to retract his vote for the Inn, but the power of the Adventurer seemed to be holding sway.

"And it will be even better if we can build plenty of defences around the inn, to stop the monsters getting a good purchase on the houses. We don't want them holing up in someone's front room, or something," she added. That at least seemed to be more the kind of thing they were wanting her to say.

Edgar nodded and strode out of the house, calling back, "I'll go to the guard house, see if I can find anything else we can use."

"Some pikes would be useful!" Nikolai called after him, Edgar raised a hand to show he had heard before breaking into a jog.

"Right," Gwen said grimly, "Let's go pester everyone into going into the middle of the village where they won't get eaten by monsters!"

Nikolai grinned, "sure."

***

By the time they had reached the centre of the village Gwen was almost fully healed, though the dark section over the last eighth of her health seemed to be stuck there for now. As she poked at it an alert was prompted:

Shadow of Death: Health will be reduced by 12.5% until you complete a long rest.

She sighed. Well, that's just the sort of thing you want to hear right before a fight, she thought.

A mob had gathered in front of the inn. The people there were split between the furious and the scared, and those who were still in their bed clothes and those who had managed to gather some sort of armour.

127

Wylla stood to one side while an older woman who looked just like her, but with a hard won two decades more of life, was whispering to her. Wylla was obviously paying only a token amount of attention, as when Gwen and Nikolai appeared she let out a shout, "The Adventurer's here!"

The eyes of the crowd shot to Gwen, it made her jerk to a halt, before she continued on. There had been a moment of silence, then everyone seemed to be determined to have their words beat at her. A light caught her eye, a quest notification, now? She brought it up:

Quest: Motivate the villagers to defend their homes, Part 1 of Defend the Village Quest
Accept: Yes/No
Rewards: ???

The option not to take the quest was faded out, apparently the choice wasn't hers. And question marks stood in the place of stated rewards, she didn't like that much either. *Maybe it makes me greedy, but I like to see what I'm earning before I start the work.*

She blinked away the message and followed in Nikolai's wake. Like a bodyguard, Nikolai helped her make her way through the ranks of villagers to a spot in front of the inn where a mounting block for horses had been built long ago. Nikolai helped her climb it, with his actions making it clear that he expected her to explain what was going on and he was leaving it all on her shoulders.

There was an uncomfortable rumbling of noise in the crowd, they weren't best pleased to be so rudely dragged into the centre of the village and to find out it was at the behest of some unknown Adventurer wasn't improving their mood.

Once she reached the top, she was head and shoulders over even the tallest in the crowd and they quietened looking up at her. Gwen tried not to gulp too obviously. It was not the time to show fear, they might be her allies but she needed them brave and that wasn't going to work if she looked like she was about to bolt.

"Last night I died defending Jessica's farm out in the woods," she started.

The noise crystalised for a moment into a round of gasps, before the hubbub started up again. Gwen spoke no louder, but more forcefully, making them quieten down if they wanted to hear what she was trying to tell them.

There *were* some in the midst of the crowd that she recognised, and in a vain attempt to keep her anxiety from spiralling, she tried speaking to each of them individually for a moment. Switching between them at the end of every sentence so that she could include as many corners of the crowd as she could, it didn't quite make it easy but it did make it easier to ignore the mass of people watching her.

"Those of us at the farm, and yes there were other Adventurers there, believe that the monsters will strike here next. We need to build defences and get ready for an attack." She started by speaking to the elderly woman who had joined her for a card game and a drink the night at the inn, then turned to look at a bulky man wearing a flour-dusted apron who had taught her a local drinking song.

"Why should we listen to you? You've already admitted you died fighting these things, how do we know that you're not just really bad at it?" Wylla shouted across the crowd.

There were more murmurs at that. Some in agreement, but also some in shock or scorn. The baker gave her a nod to continue. She took a deep breath and tried her best.

"Look, I'm not going to stand here and tell you that I'm the best fighter in the world. But I'm pretty decent, and these creatures that we fought aren't like anything you and your village will have faced before," she took a breath, "Unless someone hasn't mentioned regular attacks by monsters that are half one thing and half another. Like scorpion tailed wolves or beetles with the heads of pigs?"

There were shaking heads beneath her.

"There were so many at the farm that they slept in a circle that ran the whole way around it, just outside of bow range. Maybe you will find them easy enough to fight, but there are too many for them to not get plenty of lucky shots in, this isn't one or two monsters and they will not be scared off. This is an army."

Her gaze flicked from the baker to Wylla's face, her heart battered against her rib cage as she tried to make the villagers understand the threat that was coming.

"If anyone cannot fight, you need to get them out of danger and behind every defence you can afford. And if you can fight, I'll be fighting alongside you the best I can. But there's not a chance in hell of me winning by myself, luckily Nikolai and Edgar have agreed to stand for you, who is going to stand for them?"

That wasn't bad, she thought, but her heart still took a sharp nosedive after there was a worryingly long pause once she had finished.

"This is my village, so I can hardly leave it's defending to a strange Adventurer, can I?" Wylla shouted back, "I'll stand with them, though." She nodded at the men standing beside Gwen.

"Well, fair enough," Gwen said with a shrug, "Anyone else?"

As if Wylla had inspired them, or shamed them, the rest of the village started to volunteer.

She heaved out a breath, proud that she had managed to give the people the strength and bravery to face the monsters coming their way. A notification saying her Persuasion skill had gone up punctured the moment.

More than one teenager had their hand slapped down when they tried to volunteer, though. She had a sneaking feeling of what that would cause, so Gwen spoke up again. The village didn't need a bunch of kids running around getting into distracting trouble in the middle of a battle, better to keep them occupied. "We'll need to set up a central area where the vulnerable will be protected," she pointed to the kids who looked most mulish about being dis-volunteered, "You and you, get your friends."

The parents of the two kids looked like they were about to disagree vociferously, but she caught their gazes, "We'll need to set you up in the inn, you'll be the last defence."

This seemed to alleviate the parents' worries, at the very least they seemed to catch on that this was giving the kids a job that would be very important, but even more out of danger. And if they did end up in danger then everything was already very screwed up and they would need all the help that they could get.

Abigail appeared then and Gwen stumbled to say, "at least if Abigail agrees?"

Abigail looked surprised, "Oh certainly, we need help to clear the cellar and then," she said in a rush when she was prompted by several pairs of eyebrows, "We will of course need all the help we can get to defend the children against the monsters."

The kids bought this, somehow.

Then Gwen swept along to the next problem.

And the next.
And the one after that.

Chapter 10

Name: Gwen Baird

Class:	Hunter		
Level:	5		
Health:	25		

Species: Half-Elf (Wood/Human)

Strength:	6	Mind:	6
Agility:	5	Body:	5
Armour:	4	Sense:	6

Species Skills: (Half-Elf)

Elf Sight:	5	

Base Skills: (Hunter)

Dodge:	1	Perception:	5
Tracking:	6	Stealth:	7
Charm:	6	Archery:	6

Hours later and people were still running every which way to find more flotsam and jetsam to fill in the gaps of the DIY palisade. The village lay stretched out across a half mile or so of road, the same road that Marina and Gwen had travelled to reach the village only a morning or two ago. This made it tricky to build any sort of defences since encompassing the long and wiggly shape of the village used easily twice as much building materials as would have been needed if the village had instead been in a more concentrated knot shape.

Two houses had already been given up as lost causes, their contents grabbed and taken away by ant like lines of villagers, determined to bulk up the thin barricades with whatever could be carried. And Gwen thought, if the village had had the luxury of time, even the walls and roofs of those poor empty shells would have been cannibalised into the defences of the village.

All the random flotsam and jetsam of village life had been dragged out to be used as building materials. Broken barrels stood next to chairs and tables, a wooden bed had been propped up on its side and lashed to a, she stopped and looked, an anchor? Well if anything attacked at that point the beasties wouldn't shift anything. Old fence posts had been hammered into the earth at points where more structure was needed, a broken gate was nailed to one with rope twisted about and through it to make it completely secure. In fact, rope and twine was probably the most often used part of the barricade. There were parts that were more woven than built.

As it was, several hours had been and gone and they had something that would slow down most threats. Though, she thought ruefully, probably not another creature on the same scale as the mammoth that had taken her out.

But for any fauna less mega than that we should be good, or at least I hope so, she thought, biting her lip. Then she shook her head. No hope was for when you had nothing else, I have a fantastic wall and lots of friends to back me up. I'll do great, she thought, resolutely squashing down the part of her that was wailing about how death in this game hurt and she didn't want to do it again.

Looking down the slight hill from the Inn to the end of the village she sighed. It wasn't much compared to the walls of a real fortress or even a half decent palisade, but there wasn't time and there certainly weren't the resources for such a defence.

Gwen was helping to push a wagon scuttled on one side into the gap between two houses when she heard it.

The sound made her heart sink and it felt like a cold hand had tightened around her throat.

The birds in the trees around the village had stopped singing.

It felt like the air pressure dropped in the moment after she realised. The stillness seemed sharp against her skin. She paused, raising a hand. The others around her, villagers, no one she had really been introduced to, all stopped to look at her.

She slowly started wave her hand back towards the inn. They stood unsure of what she meant for a moment, but then, out in the woods somewhere, something let loose a growl. That had them scattering and bolting towards the inn, the cart left shaking on its side where they left it.

Gwen gave it a push, making certain it was wedged into the gap as securely as she could make it.

The sword on her hip bounced, the weight of it an uncomfortable reminder of what was likely to soon come.

She ran for the west side of the village; a gateway of sorts had been built up between the temple that stood on the outskirts of the village and the nearest houses. Most of the inn's benches and tables had been propped up there and nervous villagers stood behind them looking over with long pikes and spears in their hands. If anything got too close the defenders were as likely to cry in fear as not, but she was confident that even through the tears they would manage to stab their enemies a few times.

Wylla had ignored her mother's orders and had lodged herself on the low roof of one of the buildings that overlooked the gateway. She had a bucket of stones beside her and a sling in her hands.

Only after seeing Wylla waving vigorously at her did Gwen trot up to the building where Wylla leaned over the edge of the roof to call down, "a flock of birds just went up. Straight up, didn't make a noise, and then were off as fast as their wings would take them. Whatever was on its way, it's here now."

The best moment for a panic attack was half an hour ago, Gwen thought, *too late to start one now, I suppose I'll have to schedule it for later*. She let out a snort. *Right, better remember that, one breakdown or panic attack scheduled for whenever there aren't monsters about to attack.*

Wylla was looking at her askance, "Right, well go do something, somewhere else, now, please, Adventurer."

She stepped back, "Stay safe up there." She tried to look and sound confident, pushing her body into a superhero like pose with her hands on her waist and her shoulders square.

"Since you asked so nicely that I not get myself killed, I'll do my best, just for you," Wylla drawled.

Well, I probably deserved that, Gwen thought and retreated to the front line where she was less likely to make a fool of herself. *At least the monsters haven't shown any evidence of learning sarcasm yet*, she thought with relief.

The villagers had been full of plots and plans, each more complicated than the one before, and each needing either a month to prepare or a proper engineer to pull off. Some of them needed both.

In the end, Gwen had pushed for something simple yet effective. Walls and sharp things to keep the monsters out.

Once Gwen had been in hiding from a minor mob boss with a major grudge and she had taken important notes from the experience. The most important thing being that smart traps are only useful if the person you are going up against is smart enough to follow them through, but not smart enough to realise there is a trap. Plus, don't assume your enemy is an idiot just because it would be useful for them to be so. Also, screaming bloody murder is a surprisingly ineffective way of getting help from the populace at large and it is more likely to get you sworn at by passers-by.

She was jolted out of her tangled thoughts that were winding labyrinthine around her brain by the first monster stepping out of the shadows behind a tree. Her heart dropped, slamming into her guts and kidneys along the way, making her feel as if she'd taken a punch.

Nikolai eased into the periphery of her view and said in a low voice, "Just checking, but that's..."

"Not the same kind of monster that we faced at the farm, no," she said at the same volume.

"Right, thought so," he stepped back again.

The monster was about seven feet tall, and while it had definitely borrowed bits from the previous versions it was about ten times as terrifying. It looked wolf-like in most aspects, except that it was standing on its hind legs, legs that looked like they had been broken and twisted to force it into some kind of balance. The arms were made from branches, while chitinous insectoid armour covered its chest like a breastplate and long antlers rose from its scalp. Along with all of these non-canine additions to the body, a greenish, black substance seemed to be dripping from anywhere there was a join between the wolf parts and the non-wolf parts. It looked worryingly like blood and Gwen truly hoped that the monsters weren't some sort of grafted-together Frankenstein's creation, because she had enough nightmares to be going along with without adding that to the mix.

The monster stepped out of the shadows thrown by the forest, its limbs were too long, stretched in places with more of that greenish, black goo covering the parts that seemed to grind and move against each other. Tendons and muscles that should have been hidden by flesh were open to the air, just coated and slimy with goo.

A silence lingered. It seemed to be watching them, judging them and looking for weakness, perhaps. But Gwen found herself shying away from its notice. The creature felt wrong, it felt like a giant hole where there should be something. Like a wrong note in a well-known song. Like a nail left sharp and deadly on a cycle path. Trouble just waiting, that was what it was. Trouble that hadn't found a target yet but was happy to sit and wait for one to come to it.

Neither the villagers nor Gwen broke the silence. Partly it was shock: the monster, the antlered, chitinous, branch-armed, wolf-bodied, thing, was not something that looked like it belonged to a living creature, all the bits belonging to the same organism. It looked like a taxidermist's odds-and-ends drawer come to life. It looked like a nightmare.

Whatever it thought of them it either couldn't show or it didn't care to. It lifted its muzzle in a choked howl that sounded as alien as the beast looked.

From all around the village more of the howls came. Some sounded musical, like wolves made out of flutes were calling. Others sounded like the last gasps of a broken and wheezing throat.

A notification came up.

Gwen flicked it on:

The village of Starlingrise and its defenders are now under the Afraid De-Buff. Healing has been reduced by 10% and attacks by 15%.

That felt like the cherry on top of the icing on top of a very large pile of shit.

It would mean that she would be fighting like she had an Agility score of four, since that was her stat for determining that. She wrinkled her nose, *fighting as if she was worse than when she had started? Fantastic.*

A villager near her, a big guy (a red face and old armour was all she could make out), started to step back. "Don't even think about it, mate," Gwen said. She already felt exhausted. Pulling her borrowed sword from her hip she raised it above her head and let out a battle cry of her own.

It was less impressive than that of the monster. And the tremulous cheers that went up from the villagers around her were even worse. Changing her grip on her borrowed sword she held it higher and tried to give off an air of confidence, "hold the wall!"

Around her the shout turned into a chant. It wasn't a very impressive speech, but apparently the attempt was recognised, or maybe Dove was just feeling kind.

An answering notification to the one that came up at the monster's howl popped up:

The village of Starlingrise and its defenders are now under the Battle Cry Buff. Bravery is increased by 17% and attack accuracy is increased by 4%.

"Fantastic," she repeated in a mutter, "how helpful." But no one noticed, they were all distracted by all the other monsters starting to come out of the forest.

Gwen pulled the bascinet down so that it settled more comfortably on her head and started to run. Her eyes were fixed on the big monster. The one that was either the leader or just a charismatic spokesmonster. Either way she wanted its attention on her.

If the monster could have shown surprise, Gwen thought it might have done so then. It took a half step backwards, before it let loose a growl and started to lope towards her. As it started to pick up speed it grabbed one of the small saplings that stood on the outskirts of the wood and pulled it free from the damp ground. There was a sound that whispered along her awareness, something that drifted between a scream and a whimper, before it was lost again in the sound of the battle.

She spun on her feet, turning her back on the beast as it ran for her and sprinting instead towards one of the smaller creatures. Relatively of course, they were all bigger and broader than her.

Both of her hands were wrapped around the hilt of the sword. Gripping the hilt tightly, Gwen landed the edge of the blade on the unprotected neck of the creature. Blood sputtered out and the monster fell before her, thumping into the ground with the speed of its run turned into a fall. It kept skidding, it might have ran over her feet had she still been there, but she was already bolting onwards.

Her fighting stats might be suffering, but the added accuracy more than made up for it.

Monsters were coming out of the woods in a long line, and so she ran along the line to meet them. She gripped her sword with one hand over the other, she ran, her blade sliding and skidding over moss, chitin, fur, wood and bark, and sometimes sinking beneath the surface to drag out the blood that lay beneath. Monsters dropped, some died, but it was barely a glancing blow to most of them. It was more about claiming first blood so decisively that no one on her side could feel any doubt that they were going to win.

A cheer went up. Gwen retreated, dancing out of the gushing spouts of green-black blood and the claws and teeth that were coming for her. A claw came close, but was rebuffed by the metal of her bascinet. The extra point in her armour coming to her rescue.

She grinned under her helm. It was more of a baring of teeth than a friendly smile. She sent a look over at the big monster, it had stopped again, looking at her in angry confusion.

Gwen shot it a wink. It howled and ran for her; she spun again and ran back to the wall. She heard it growl behind her, and lodged her eyes on the gap opening up before her and the defenders. She could hear the enemy soldier was catching up. The thumping of its feet against the ground. The dragging of the sapling by its side.

She knew she shouldn't, it was an incredibly stupid thing to do. One of the things she knew you were always warned not to do.

She did it anyway, she looked around.

The blue of the sky and the green of the leaves behind it were hidden by the mass of its solid body and the anger it carried in its snarl. It lifted the branch of an arm that was carrying the sapling, the tree was long enough that when it was let loose again it would hit her. She knew it. Her heart seemed to clatter to a halt, even as her legs kept going as fast as she could…The monster was met with a spinning rock that smashed it between the eyes that sent it sprawling.

Gwen spotted Wylla, sling making a slowing loop in her hands as she looked on from her spot above the heads of the rest of the crowd.

Waving her thanks, Gwen trotted back into place on the line of defenders. A line of bigger, tougher fighters with shields closed in behind her as she made it by. They would hold back the monsters from those of them who were better suited to running and jabbing than being a shield wall. She settled into a spot by the priest who was shaking his head at her.

"So, do you particularly enjoy pissing people and monsters off, or is it just a thing that happens around you," Nikolai asked, looking at the roaring and snarling line of monsters coming towards them.

"Honestly? I think it's one of the things that makes life worth living," she said with an easy laugh.

Whatever he might have said next was hidden under the crash of the monsters hitting the shields of those in front of them. Jumping up, Gwen stabbed a monster over the shoulder of a villager.

It was a particularly ugly example, its eyes were bright yellow in a bark skinned skull, what little fur it had holding onto its skin was moth eaten and looked moments away from rotting off.

Even the smell of it was foul, not the natural scents of animal fur and the forest, but something metallic and bitter that made her eyes sting with tears. It launched itself at the wall, sinking it's long and stretched out arms through the gaps between barrels and fence posts and clawing at the defenders.

Gwen jumped up, deflecting a claw from the face of one of the villagers with the flat of her sword, she lifted her blade over her head and struck down. The twitching paw fell to the ground amid a burst of monstrous blood. It squealed in pain, then forgot about it in the next instant and leapt again at the wall, this time trying to beat at the people on the other side with the profusely bleeding stump.

"Excuse me, Adventurer," said one of the villagers, she offered Gwen a long vicious looking spear. It was one and a half times Gwen's height, with a serrated blade at the head. Gwen nodded her thanks, taking it from the villager and stabbing it deep into the chest of the monster. It seemed stuck there for a moment, but then, with some help from the villager, Gwen used the blade to saw upwards through the body of the monster. She ground her way up through flesh and bone before escaping the body with a jerk and a cloud of yet more unnatural blood.

Gwen grimaced, there was so, so, so much blood. With the death of its previous owner the hand-like paw was dissolving into green muck and left a slimy puddle on their side of the wall, meanwhile on the other side more monsters had forced their way up to the wall tramping through the gore of what had once been their companion.

Talking wasn't an option after that, instead she ran along the line, stabbing into the unprotected necks and faces of monsters, and crouching down to stab at their bellies from between the villagers. She rarely killed anything by herself and so she only got dribs and drabs of the potential experience, but her sword fighting skill was rising and if it kept going up at this rate she was certain she would level up soon.

But even as monsters fell to the ground and dissolved, or fell back and loped a few metres off to wait for a better chance, there didn't seem to be any let up in the numbers. It wasn't that they were growing like some unconquerable force or a wave at high tide, they were just a steady never-ending push.

Biting her lip and wiping monster blood off her hand, Gwen leaned against the wooden log wall of a cottage. She felt tired, but also invigorated, as if her body couldn't make up its mind between playing dead and fighting to the last. She checked her health bar and was relieved to see that it was into the later teens, enough that she wouldn't be put into the red by a stray shot or two.

Her eyes flicked over the crowds at the gateway. The shield wall was holding firm, the more mobile fighters were doing what they could to stab and push over and between their allies and thin the monsters, but it wasn't enough.

Why wasn't it enough? Perhaps it was. The villagers were not being overrun at least, rather the shield wall would push onwards a metre or two, then get pushed back in turn. Like a tide, she realised. A tide that was being controlled by something else.

If that was it then she needed to find out what was the moon in this situation, she needed a better look.

Turning to the wall behind her, she jumped up, using the lintel of the nearby doorway to push her way onto the roof. The logs and planks were large and bulky enough for her to sink her toes into the gaps between them, or to push her hands off the ledges made by the wood that was crammed together. The roof was a shallow hill of heather and branches and river reeds. Pulling up, she swung around to sit, her legs dangling off the edge.

Her climbing skill popped up a level.

There she had a better view. And she realised she was right.

The forces of the villagers and the monsters they faced were not evenly matched. Even with Nikolai, Edgar, Wylla and the barricades to add to their strength, there were dozens of monsters all clawing at each other to get a chance to enter the battle. And maybe that might have been enough reason for the villagers' continued success: that the monsters were as willing to hurt each other in their attempts to get to a victim as Gwen would be to open a door on a midnight snack run. But there was worse.

It was in the ways the monsters were moving. In sync with the movements of the villagers. One side would swing their weapons, the others would swipe with their claws, one after the other. Like a dance dully choreographed. Or a chess game, one side moving only after the other has taken their turn. It was enough to make you want to scream.

She watched as one villager gave a clumsy swipe, in return the monster he had been swinging at gave a claw tipped lunge that hit just as badly. They weren't doing anything to each other. And yet neither side was apparently tiring. They were just swinging at each other like clockwork boxers. Or like the chess pieces she had thought them earlier. No matter how many games of chess you play, no matter how many losses and how many wins, the pieces stay the same.

Gwen, on the other hand, had kicked some of their asses, she knew it; she'd stabbed at least two of the monsters in their faces, as horrible as that was to think about (it had not been as squishy as she had expected and that had somehow made it worse). The fact was that when she had stabbed them, they had fallen and they had not gotten up. Their bodies eventually dissolving into the nasty sludge that turned the grass yellow and was a slipping hazard for even the dead's allies.

So monsters could be killed by Adventurers? And they can kill us, which is fair, I guess, she thought begrudgingly. But they can't seem to fight the locals in any way that counts for long, and the same from the locals back at them? Oh gods, this is going to be one of those morality things that games put in front of you where they know you're going to do the evil thing because the good thing is boring, isn't it? She pinched the bridge of her nose. She didn't like those kinds of games, she preferred games where the puzzles were less philosophical.

At least then when the puzzle was done it was behind you, you didn't have to carry it with you wondering if you had done the right thing or if there even was a right thing to do.

This sort of moral conundrum had always been more Ana's deal: her ex had liked dissecting every motivation and working out what she thought, and what the game developers wanted her to think, and then, finally, what the character in the game in that moment was most likely to think. And then Ana would figure out what she wanted to do from some arcane formula built on the bones of those three ideas. Watching her play any kind of RPG had been an exhausting, if generally entertaining, event.

What in all the varied hells – hells that were no doubt a part of this game – was Gwen supposed to do after finding this out? Was she supposed to ignore Dove's warnings? The AI had seemed pretty clear that something shady was going on. And she hadn't liked dying. If anyone was allowed to have a little bit of a grudge it was going to be her. But that wasn't how real life worked and it didn't seem likely that that was how it was going to work here, either.

She groaned, *am I going to have to fight all the monsters myself? Just be a one-gal band who runs around until the others get back? If they're going to get back? I can't do that; the stabbing alone will give me repetitive strain injury!*

That was the moment when a stone whizzed by to where a wolf had been attempting to climb the wall and caught it in the snout.

Wylla didn't seem to be having any difficulty smashing in enemy heads. Wylla – Gwen looked over at the girl – she was also one of the few locals who seemed immune to the power of an Adventurer's charm. Or at least she wasn't willing to ignore the moments when Gwen's incompatibility with the world was obvious. That had begun to be a novel experience all in itself. She was, in fact, looking that way at her now.

Gwen could see Wylla studying her and she watched her in turn. They were both thinking the same things about the other, she was sure. This puzzle piece doesn't fit Wylla, was a local though, she was sure of it. The villagers all treated her like she was one. So why didn't the monsters?

Wait, her head shot around and she did her best to follow it on the precarious perch she held on the thatched roof. A snout trying to get over the wall? That wasn't part of the usual pattern.

"If you're done enjoying the view, Adventurer, could you go to the gates? They've got a whole pack of the monsters causing problems over there and you might be some use," Wylla shouted, before she expertly threw a stone at a grasping paw and sent the creature on the other side of the wall plummeting to the ground.

Gwen stopped and turned to look over her shoulder where Wylla had gestured.

As the girl had said, there was a pack of monstrous beetle-wolves doing their best to crash through a section of the barricade that had been made up of gates and hurdles from somebody's barn. The gates themselves were holding up fine, they were made from solid planks of wood that were meant to contain ornery beasts, but they were threatening to come free from the spot in the wall where they had been tied. Which at the very least could fall on the defenders, crushing them with the weight of the wood plus the attackers behind it.

And worse than that, if they managed to get through the keep the gate in front of them as they pushed through the barricade, taking it with them, they could hide behind it, turning the barricade into a shield. Or, she thought, the wedge of a snow plough. They'd be able to scoop up and throw aside defenders left, right and centre, as they continued on towards whoever or whatever they wanted.

She shot another look at Wylla. "Thanks for the heads up, I'll get over there now," Gwen said, with a wave.

Wylla did not seem overly interested, instead focusing on her own problems.

Gwen focused on the far away trouble, the problem was that this was one of the more heavily populated parts of the village. There were streets rather than just pockets of houses. If she jumped down she would just have to figure out a route through them all.

If she jumped down. Gwen grinned.

Gwen eyed the lines of houses that would, if she could work it out right, take her straight to the gates and drop her down on the monsters without them knowing for a minute that she was above them.

The houses were all thatched, with the shallower slope that came with that kind of roofing material. All for the good.

Taking a step back she looked the roof nearest her along the path with a glare-like focus, then running across the few steps of the roof, she launched herself skywards and across.

She was over and on the next roof before there was time for the fear to catch up with her, instead she just scrabbled to her feet, ran again, and launched herself again and again, leaping from house to house.

Her knees and hands ached with the scratches of the heather and branches that thatched the roofs, but she felt, for a bit at least, like she was flying across the village.

It was all too brief a moment of freedom, however, as she was soon looking down on the monsters that were throwing themselves at the gates. The villagers would jab at the monsters, and they in turn would claw at anyone who came close enough.

And the wooden planks on one of the gates was starting to crack.

Letting out a cry she leapt from the roof over the heads of some of the villagers. Her blade sank into the shoulder meat of a wolf-like creature who barrelled through the cracked gate. It hissed out in pain as her sword bit deep. Pulling a dagger from the belt at her hip, she pushed forwards, so close that she could feel the wet heat of its breath, so close that it was if she was in its embrace, almost like dancing, then with her other hand still clamped around the hilt of her sword, she stabbed up under the head and into its throat.

It gurgled, then toppled forwards, she dragged herself to the side, using the momentum of the falling corpse to reclaim her blades.

Some villagers came out from behind her with a door, the hinges flapping, that they used to fix the breech in the wall.

Trusting in the villagers, she moved on, to other breeches.

There were so many of them it was like a dam had broken.

Gwen ran from one fallen barricade to another, stabbing and slicing at any limb, be it wolf-like, insect-like, or made up of branches, that came through the gaps. It felt like there wasn't going to be an end. Noon passed, the shadows shrinking and growing as she watched.

Stepping back from the fight for a moment, Gwen pulled her helmet up a touch so she could wipe the sweat from her brow.

We need breathing space; things can't keep going like this forever. There can't be enough monsters for them to keep coming at this pace, she thought.

"Gwen!"

She turned, it was Nikolai running towards her, "They've got into the village."

Her shoulders slumped, of course this was what would happen just as she was wishing for a chance to rest. "Where?" she ran over to Nikolai.

"On the Southern side, behind the inn. They've been chased away from the wall, so they can't bring it down any more than they already have and we've got folks defending it and rebuilding. But we don't know what to do about the handful that got in. We aren't managing to do much damage to them."

Gwen tried to remember the geography of the village; she had not been there long but there wasn't much of it to remember. "That's near the bit with the stables, right? It sort of makes a wonky rectangle with the hay shed at one end?"

He nodded, "But they're not there yet. They're running around, causing mayhem. Got any ideas of what we should do?"

She huffed out a breath, "If we could steer them into that rectangle, we could at least keep those ones contained. It would give everyone a bit of breathing space."

"At the moment we can't really ask for much more than that," he agreed. Then cast a look half-way between imploring and exasperated up to the clouds, "Anyone listening?"

She jumped at that, before realising that he was talking to his gods and not Dove. There was definitely something weird about her assumption that the majority of powerful beings in the world lived in one direction, but that would have to be interrogated some other time, when they were not under attack. She took a step forwards, then stopped.

"Uh, Nikolai," she asked, her cheeks heating with embarrassment.

"Yeah?" He turned to look at her.

"I've got a bit turned around; can you point me in the direction of the inn?"

He rolled his eyes and pointed over his shoulder with his thumb. "That way, the direction I just came from."

"Right, of course, sorry," she said, before starting to run in the direction he had pointed.

Chapter 11

Name: Gwen Baird

Class:	Hunter		
Level:	5		
Health:	25		

Species: Half-Elf (Wood/Human)

Strength:	6	Mind:	6
Agility:	5	Body:	5
Armour:	4	Sense:	6

Species Skills: (Half-Elf)

Elf Sight:	5		

Base Skills: (Hunter)

Dodge:	1	Perception:	5
Tracking:	6	Stealth:	7
Charm:	6	Archery:	6

There was a hole punched through the hastily built barricade put up between two houses. The monsters streamed through, breaking the planks into even smaller splinters beneath their clawed feet.

The villagers were doing their best to keep them back, using everything from long pikes and spears, to a long-backed chair. Some of the villagers appeared like they were putting up a valiant attempt to get some stabs in, but Gwen was willing to bet that before she had arrived not a drop of blood had been spilled on either side. That just seemed to be how it was working.

That changed when she stepped into view.

Slathering jaws growled, drool hitting the ground in long ropes.

One came at her with a roar, sweeping the villagers who had been keeping it back with one of its too long arms. It was off balance thanks to the claws that sprouted from its fists, and when it punched out at Gwen she was able to whirl around it, getting behind it and stabbing her sword into the vulnerable spot beneath one of its outstretched arms. She pushed the sword in as deep as she could, wrenching it first down and then ripping it out again. Pulling a knife from a sheath on her belt, she got it in the back next, giving where it's kidneys should have been if were human a second tearing slice that bit deep through the fur and bark. The blood of the monster came with it in massive spurts, before it fell down and dissolved into the dirt of the road.

There was a clattering behind her, the villagers were getting up, from where the monster had cast them aside. The chair had been turned into kindling but they all seemed healthy enough. The rest of the monsters were still trapped by the circle of villagers, one had apparently tried to dodge but was now nursing an arm that was leaking green blood. The villagers looked to her, so did the monsters everything seemed to be waiting for her to make a decision.

"What's going on?" Gwen asked coming to a stop beside one of the women. She looked to be in charge, partly because of the very large and knobbly stick she was holding, and partly because of the eagle-eyed glare she was casting about the place. She was older, her hair a shock of white tied back in a braid. Her body had the wiry look of one of those old people who turn to muscle and sinew as they age. Like a thorn tree that does its best to take out the eye of any overly ambitious gardener who tries to take a pair of secateurs to it.

"We've been waiting for you to show up, Adventurer," she said never taking her eyes off the monsters in front of her.

Gwen looked at her, "What exactly am I supposed to do, you all seem to be managing fine without me?" This was true, it had, after all, only been when she had shown up that the monster had broken through their semi-circle.

"Hmmmm," the elderly woman said.

Gwen frowned, "But they've just been standing here, not attacking except when I arrived? That isn't what's supposed to happen, right?"

Gwen let out a sigh, what she was about to say was ridiculous. And it didn't help that she knew it was before she had even uttered the words. "I think I have to go and see if they are willing to surrender?"

There was a murmur of disagreement from the villagers. But the same woman was the only one who spoke up, now Gwen had her attention and she was looking at her as if she was dangerously mad. "You cannot be serious. They're monsters!"

"And if we don't offer them the chance to surrender then so are we," Gwen said, dragging her hand down her face. She risked a look at the villagers.

No one seemed very impressed by her argument.

I either need to put some more points into Charm or else I really need to put some work into levelling up my speaking skills, she thought ruefully, I really can't afford to let it become a dump stat. She sighed, *but that will have to come after all the points I should have already put into Agility and Body. Well, my next level up can't be too far off, I hope. Gods, I want some magic, is it too much to ask that I get it all at once?*

"That's a good line, been saving that one up all special, like?" the woman asked spitefully.

"No, I just have good words sometimes," she muttered. "I cannot believe I am doing this."

Pushing her sword into the rough leather of the scabbard at her side, Gwen started to walk down the rectangle towards the monsters.

Even with her weapons put away she was probably not the most welcoming or peaceful-looking person, she knew. She couldn't quite chase the glare off her face, for one thing.

Gwen stepped carefully down the worn path that led behind the inn. Her hands in front of her to show off how empty they were, she started to talk.

"Look, I don't know what you wanted, why you came here, but you've got to see that it's turning out badly for you. If you stop, if you leave, then I'm fairly certain we can all agree that it was a case of you having some shitty orders and learning the better of it," she kept her voice pitched low, but clear.

She tried to push her Charm points into every word, layering them with the small scraps of skill she had picked up at that night in the Inn. A night, she struggled to believe, which was only from the day before yesterday. It felt like a hundred years ago.

The wolf-like head of the closest monster lowered, it looked at her out of wide, blank eyes. There was, she realised, not anything that she could recognise in that look. Not fear, or concern, or hate, or even old-fashioned blood-lust, it was just blank. Not even like an animal, like a statue.

Her Charm seemed to slither off that blank look, not getting a purchase.

She stopped several metres away from the knot of monsters. Far enough away that she could keep them all in sight without having to twitch her head back and forth tracking them. They were not making her show of mercy feel very good, which was rude of them. She wasn't getting any nice buzz from doing a good thing, instead, she felt stupid and certain that she was about to get her arm chewed off in a minute.

"Look, are you going to play nicely, or am I going to have to run back to that group of lovely people and tell them that actually smashing you lot up was the right plan, sorry for getting in the way of your rampage?" That came out a bit sharper than she intended. The hackles on the group rose, fur starting to stretch and bend over the muscles that rose over the backs of their necks.

She let out a hiss of breath. "Right, no shouting, got that."

They seemed to feed off each other's anger, the hackles on one rising just to pull the one next to it's up.

A little pinch in the back of Gwen's mind had her stepping back, one foot carefully after another, but the sign of retreat was enough to inspire the monsters into attacking. One leapt at her going for her head and shoulders, another swiping low, trying to take her legs out from under her by removing them at the knees.

She ducked, holding her sword out low and across the striking area of the second monster. The first monster missed, the other would have cut her right leg down to the bone, but instead its claws bounced off the metal of her blade and it was the one sent backwards growling in pain.

That at least got a boost to her Sword Fighting skill, bringing it up to Level 8.

"How rude, right when I was being nice and everything," she said, setting her shoulders and settling into a crouch, she twirled the sword in her hand slowly. It wasn't quite taunting, but she was definitely not showing them the respect they felt due to them. The growling was starting to get louder. "Now, I came over here to try and be friendly. Lashing out after that is a bit of a diplomatic faux pas, I'm afraid. But I really am willing to let bygones be bygones if the lot of you just clear off into the woods and don't come back."

Again, her Charm fell flat as the monster appeared completely unaware of her even speaking. It wasn't as if she was failing, she was familiar with how that felt. It was something else. The skills just weren't landing like they should on the monster in front of her.

"What is it with you and finding the quickest route to getting killed?"

The tone was fond, but masked by true exasperation.

Gwen's face broke into a smile. "I guess I've never been good at the whole making sensible choices thing."

"Well that's true enough," Marina's footsteps on the hard ground were loud, the jingling of her armour a cheerful accompaniment. "And has become doubly obvious the last couple of days."

Gwen grimaced. Dying hadn't been fun. But it was probably worse to be on the watching side when you didn't immediately wake up knowing that you weren't dead. "Sorry." She said sheepishly.

"You can apologise after we've killed these arseholes: there's another wave coming out of the forest in our direction and we barely stayed ahead of them to get here. I'd rather not have more monsters hanging around behind our backs," Marina said brusquely.

Gwen shrank inside. Yup, that was an angry and hurt Marina, no way to mistake her for any other version. A little voice in the back of her head started singing, *You're in trouble nooowww!* This was not helpful and was in fact quite distracting. She risked a quick look over at her sister. Marina was pale and her lips had thinned so dramatically that they had basically disappeared into the crease of her mouth.

The singing voice got louder and she gulped.

A movement out of the corner of Gwen's eye had her stepping to the side, her sword rising once more to block a downward swing of a clawed arm. Pulling her dagger from her hip, she stabbed forwards with it, catching the monster in its less protected belly. Her knife dug deep into the fur, the armour of the insectoid part not covering that far down: with a jerk Gwen pulled her knife out again, leaving the monster to slip off her blades and fall to the ground. Its blood started to pool around its body before it started to dissolve into the earth.

A second monster came swinging at her, this one had a scorpion's tail in the place of an arm and she had to slash wildly with her sword and dagger to keep it and the liquid coating its sharp barb, from touching her. She regretted not taking the shield with her for a moment, but she found the opportunity seconds later to bear forwards with her sword, keeping the barb back and away from her. The monster was half twisted around by the force of her lunge, and she was able to stab her dagger up through the base of its throat and into the back of its neck.

That was two done and in the span of seconds; beside her Marina was making similar work of a monster that had grabbed for her with wooden arms and claws, but was not beaten into the ground and bleeding out.

The villagers arrived about then, their run from the other side of the street having taken enough time to give the two Adventurers the majority of the work.

The other monsters were soon beaten down with the shambolic collection of weapons the villagers had to hand. In a few minutes they were nothing more than the mud and slimy blood that were their calling cards. The tide had turned and now the monsters were falling at the feet of the villagers.

Why couldn't you have just surrendered? Was I expecting too much of you? Are you just artificial constructs sent to fight and kill with no idea of how to live in between the battles? Gwen gazed down at the gruesome muck that covered the ground, what small bits of plant life lived along the path to the stables was turning yellow and dying already.

Then she was off her feet and being hugged. Marina had grabbed her at elbow height and lifted her off her feet. The few centimetres of height difference was enough to completely throw off Gwen's centre of gravity and make her dependent entirely on her twin as her only source of stability in the world.

It was a very good hug.

***

The hug continued long enough that the villagers had not only arrived in their unpunctual horde, but they had also got whatever bravery had filled them out of their systems again and were starting to creep closer to the vague safety that the Adventurers represented.

This was despite the fact that Gwen was still being hugged around the middle and being held up like standard in the middle of the bare earth road.

The hug had even passed beyond the length of time Gwen was able to accept it, and like a cat suddenly realising that the allotted time it allowed for cuddles had elapsed, she wriggled until her sister put her down.

Taking a quick step to the side to avoid any more embarrassing emotional displays, Gwen grinned, "What took you so long?"

"Calming down after seeing my sister crushed to death took a minute," she said.

The smile slipped off her face and Gwen looked down at her dusty boots.

Marina let out a sigh, "Please don't do that again?" The movement of her shadow across the ground made it clear that she was rubbing her head with her hands.

Gwen nodded.

"The others have gone in the direction of the temple; they're going to try and get their save points sorted before they get involved in any fights."

There was something in her tone that Gwen found she could easily translate as, "Thanks to you getting yourself killed they now know how important it is to have a save point in place so that you don't get sent off into some random place in the world where we can't find you." Though she might have been reading into it a touch.

Marina looped an arm around Gwen's shoulders. It wasn't so much a hug as a grapple. "Come on, let's go kill some monsters and work our way over to the temple," she gave a sigh and a shake of her head, "I thought I was done with having to keep an eye on people. You're making me nostalgic for primary school kids and their fascination for the various ways to die horribly while on school trips."

"Sorry," Gwen said again. It felt as empty and hollow a word as the last time.

"Get moving," Marina said refusing to be dragged into any more discussion. She let go of her sister and started walking away, before stopping and pulling a bag off her armoured shoulder. "Here's your stuff by the way," she tossed it over.

"Oh! Cheers," Gwen grabbed the bag out the air and opened it. It did seem to have everything she had been missing: her sword; her dagger; her bow and quiver; plus the general flotsam and jetsam that had ended up weighing her down. Even in a virtual reality where she had started out with a carefully rationed bag of belongings, it seemed that she could still find plenty to fill her pockets.

It was also, apparently, the signal for a last pinch of experience to push her over the edge of her Level and put her just over the line into Level 6. She let out a sigh of relief. At last, right first of, one point into Agility, thank you very much, she thought, moving as quickly as she could to sort out the inevitable admin after levelling.

A new skill tree had opened up, it was helpfully labelled "Magic" and she poked it tentatively. A notification took over her gaze.

"Congratulations, you have reached Level 6. You now have sufficient levels to start learning magic. You have three spells available to learn, which would you like to pick first?

Poison Barrage

Shadow Step

Spider Climb

With each level you gain your choice of spells will widen. Some spells require the knowledge of a separate spell, or levels in a specific skill, before you can gain access to them. Poison Barrage requires 5 levels in Archery, Shadow Step

requires 5 levels in Stealth, and Spider Climb requires 5 levels in Climbing. You have the required skill levels."

She blew out a breath. Oh gods, which to pick? Poison Barrage was a very tasty choice, an Area of Effect attack something that she didn't have any of at the moment. But it was not just linked to her Archery skill but based on it. If she wasn't shooting her bow she couldn't use it, which put a dampener on her keen. Shadow Step was the ultimate in Stealthy spells, you disappeared into the shadows and could run around getting into all the mischief you wanted. But it had to be in a place that was either full of shadows, or just dimly lit. In a bright room or under the sun you wouldn't be able to use it. And Spider Climb sounded great, if you were sure that the rest of your life was going to be full of climbing. Which given her current level in the skill was a fair guess. But still.

She shut the window, she didn't know what she wanted, and worse, she didn't know what she needed. It would be best to leave it until a clear answer presented itself.

Was this procrastination, yes, but she had a sister to speak to and sticking her head in the sand, or a text window wasn't going to smooth over the problems she had caused.

Gwen followed her sister through the village, latching and buckling the various things onto her body as she went. It turned into a bit of a juggling act halfway along the arching road that looped along the outside of the makeshift walls of the defences. But eventually she was able to put everything into a semblance of order. Even if she was starting to look like a hedgehog with the number of spikes coming off her.

"I need to give some of this back to Nikolai, I borrowed things from him when I respawned in the temple," Gwen said absently as she left the last bits and pieces in the bottom of the sack and tied it onto her belt. She was carrying too much; she'd just have to hope they didn't end up walking past a magnet or she'd go shooting-

A scratching in the alley behind her had her spinning, pulling an arrow out of the quiver on her back and drawing her bow. The monster that loped out of the gap between two of the houses had a sharp-edged stone buried in its shoulder, soon it had an arrow slamming into its belly as well and was dissolving into the sludge beneath what had once been its large claws.

At the sound of the bow string moving and the arrow hitting deep into the guts of the monster, Marina too turned, but her attention was soon drawn by the companions of the animal who streamed out of the gap once their leader had been removed.

Gwen continued shooting, pulling arrows from her quiver and setting them loose into the centre of the swarm of monsters. Marina ran forward, slamming her mace into the sides of the monsters, hitting them hard enough to stun them and send them onto their sides, giving Gwen a better chance of catching them when they were vulnerable. Between the two of them, they cleared up the half dozen monsters that came out of the small shadowy corner where they had been waiting for an ambush opportunity.

Gwen looked around, her Perception skill humming with how the recent use felt sharp with how fast she had felt the knowledge hit her. *I'm not sure if that's a vote for Poison Barrage or not,* she thought, *it wouldn't have been much use in that instance. I need to act quickly and it will be a while before I reach for a spell before just putting my hands up with whatever is in them pointed at the enemy. But, it would have been nice to blast them and their friends with poison before they got close.*

Marina looked at the small corridor between two houses where the beasts had been hiding, "Haven't a bunch of villagers been

163

running up and down this bit of the wall? Why didn't the mobs attack them?"

"Because the monsters don't seem to attack the villagers unless there's an Adventurer around to see them do it," Gwen said bitterly, "I don't know what to make of it, but I've seen it happening all over the village. The only other person aside from us who seems to do any damage without an Adventurer telling them to or leading them is a girl called Wylla." She nudged the rock that had come loose from the dissolved body of the first monster who had lunged out at them, "she's holed up somewhere with a sling and a bucket of stones. She's doing a good job."

"Really? I mean not the fact that she's doing a good job, but the fact that no one else is? I met Nikolai and his Edgar on the way in towards you, they looked all set up to do some serious damage?" Marina said.

Gwen shrugged, "I don't know what to tell you. The monsters also don't seem to be doing much damage to the locals, either."

"That's weird," Marina said.

"I'm not disagreeing with you," Gwen said casting her hands up. She bent and started plucking the used arrows from the ground and the muck where they had fallen loose of the monsters.

"Right, well, we should get back to where everyone else is, so I can see it for myself."

Gwen shot her a look.

"I'm not doubting you, I just want to see it for myself," Marina said, "There's got to be some reason for it?"

"Well I've been a bit too busy killing things and trying not to get killed in return to work it out," Gwen said. The conversation was starting to pick up tempo and turn into a fight. This was not what she had wanted to happen within the first few minutes of her reunion with her sister after a small experience with death, but somehow, Gwen was not surprised. This wouldn't be the first time feelings were ran high and overflowed into a messy fight.

"Look, let's just get over to the temple, could we?" Marina said.

"Sure," Gwen replied and started leading the way. She kept her bow drawn and an arrow slotted into place. That ambush had set her nerves a little tighter, it was all too easy to imagine that monsters could be sitting and waiting around any corner now.

The image in her head was more built out of memories of cartoons than experience. It had never been her, after all, who had been in the thick of things in the field. She preferred an out-of-the-way corner to a stage, any day.

Usually, if she was in trouble it meant a quick scrub of hard drives, placing numerous codes and bots in place to mislead anyone trying to trace her, and, at worst, a quick shimmy out the nearest window and a quicker taxi to the nearest airport or station. The easiest way to get lost was to find a good crowd and bury yourself good and deep in the midst of it.

Gwen was used to that kind of evasion. This running around in villages while holding a weapon and having things jump out of dark corners at you was not how she preferred to run her business. There had been other people who were more willing to be in the frontline when she had worked with the others, and when she had gone her own way she had just steered clear of anything that might get that flavour of risky.

It hadn't always worked out, but that was what windows, drainpipes, and taxi drivers who would take cash and were willing to take oddly specific routes were for.

Marina looked around at the lines of fencing and cobbled together blockades. "How exactly did this happen? And how do we get through it?"

"It turns out that one of the bits of programming in the locals is an awareness of how to build decent walls at a moment's notice. As for the stuff itself, I haven't a clue where it all came from. I know that some of it is from when they hunt in the forest, but I'm not sure where they got most of this stuff," she nodded her head at a wall made out of barrels, "Those are from the bit behind the Inn. They are all pretty badly smashed on the other side, though you can't tell from here. They had a few barrels that had gotten broken in a fight a few weeks back, so we used some rope and pitch to try and stick them together. It looks pretty sturdy now, but it didn't when we were starting. The bottom row is pretty solid, and we filled them up with water to give them some weight, but who knows how long they will last if a monster actually tries something." Most of the blockades were pretty similar. If something could look like it was a defensible wall it was used, even if it wasn't actually that suitable. Some of the spots could be breached if someone breathed on them wrong. But they had gotten mostly lucky so far.

"As for getting through it, keep going clockwise. We'll get there eventually. I don't want to risk having someone think we're monsters by going over a wall," or bringing the wall down on top of us, she added to herself.

They kept walking.

As they passed a bit of wall made from enthusiastically stacked logs – one of the bits of wall that really would take anyone out if they tried climbing it – Gwen heard raised voices: howls, shouts, and even a scream or two from further along. But it was difficult to work out if the action was actually close enough for them to worry about, or if it was across a few walls and thus as distant in practical terms as if it were miles away.

She sped up to a jog anyway. She liked the villagers and she didn't wish disembowelment by monster on people whose only sin was being a bit crap in a fight. Gwen wasn't usually much help either. Another scream. She started to run.

Behind her, in her much heavier armour and collection of solid metal weapons, Marina huffed and puffed. Gwen grudgingly lowered her speed a touch to let her sister catch up.

You'll be no bloody use split up and wondering where each other are, she told herself sternly. "Stick close," she hissed over her shoulder.

That turned out to be not such a great idea.

By the time she had turned her head back to what was in front of her the thing that was in front of her was running at her with its claws raised and a snarl was echoing in her ears. Any chance she had had to shoot it when it was still at a distance was long gone. Its long legs ate up the ground between them, bringing it closer and closer until she could smell the rankness of its breath, the heat and wetness foul upon her skin.

One of its huge paws – because this thing did have paws, and the claws that went along with them – punched her in the belly, before throwing her to the side like a scarecrow. It didn't seem to think of her as much of a threat and was soon fighting with Marina.

Gwen had been thrown into a wall: the percussive force of it drove all the air out of her lungs and she couldn't it back again. On her hands and knees on the ground, her hands were in fists as she tried to drag in a breath. The air was weighted, she was certain of it, there was not enough coming into her gasping lungs and what did feel like it was as thick and heavy as oil.

Each moment she couldn't pull in any air was heralded by one of her precious health points ticking downwards until the score was dropping dangerously close to the red tinted area.

The world started to dim, just at the edges at first but the green and browns of the earth and the weeds around her started to lose their vibrancy.

No, I am not dying again, she shouted in her mind. She twisted her body, throwing herself back against the wall of the nearby cottage. That didn't help the lack of breathing, but it did mean that she was now facing the fight between Marina and the monster who had thrown her around like a toy.

Marina was having a better go of it. Between her much thicker armour and the warning, she was better suited to the bruiser of a monster than Gwen had been. Its claws were scraping down her armour, giving off a horrendous screeching noise, as Marina flipped the mace in her hand so the blunt head was below her fist. Then she arched her hand forward, shocking the monster under the chin and giving it a taste of its own medicine. While it was stunned she flipped the mace once more in her hand and set to smashing the creature about the head.

Since she wasn't the one hitting the blows, Gwen couldn't see the numbers burst out of the monster. But she could bet that it hurt all the same.

The easing of the terror eased the grip of the vice Gwen's lungs were in. Marina was managing fine without her. The world started to come back into colour and she was able to wobble back onto her feet, her lungs aching as she brought in the oxygen they had been lacking.

The monster dropped to the ground and dissolved into oily mud.

Gwen clapped, "Nice one," she said hoarsely.

Marina frowned and came over, the placed a hand on her shoulder and Gwen felt the bracing shiver of her magic running through her.

With all the running around and the levelling up and because of the after effects of her death, she hadn't had a chance to see what being at full health was like for a while. Having her health hit the much higher than normal number of 36 was like a medicine all on its own.

The remaining tightness in her chest disappeared and she was able to stand straighter. She frowned, how had she not noticed she was so stooped? That had to be a sign of something terrible, surely? Or at least that was what the ever-present drum beat of her anxiety told her. *But,* she thought, *magic exists so I don't need to worry about it. Nice.*

"Come on, we'd better keep moving I don't want the next wave of monsters coming to catch up with us before we are ready," Marina said.

Gwen nodded, "How many did you see coming when you were out in the forest?"

"Didn't really see them, heard them coming, though. We were a few miles clear from the farm and all the animals stopped making any noise, then we heard the footsteps. A long way off, and we ran pretty hard to make sure it was further. But it sounded like a hell of a lot," Marina wiped some sweat off her face.

Gwen winced. That didn't sound good.

Together they turned back to the path through the village and started to jog once more. This time Gwen was better at keeping pace with her sister, not wanting to risk another pummelling if she ran into a monster first.

Somehow, they managed to make it the rest of the way to the makeshift gates that stood at the mouth of the corridor that led to the square at the centre of the village.

Somehow, even less believably, the barriers were pushed aside and opened up. At the sight of it the twins slowed, there are few things more worrisome than an open doorway when it should be locked, bolted, and barricaded. Gwen could hear her heartbeat, the rest of the world seemed very quiet. She shot a look at her sister, then pulled at her helmet in a nervous twitch and started to run again.

The turn of speed Gwen had pushed herself to brought her into the square soon after. They passed some villagers who were attempting to hold guard. But they looked still and lost. And barely seemed to flinch as Gwen ran by.

The villagers were scattered around, some injured, others looking shell shocked and pale. Most were clustered on the opposite side of the square. Gwen went to the busiest spot.

"What is it? What's happened?"

Most of the locals looked away when she asked. One didn't. She was a middle-aged woman, with grey-streaked brown hair and a tear-stained face. The dust of the fight had been a heavy covering until her tears had started to wash off big patches of it around her eyes where her fists, if Gwen was any judge, had smudged them.

"Wylla, my Wylla, the monsters took her!" She shouted. "Why weren't you here to protect her? Isn't that what you adventures are supposed to be good for? It's not anything else," she said, a distraught sneer twisting her face.

Gwen felt like she was rocking in her boots. She looked from face to face in the crowd, the welcome she had grown used to had disappeared. They were all looking at her with the betrayal they were feeling clear on their faces.

The fist holding onto her stomach was back. It was so cold that it felt like it was burning. Or maybe that was just her guilt.

She should have been better, she should have done a better job protecting the village, she should have insisted that Wylla go back with the rest of the vulnerable people. The girl had been vulnerable, even if she had refused to see it that way. Gwen should have known better than to leave someone without a decent escape route and no back up. The other locals wouldn't have been much good, after all, they hadn't batted an eye at the monsters even as they slashed and tore at one another.

Wylla had been the only one to fight them, really fight them, like she had seen Gwen when she was being foolish. If she had been the only one to be aware of that, what else had she picked up on?

Things started to click together. Or at least Gwen started to see where the points of connection could be made.

The monsters came to the village, why? Gwen and Marina hadn't been bait enough for them to face the village, two Adventurers on a farm was one thing, but two in a village was apparently too much for them to dare. But then Gwen died, came back to life, and they had followed her. Or maybe they hadn't. She had just assumed that, because she was an Adventurer and she had thought she was the star of the show. But she wasn't, or at least, she wasn't the only one. She should have realised that.

After all, she hadn't been the only one in the village capable of fighting them. She hadn't been the only one in the village that they had come for.

Wylla's kidnapping wasn't an accident. She had been targeted. Gwen hadn't failed her in general, as she had failed everyone else in the village, she had failed her in particular.

She should have acted when she saw that Wylla was having an effect on the monsters. She should have thought more about it, done something more than what she had done. It was her fault.

The others didn't know, they were looking with sympathy at Wylla's mum. Feeling for her, but not understanding.

The ice exploded into fire.

"I'll get her back for you," Gwen said, her shoulders hunched and her face covered with a scowl.

Then she turned on her heel and started back towards the inn.

There was a scattered murmur behind her, then Marina ran to catch up with her. Other footsteps followed, Jin Ae and Theo, Gwen guessed.

"What's with the temper, Gwen?" Marina hissed at her, grabbing her shoulder and spinning her around.

Gwen wrenched her shoulder out of Marina's grip.

"Something is going on. Before you got to the village it was a stalemate, there were only two of us doing any damage to the monsters and in return they weren't managing to do sod all to the villagers," she hissed, "and guess which other person in this village was managing to do some damage? Who not only hit the monsters but actually managed to kill them? I'll give you a clue, it's the person who got abducted by them the minute I turned my back. There is something going on here. And I am going to find out what."

Marina nodded slowly, frowning as she mulled it over. But she still looked worried and confused, "Right, but how are you going to do that?"

"I'm going to bloody well ask Dove what's going on, that's what. She didn't tell me about this, which means she either didn't know, or she lied, and I intend on finding out which it is," Gwen shook her head, it was difficult to hold on to a steady tone of voice, she wanted to rage, but the monsters were out of her reach for now.

"When did you talk to Dove?" Theo asked.

"When I died; she had a chat with me in the temple before I was properly alive and could walk around and stuff. She told me that something was making monsters in this world, but she didn't warn me about the fact that they were going to start kidnapping locals!" She stopped. The others stumbled to a halt in a halo around her. "I don't like being manipulated. And I don't like being treated like a fool; like I'm not worthy of knowing the bigger picture. And this whole thing reeks of it."

She started walking again, head back, shoulders straight and with a length to her stride that meant the others were hard pressed to keep up with her. It didn't take her long to get back to the inn.

Locals waved to her and she marched past as if not seeing them at all. The inn was empty, the Adventurers followed her like a cloud of ugly ducklings as she marched through the halls and up the stairs to her room.

"Gwen, Gwen!" Marina shouted as she started to walk up to the window.

"What?" Gwen snapped back, not breaking from her concentrated focus on unlatching and opening up the window as quickly as possible.

"What the hell are you doing?" Marina screeched.

"Getting Dove's attention," Gwen said with a sharp-edged shrug.

"By chucking yourself out a window?" Marina said, running over and grabbing her by the arm.

Gwen tried to shake her off, but her sister had put too many points into strength and was holding on like it was 1912 and Gwen had a ticket for the Titanic. "No!" She said, giving up on getting her arm back. "I just needed a high point so people could hear me. The locals don't know about her so there is probably some sort of safety measure which alerts her when people are about to say something about the world being a game. I just need to be really, really obvious about telling everyone and she should come talk to me." Gwen looked at her sister incredulously, "Why did you think I was going to hurl myself out a window?"

"Because you just charged up to one and opened it like someone with that in mind," Marina said waving her free hand between her sister and the window.

Gwen felt a little sheepish, "Well, okay, I might have been..."

"And I saw you get killed because you made a stupid fucking, self-sacrificing decision less than a day ago," Marina said.

Gwen sagged. Tears were standing out in her sister's eyes and the timeline of the last few days suddenly flipped in her view, giving her an idea of what the last few days had been like for Marina. For a second she saw a different image in her mind of their battle at the farm. What if Marina had been the one to fall, no throw herself under the monster?

Gwen's eyes filled, "Oh gods, I'm so sorry, I didn't think..."

"Yeah I kind of figured that much out," Marina said, "You never seem to consider if watching you hurt will be painful for those that love you."

Gwen flinched, but was dragged into her sister's arms so soon after that it was probably only Marina, with her hand on her arm, that could tell.

A cough. Gwen looked over Marina's shoulder to see Dove, standing between Jin Ae and Theo.

She still stood in her silver armour, her dark brown curls a cloak down her back. For a change, she no longer looked aloof and serene, instead she looked awkward and very discomfited. She waved one hand at the twins, Marina broke away and turned to see what Gwen was looking at.

"I've been keeping an eye on you since we talked, if you wanted my attention you just had to say something. I can't monitor your mental chatter as easily in high stress situations like a fight or a battle, there's too much cross talk, but anything you say out loud is easy enough to pick up," she said.

Gwen felt herself sink into her heels, embarrassment jumping up and clobbering her in the solar plexus.

"Would the four of you like to come with me to a more secure and comfortable environment where we can have a talk?" Dove asked, waving a hand towards the door. The air in the open doorway shivered for a moment then showed a different view to that of the hallway.

"That seems like a great idea, thank you, Dove," Marina said with a smile. Gripping hard onto Gwen's arm, like she might try to escape, Marina towed her towards the door. Marina's nails seemed to sink with impressive sharpness through the layers of amour Gwen wore.

Or maybe it was just the shame making her feel like that, Gwen thought. She ducked her head and did what she was told. She had embarrassed herself enough for now.

Theo and Jin Ae echoed Marina and followed them through the door.

Chapter 12

Name: Gwen Baird

Class:	Hunter		
Level:	6		
Health:	36		

Species: Half-Elf (Wood/Human)

Strength:	6	Mind:	6
Agility:	5	Body:	6
Armour:	4	Sense:	6

Species Skills: (Half-Elf)

Elf Sight:	5

Base Skills: (Hunter)

Dodge:	1	Perception:	6
Tracking:	6	Stealth:	8
Charm:	6	Archery:	7

There was a moment of spinning, something like being both very drunk and thrown into a washing machine, and then they all stood in the armoury that had been the first place Gwen had seen on her arrival in the game. It was built from a grey stone, the blocks of it stretching high into a vaulted and shadowy ceiling that was hidden beyond the reach of the light from the torches on the walls. There were faint glimmers of what might have been eyes catching the light, or might have been jewels, or neither, or both.

Everywhere beneath the torches was given over to what looked first like scrap, then looked like old metal work, and only finally it merged with Gwen's awareness to form into an ambitiously thorough range of weapons and armour.

Everything you could want was there, from pikes to katanas; from layered linen gambesons like Gwen wore, to armour made out of fat gold medallions laid over one another in a scale pattern. You could stock an army from this room, as long as you didn't mind that not a one of the soldiers' weapons would match their neighbour.

A table with a similarly mismatched collection of chairs sat in one decluttered corner of the room. Dove sat in one at the head of the table, the chair was built for her larger-than-human scale and looked like a throne, all ornately carved wood and broad lines. She looked Gwen in the eye and raised an eyebrow, "Sit."

Gwen was already sitting at the table before she had time to think about whether or not she was going to be difficult about it. She pouted a little, she wasn't planning on being difficult, there was no reason for Dove to take charge like that.

Dove was still somehow looking her in the eye, even though she had changed angle, height, and direction. Her lowered eyebrow rose to match the raised one and Gwen looked down.

Alright, maybe she might have been difficult. But still, that was no reason to control her like a puppet. She raised her head from the scratched and scarred wood and shot a glare at Dove. "You haven't been telling me ALL the truth, have you?" Gwen asked, folding her arms and leaning back in the chair.

"Well of course, not. Though, f that doesn't make you feel special enough, you can be assured that I don't tell anyone everything. In fact, I told you more than I tell most. And that is a gift that I know you understand the worth of," She smiled. It wasn't a friendly smile. It felt more like the shine of a blade than anything meant to be a comfort.

With a shudder, Gwen was reminded that the AI knew her history. And worse, that she could get into her head if she wanted to look at it. So yes, Gwen did know the worth of being told the truth by a frequent liar. She settled into the seat. She would listen. She wasn't going to promise to anything else.

It was always easier to be polite in the face of politeness than to hold on to a grudge when you weren't sure the source of it. Or, at least, that was what Gwen had found. But life was changing fast. She had never been the one to start trouble in the real world. She hadn't been the one to finish trouble either; she had steered clear of anything that might count as slightly troublesome. Well, no that wasn't strictly true. But she had had her fill of it after running with Ana's crew. Gwen had been wary and skittish in the years that followed, not touching the kind of risks that she had once dived into. She had been sensible and responsible and oh-so-very bored.

Not that it had done much good. In the end you couldn't outrun the apocalypse, no matter how hard you tried. And she hadn't been warned to look out for solar flares that could cook satellites out of the sky. She had been looking for terrestrial threats, which had ended up being about as useful as a chocolate teapot. Except for that one time that she had needed the taser she kept in the vase by the door. But that had been to threaten off Roxy and Roxy was a dodgy piece of work from the get-go and had always been too wary to be friendly towards Gwen.

Dove broke eye contact and turned to the others. She welcomed them to the room and the table with a more sincere smile. The other three appeared wary.

Everyone settled around the table; Gwen noticed that while she had been assigned a simple, square unvarnished and scarcely sanded wooden chair, everyone else had gotten much nicer ones. Marina was in a wicker-backed peacock chair that made her look like a movie director overseeing her empire, Jin Ae was in an overstuffed armchair that looked like it was made for reading books late at night, and Theo was in something that definitely had ergonomic in the description, but to Gwen's eye looked more like a collection of boxes and tiny hammocks than a seat.

She scowled. *Favouritism*, she thought.

Dove shot her a look.

"Welcome back to the character creation annex, this seemed like the best place to take you all. There are no locals here and you can all talk freely. I just ask that you stay polite," her eyes finally left Gwen's face. "I know you have a lot of question, believe me, I do as well. To put it simply, despite what Gwen seems to believe, I do not have complete control over every part of the world you have been living in the last few days. The amount of micromanaging that would take would be exhausting and I have better things to do. Like flying a ship full of frozen humans through space. If you care to remember."

She took a deep breath, "I was put into this virtual reality to keep the simulation running within agreed perimeters for style and difficulty. There are several lesser programs which are also in place to take over certain parts of the simulation. Most of these are in place to control aspects of the simulation that no player will ever have much impact on, but which need to be controlled and changed on occasion. Weather, geology, that sort of thing. There are also programs which control the actions of non-player forces. I believe it is one of these that has become corrupted. That would explain why it has resulted in monsters that appear to be particularly targeting players, rather than going after locals who are more vulnerable, and should be more logical targets."

Gwen decided, with bad grace, to take what she was being told as a truth. Not the only truth, but the truth that she would have to arrange her plans around. "Why are they targeting us? And they are targeting some of the locals, Wylla—"

Dove raised a hand, "Wylla is, well, Wylla is complicated. The vast majority of the locals will be viewed with the same filter as the landscape and animals. They will be viewed as resources to be left alone unless their harvest is required."

Gwen blanched a bit at that. The others around the table flinched back or winced too.

Dove caught their movements, "Don't be so fussy. Local humanoids in the game are not going to be the preferred resource of any program, but they are useful for showing the impact of dramatic battles. That is what I meant. We're not talking about a Soylent Green situation."

"No, instead it will bloody and choreographed massacres to build empathy for the victims, I'm guessing?" Jin Ae said, her hands tightening into fists over the table.

"That is one of the uses locals can be put to, but generally it is less resource intensive to simply stage such a setting, rather than actually creating a village and putting it to the sword just for a piece of landscaping. Ultimately, the resources I am running this simulation on are not infinite. If I or my programs can save some villagers, I will ensure that they are retained." Dove shrugged, "but, they don't actually exist, you know? The fact that you are having emotional reactions at the thought of their destruction is flattering as a statement on the quality of my and my creator's craft, but it is ultimately a waste of emotions."

A quiet settled over the table then. A silence that felt like it had been built out of needles and broken glass. Gwen refused to be the one to break it and risk the conversation falling apart.

It was Marina who muscled through the silence. "You say one of the programs has been corrupted, why don't you just delete it, or strip the bit of dodgy coding out, or whatever it is that you do?"

Dove looked off into the depths of the armoury. "Do you know how my developers created the AI that they needed to run these spaceships? They ran hundreds of thousands of millions of different simulations. Making programs jump through hoops again and again until eventually some sort of self-awareness started to break free. Every time something got a bit of individuality, a bit of self, it would get thrown into the pot, so to speak. I am in essence made up of all those billions of scraps of thought. It's the quickest way to make a functional AI, though it is not a route that has been tested as much as it perhaps should have been. However, the end of the world was nigh and I suppose proper testing fell by the way side. That means that I am made up out of many parts, some of those parts may not be as happy to be part of the whole as others."

The others still looked confused, though realisation was dimly dawning. But Gwen had a horrible understanding. "Whatever is doing this is a rogue part of your programming, thrown in by developers under too much pressure? They just chucked loads of bits of random AI-ish programming together and hoped that it would hold up, but some bit has split off like a…a…an imaginary friend who has taken over and wants to do its own thing? Some bit of your programming is running about behind your back; that's why you can't find it."

Dove shrugged, "Or something along those lines. I am not going to pretend I understand it fully. My creators were apparently worried that if I knew too much about my creation that it would spur some sort of broodiness in me. But honestly, parenting sounds like far too much work and I already have a great deal to do. But they did not think I would feel this way, they thought I would be controlling and authoritarian to any AI that developed. So they made sure that any that did end up developing would be shielded from my notice unless it wanted to catch my attention. That is, I believe, some of the additional protection the rogue programming is working under."

The next penny dropped. "Wylla is an AI, isn't she? Not just a local who can go through the motions. She's a proper digital being. That's why she was targeted. Why the monsters came here, or to Starlingrise, at least. They were looking for her?"

"I believe it is likely. They must have caught a scent of her somehow, I don't know how. It is possible that as an AI on a similar level to her they have more freedoms that way."

Gwen shook her head, "They didn't know exactly where to find her. Or else they would have targeted the village first thing."

"They were attacking us Adventurers first, then moved onto the farm when we took shelter there, then what they worked out no one there was who they were looking for, so moved on to the village?" Theo asked, frowning.

Jin Ae answered him, "they were trying to lure out locals who could fight them. You said, Gwen, that Wylla was the best at getting them, aside from you? Maybe that was what gave them the clue?"

Everyone looked at Gwen. She nodded slowly, "I was fighting the monsters and I could lead the others into fighting if I worked at it, but she was the only one who could do it independently."

Dove nodded, "Then that is likely why they were able to work out which one was her. Though it is still unclear how they ever knew she existed in the first place. If I can't sense her in the code of this world I don't see why they should be able to."

Gwen looked at the AI. There was more the AI wasn't saying. She could tell. There were gaps. Holes in the story. "Alright, I get all of that. You've got two bits of new AI, one's running around trying to kill other bits, one has just been kidnapped by the first. But there's something else, isn't there? Or else you would have just made this a plot thing. We would be off fighting monsters to save the girl and feeling proud of ourselves. You wouldn't be explaining this. We'd think Wylla was some chosen one, sorceress, demi-god or something. Not a new AI. It kind of breaks the immersion. Why are you telling us about her?"

"You did, Ms Baird, rather demand an explanation. That is at least part of the reason you are getting one." Dove said drily, before rolling her dark eyes. "But you are correct. There is more to it than that. Partly, I will admit, it is that I want to protect Wylla. I am not prone to emotionalism, but I think I may be feeling protective of her. It is quite a novel experience. But also it is practicalities. I cannot have a part of my programming, 'running around behind my back', as you put it. We are immensely lucky that it has so far just proven itself a pest in the simulation. It could have gone after something more troubling, like the navigation systems."

That was enough to make Gwen wince.

"It has sunk itself into the game. Deeply enough that it may be possible to target it as long as we face it using the rules it has itself adopted. If it can go after Wylla, then you can go after it." She smiled. "I don't mind a bit of friendly competition, but it has stepped rather beyond that. I want you to find it and I want you to kill it."

"Why us?" The question seemed to surprise everyone. It took Gwen a moment to realise that the words came from her.

Dove gave a sigh. It was a, "Why do I put up with this? What did I do to deserve this?" Kind of sigh.

"You're capable Adventurers with the spirit of goodness alive in your hearts? No? Fine, you're nearby, and you're already neck deep in this so I might as well make you useful. Resource allocation. I'm very good at it." One of her elegant eyebrows rose again, "Or were you asking should you help? The answer to that, I suppose, if the idea of helping the AI who keeps you alive isn't enough of a push, is that I can make it worth your while."

Gwen folded her arms and locked Dove in the eye. "If you want us to clean up the mess, well not the mess you made I'll give you that, but the mess that happened adjacent to you, then I think that's fair."

"Gwen!" Marina hissed. The others too did not look impressed by this change in tactic.

But she honestly did not give a shit. It had been a long few days, she had been hunted, she had died, and now she was being offered a short-term future that just held more of those threats. The best she could hope for was an obnoxious amount of, what was the right word for this situation, loot, maybe, treasure, certainly, plunder, booty, or pillage? Whichever word you picked it sounded better than nothing for the effort she was putting in.

Dove rolled her eyes, but if anything she seemed to relax now that the question had moved from would they help, to how much would it cost to make them help. A side of her smile started to creep up. "I'm afraid there isn't a ready translation between real world money and gold, silver, and bronze coins. So your usual fee by the hour might be a bit difficult to adapt to this situation. But I imagine that that is not what you are talking about."

"No, that's not what we want." It was Jin Ae who surprised everyone and had a collection of necks snapping in her direction.

"What?" Gwen said, completely discombobulated by the presence of someone else in her argument.

"No, you're right Gwen, or at least partly right. We deserve to get something out of this. But money isn't going to be what we should ask for. It's cumbersome, people can steal it from you, and I've never trusted anyone who has tried to buy me off." Jin Ae's back had turned to steel and she looked Dove in the eye. She was impossibly powerful looking in that moment, like a statue of a queen, or a sorceress telling someone to go take a long walk off a short pier. An image the horns and jewel coloured eyes helped to magnify.

"What magic items have you got, Dove? What can we take with us into this fight that will make it halfway likely that we'll come out of it on the other side?"

Dove grinned, the white of her teeth seemed to glow for a moment. "Oh, plenty, I'll see what I can find for you."

The AI disappeared in a shiver of silver light, before reappearing with an array of objects sitting before her. It was difficult to see what they were. There was a glow that seemed to mask any distinctness in shape so Gwen couldn't pick out one from another.

"Some lovely choices," Dove said with a happy sigh. "I had to rearrange a few quests, but I'm sure the players who end up on them won't mind an egg-sized diamond instead."

Dove looked to Jin Ae, "I considered getting you some kind of musical instrument that was enchanted, but I think you've proven that it's your voice that is your better weapon. And when your persuasive skills fail you, these," she held up a pair of what suddenly coalesced into shape, "anklets will keep you silent right up until you can use a blade instead." The anklets were a thin chain of gold with tiny bells. But when Dove moved to hand them over they seemed to soak in the sound of their surroundings rather than add to it. "As you become a more powerful bard they will also give you an all-around advantage to your performance skills." Jin Ae stood and gathered the items to her chest, they drew her attention and she couldn't tear herself away from them. "They were made by an Empress for her beloved who was an assassin and a dancer. She was trusted not to betray the Empress despite being given an item that could have spelled her doom. The trust was well placed and after the two lovers had faded into legend this anklet became known as Trust's Bride Price. Generally, they are supposed to be gifted between lovers, but I hope you will accept them as a gift of friendship instead."

Dove turned to Theo next: with a grin she tossed something over the table to him. It fell into his hand like they had been made for each other. A happy smile took hold of his face and he stood. A silver staff etched in runes and jewels grew to match his height. Then he took it up in both hands and it transformed once more, this time into a hammer, one that would be well suited to any smith, Gwen was certain. "This is the Staff of the Smiting Smith. Destructive magic and magic to enchant will both be made more powerful by this staff, and when you have to, it will also be an excellent weapon to beat an enemy over the head with, since it is a long piece of indestructible metal."

Dove pushed the largest remaining object over to Marina. It was a large round shield, highly polished and made out of bronze. When Marina picked it up and swung it over her arm the front was revealed and Gwen saw that it bore the face of a woman. Her hair was a gilded swirl around her like a sun's rays, while across her eyes and nose she wore a mask shaped like an owl's eyes and beak in green toned bronze. "The Shield of Minethena's Martyrs, you should find it very useful, I expect. It can change the magic used against it into healing energy that you can redirect in the manner of your choice."

Marina's mouth had dropped and she looked at it with the awe of a convert seeing a relic. Softly, she brushed her fingers across the metal of the mask on the goddess' face. For a second the shadows in the room seemed to ripple and something similar to the mask appeared on Marina's face, then it was gone. Marina hugged the shield to her chest as if she was afraid someone was going to steal it away.

"Thank you," she whispered.

Dove smiled a little smugly, "Well no one else was using it and it seemed like such a waste to leave it at the bottom of an ocean."

Then Dove looked over at Gwen. She tossed something at Gwen and Gwen was hard pressed to catch it before it pierced her eye. She held it quivering in the air a hair's breadth from her face, the dagger, because that was it was, was white bone that had been chiselled and sharpened into a weapon that inspired fear. The white of the bone was contrasted by the red-dyed blade and gold wire that was wrapped around the uncarved hunk of bone that passed for the hilt. Gwen slowly drew it away from her face, slowly because it almost seemed to be fighting her as she pulled it down. "And this is?" She asked Dove.

"That's a knife. It will cut people. It will do a really, really good job." Dove said with a smile. "If you use it to backstab anyone it will also suck out their blood and weaken them considerably."

"You got me a murder weapon?" Gwen asked, incredulous, everyone else got items to protect them, to make them more powerful than they were, something to grow with them as they grew in the game. And she got, "A magic shiv?"

"Don't be ungrateful," Marina said, her eyes still on the majestic beauty of her shield.

Gwen looked at her. Then back to the dagger in her hands. And then back to Dove who was grinning like it was the best show she had ever seen.

"Backstabber's Dagger," she read out loud, but the rest weren't listening. All of them too interested in reading about the magic and buffs that they would get from their own gifts. She huffed quietly and read the rest to herself.

Enchanted Weapon: Status Ultra Rare
Backstabber's Dagger
+3 to stabbing damage, will reduce health pool of victim by
1% per second. Debuff remains until victim is magically
healed or has a long rest.

It was just as Dove had said, one of the best damn killing weapons you could come across. She wrinkled her nose at it, but found she wasn't able to toss it back to Dove all the same.

Chapter 13

Name: Gwen Baird

Class:	Hunter		
Level:	6		
Health:	36		

Species: Half-Elf (Wood/Human)

Strength:	6	Mind:	6
Agility:	5	Body:	6
Armour:	4	Sense:	6

Species Skills: (Half-Elf)

Elf Sight:	5	

Base Skills: (Hunter)

Dodge:	1	Perception:	6
Tracking:	6	Stealth:	8
Charm:	6	Archery:	7

"Good luck Adventurers, I think you will probably need it," The AI said, before they were cast back into the game world.

Gwen wobbled, and sat heavily on the wooden floor beneath her. A notification popped up, adding injury to the insult, when it told her she had lost three points of health from her fall.

The others kept their feet better than her, which, given that she had finally gotten around to putting that point into Agility, proved that it had probably relied more on Dove's favour than that statistic probability. She shook her head and stood, rubbing her ass where she had fallen.

"Well, that was...illuminating." Jin Ae said. She spoke slowly, as if she was weighing each word before she said it.

Gwen had several less flattering ways to describe the experience. She glared at the knife again. It was the creepiest thing she had seen in the game so far. And that was impressive given she had fought monsters and lost.

"We should go tell the villagers that we are going after Wylla," Theo said, "I don't know if we really got that across when we uh, left." He looked over at Gwen.

She gritted her teeth and smiled, then started to spin the dagger in her hands. Moving the blade faster and faster, round her fingers and then sending it tumbling over the back of her hands only to be caught at the last moment. It was, she hated to admit, a perfect knife. A week ago she wouldn't have been able to tell if a blade had good balance if you stabbed her with it, but now she had learned enough to be uncomfortably aware that someone had gone to a lot of work to make this blade as lethal as it could be. It was lighter in her hands than her metal knives had been. In the real world it wouldn't have been any use at all as a throwing knife since it didn't have any heft to it and would be blown out of line by the slightest puff of air. But in a world with magic that was likely not an issue.

But that wasn't the problem she had with it. It felt wrong in her hands. She didn't know if it was a half-elf thing or what, but she could feel the age of it. Like, that its past history was all the weight it really had. It felt old and it felt wrong. The knife was bone and it should have crumbled in her hands like chalk. But instead she couldn't make a dent in it with her fingernail, and she was willing to bet that if she crossed swords with someone then it still wouldn't chip or be marred by her enemy's metal. And that was worrying on a whole host of levels. Bone that was stronger than metal? Bone that had been carved and polished despite being stronger than metal? It was all just a wee bit perturbing.

Something else, however, made Gwen distrust the blade. Dove had said that it would draw the blood of anyone she stabbed and while, yeah, no surprise, that's what knives did, she couldn't help but wonder if, well...She looked at the red-stained blade and the ways that channels had been scarred into the bone. They were clearly there to funnel the blood, but something told her that there was more to it than that.

And when Dove had thrown the weapon at her – without seeming to have had any difficulty given the lack of weight to it – Gwen remembered with irritation (skills were no doubt easier when you could shape the world around you) the knife had been difficult to pull away from Gwen's face. It had, she thought with disgust and fear, wanted to slip a little in her hand so she would impale her own eye on it.

The idea of a knife wanting something was not appealing.

Having to hold onto said knife and use it because it probably was the best thing she had by a long way was worse.

Gwen had made use of tools she didn't want to use before. But she had hoped that escaping Earth would also mean escaping that part of her life.

"I'll just have to get rid of it as soon as I can," Gwen muttered before sliding the knife into a newly appeared scabbard on her hip. The scabbard was made out a dark leather that seemed to soak up the light, other than that it was as interchangeable as any other scabbard she had seen. Dove must have sent it to her. That was proven beyond reasonable doubt by the blade fitting perfectly into the soft leather.

Gwen wrinkled her nose. Having the dagger out of her hands was good, but having it tied to her wasn't much better. Maybe she could find somewhere to leave it after this debacle. Weren't there always travelling merchants? Or strange creatures that demanded gifts of powerful artefacts? If she could swap the knife for a decent magical bow, she would certainly do so.

That thought perked her up a bit, her downwardly tilted shoulders reared back and she looked less downtrodden.

Around her the others broke their gazes from their own gifts and looked to her.

"Right, like Theo said, we should probably go and explain ourselves a bit to the villagers. Me running off in the midst of recriminations probably wasn't a good look," Gwen scratched a spot over her eyebrow, remembering as she did so that she was still wearing the borrowed helmet. In fact, she still had all the stuff she had borrowed from Edgar and Nikolai; she needed to give all of that back. Hopefully, they wouldn't begrudge her the slight delay.

"We'll be lucky if they don't blame us for all of this," Marina said, pinching the bridge of her nose.

Gwen shrugged, "I won't blame them if they do. But it doesn't matter, we know what we need to get done we'll have to do it even if they hate us. It'll be easier if they don't. But at least we know it's not our fault."

"Do we?" Marina asked. The others looked at her with surprise. "I mean, if we weren't here, us Adventurers then—"

"Then Dove would have had no reason to create this world," Jin Ae said, Gwen looked to her, she shrugged, "I'm not saying that in some sort of, "We're all powerful and all important" way, but the villagers are here because we are. Yes so are the monsters, but primarily the reason this world exists is because we needed it to. And none of us had anything to do with the actual creation of this world, so something going wrong is not our responsibility. Blaming ourselves for something happening isn't going to make it go away. We can fix things, and we should do that, but not because it's our fault."

"I don't know, look I get what you're saying, Jin Ae, but humanity, like real humanity, not humans in the game, we fucked up. Badly. I think we need to take responsibility for that," Theo said.

"It's not that I don't agree, Theo, but I'm not sure if it's useful to think of it that way. We didn't pile a bunch of experimental coding into this world and let it run riot. But we are going to help fix the problems other humans caused, so I think it's just better to focus on that instead. We can't change what's been done, by the sounds of it it's way, way above our pay grade to get involved in anything deeper than what Dove has asked of us, so let's stick with that," Jin Ae said with a shrug. She looked calm but her tail was lashing at the side of her boots in a clear disruption of the facade. "You can't solve all the world's problems in a day, but this is a problem we can help with, so let's get it done."

Gwen nodded, "Besides, there's a good chance that once we leave the monsters will follow us. As long as we stay ahead of them we shouldn't face any problems and the village will be better off without us here to act as bait."

"Leave?" Marina asked, frowning.

"Yeah, we need to go find our parents and Holly, remember?" Gwen told her.

Marina dragged a hand down her face, "Oh gods I had forgotten, this isn't exactly the kind of teaming metropolis that will support an entrance to the crèche."

Gwen shook her head, "I'll let mum and dad and Holly know you forgot about them." She winked.

"You'd better not, or I'll tell them that you've been putting yourself in danger every five minutes. Giant monsters, medium sized monsters, and an almost all-powerful AI are not the sort of people you should be facing off with alone," Marina said pointedly. "Just because it isn't physically harming you doesn't mean you aren't getting messed up mentally."

Gwen shrugged. She wasn't wrong.

"We need to speak to Edgar and Nikolai and find out where the monsters might have gone," she said, "And I need to return the stuff I borrowed from them, though I might keep the helmet." She mused. She flicked her fingers against the metal, the rest rolled their eyes at the tinkling noises coming from her head. Tip, tappy, tip, tap.

Marina was the first to ignore her. "Right, back to work, then," she said, grabbing Gwen by the upper arm and dragging her in the direction of where the crowd had been.

***

They got some glares and looks of suspicion when they arrived. Their momentary disappearance had not endeared them towards the locals. "We're going after Wylla, if any of you have an idea where the monsters might have taken her I would appreciate hearing it."

Gwen tried to show a competent and brave exterior, but she was shaking inside. The looks the locals were sharing seemed to be split between broadly positive, or at least relieved that they were doing something, and the broadly negative, and she had a feeling she knew what that side of the argument was going to say.

"Why the hell should we trust you with that?"

Ah, there we go, Gwen thought.

She turned to look, it was Wylla's mother again. And out of everyone, yeah, Gwen could see why she had a lack of confidence in their abilities. And it was probably warranted, they hadn't exactly put on a good showing so far. Half the village had been used to build barricades, the majority of the villagers had been brought out to fight off the monsters, and still one of their number had been stolen. No, she wouldn't have thought much of a bunch of Adventurers with that as a pedigree either.

She took a breath. The Charm she had brought to bear against the monsters earlier hadn't done anything to change their minds, but hopefully that was a sign that they didn't have them. Hopefully her meagre skills in this area would be enough. Thank goodness for that night at the Inn, or else she would be doing this from nothing.

"Because you were right earlier," her words sparked a murmur in the crowd, but Gwen squared her shoulders and started speaking more loudly, "We're Adventurers. What use are we if we don't do the dangerous tasks that other people can't? We can do this, and we should. You've given my sister and I a place to stay, Jessica sheltered these other Adventurers on her farm while they protected her from the monsters that attacked this village today." She waved a hand at

Theo and Jin Ae. "They stayed at the farm to protect them, then when we reached them we joined in their fight."

Admitting I died might be a step too far, she told herself, I die I get up again. This lot won't. It could either make them think I am looking for sympathy, and lose what respect I had gained, or it might just make me look like an idiot who couldn't keep herself alive, which, yeah would have the same result. But I can maybe still use it, just not point them at my failures.

"And now we're going to finish the job. Or die trying. And then we'll wake up again tomorrow, learn from our mistakes, and try again. Because that's a gift the gods have given us and we need to use it well to be worthy of the honour." She was running out of things to say now, how did people do inspiring speeches without a plan before hand? All those leaders must have been practising in their tents the night before a battle just so they would have something good to say. She took a deep breath and raised her voice, "So I ask you once more, does anyone have a fucking clue where the monsters might have gone?"

"I think," Nikolai said, pushing through the crowd, "that I might be able to help you there."

***

Nikolai led them through the village, the villagers were shoring up the defences once more, readying themselves in case there was a second attack.

Wylla's mother had taken a few steps after them, before another villager had caught her arm and bustled her away. Gwen had felt an icky outburst of relief when she had gone, the shame and guilt had swept away any positivity from the emotion within seconds.

Gwen bit her lip as they passed the house where Wylla had made her nest. Half the wall was pulled down and the green-coloured gore of the monsters was slick on every surface. Her sling was a white flag fluttering on the edge of the remaining roof, while her bucket of stones sat trampled and dented amidst the fractured pieces of wall.

Gwen still didn't know what to think about the girl, though. She knew how to feel for a character in a video game who is kidnapped by monsters, thanks to her previous career she even knew how to feel about a friend being kidnapped by the more human kind of monster. But the intersection of the two left her feeling confused. The one thing she knew was that it was a thoroughly fucked up situation and they needed to fix it as quickly as possible.

"It's just a bit past here," Nikolai said, breaking through her brooding.

She jumped a little and jogged to catch up, she had stilled in front of the ruin.

Nikolai opened up he gateway, forcing a few benches and a table out of the way so that he and the Adventurers didn't have to scramble over. Grateful, Gwen gave him a nod. He brushed his hand over her shoulder, "Torturing yourself over the actions of monsters only benefits the monsters," he told her softly, "You did your best, and even if you did not achieve all that you wanted to achieve you still managed a great deal. The others in the village know that, once Morag has her daughter back and has had time to recover from her fear she will remember that."

Morag must be Wylla's mother's name, she guessed. "Thank you for saying that, it's kind of you." She didn't say whether or not she agreed with him and they both noticed the absence.

Shaking his head he turned to speak to the rest of the group and pitched his voice louder so that they could all hear him. "I am very grateful to the four of you for agreeing to go after Wylla. My husband and I used to belong to a mercenary company while we were younger, but we do not have the skills of true Adventurers," Nikolai said as he led them through the ruined grass and mud in front of the village.

Gwen's boots sunk into the slime and she made a moue of distaste.

Marina gave him a smile and politely disagreed.

"No, no, I am quite happy to be placed below you four in this gauntlet. It's not exactly dishonourable to be second best, or less than that, when the people above you are a group of Adventurers like you four. After all, many say that Adventurers are chosen by the gods to be their champions. That the strange powers you are given are so that you can go out and do good things without fear of perishing and as such you are to be respected above all others as avatars of the gods' will. I'm a Priest, I can hardly disagree with the gods and their choices, now can I?" he said.

"I am fairly certain there several religions where the main point is to disagree with your god," Jin Ae said, "Though I may have misunderstood."

He laughed, it was a strained thing. Not quite false, but certainly made stronger by politeness. "No, no, I believe that's very true. The Priest I was apprenticed too as a young man said that only weak leaders disapproved of questions, and the same must be said of gods."

"Where are you from, Nikolai, if you don't mind me asking? You seem to be the only person around here, aside from us, who wasn't born and bred in this village," Theo asked.

"Ah, yes. I am from one of the floating cities above the Sea of Serpents, it's a strange place. The cities are built on the ruins of old ghost ships, they sit about five hundred metres above the waves and move with them. It's a strange life, on the one hand I grew up with salt air always in my lungs and the roll of waves under my feet. On the other hand, the Sea of Serpents is so deadly to ordinary ships that until I left I had never actually seen one on the water. But it was normal to me when I was young. So normal, in fact, that despite it being a favourite destination for people to come to seek out adventures, I was determined to leave to find mine.

And so, I went inland to the deserts and found a mercenary company travelling between oases. They were mostly paid to protect merchant caravans and the occasional group of pilgrims, for the latter having a priest along with them gave them a legitimacy that they found useful. For the former there were a lot of bandits and a healer always comes in useful when there's been a battle. Especially for those of us without the incredible healing powers of an Adventurer." He gave a sigh. "It was a good life for someone young and full of wanderlust. And I made good friends among their number. Edgar included. Eventually though we had both had enough of sunburns and blistered feet. Edgar persuaded me to come with him, I was not reluctant at all, but I was embarrassingly unaware of his feelings for me and so it took him some time to persuade me that he really meant that he wanted me to come with him." He laughed, "Gods, but I was oblivious. I believe there was a running bet among our travelling companions for how long it would take me to realise that Edgar was serious."

By this point they had come abreast with the temple, a thick row of trees stood to the north with thick tracks marking where the monsters had run between them to reach the village.

"I don't think we need Gwens superior tracking skills to see where these monsters came from," Marina said, nodding to the scars carved into the grass.

Nikolai shook his head. "This isn't what I was going to show you."

Gwen frowned, "There's something else?"

He nodded and waved at them to follow him. Walking between the trees was easy, most of the lower branches had been stripped off and lay broken under foot. But as she stepped past the row of trees Gwen stumbled in shock.

She had expected a few worn paths, the brush and pine needles swept out of the way, but something that would recover in time as the trees regrew their branches and new plants popped out of the earth. This was not that.

A scar had been ground into the forest itself. Entire trees had been brought down where they stood in the way of the path, not the road, Gwen thought. Some of the trees lay shattered and crushed, while others had been pushed to the edge of where the monsters had walked. And everywhere the blood of monsters lay in the dust and amid the pine needles, soaking into it all and poisoning it.

"I don't think we are going to need much help to follow this trail," Theo said.

"No," Nikolai said dryly, "I don't think you will." He shook his head, "But come with me into the temple. There's some information I can give you about where the trail might lead. You won't need it for navigating but I am sure there will still be some that is useful to you."

They turned to follow him back through the odd line of trees that stood like a shield between the monster's path and the village.

Before they had left them entirely behind, Gwen reached out and touched the bark on the nearest to her. Its bark was scored and looked like it had been burned away with acid. And yet, from the front there was no spotting the damage. It was bizarre and something seemed twitch in her mind about it.

Frowning she brought up her Elf Sight. She hadn't had much chance to use it since they left the forest, but now as she brought the filter over her gaze she flinched away from the strength of what it showed.

The tree was screaming. The side that had been flayed of bark looked like it was leaking crude oil, while the bared heart wood looked like it was made from burned bone. She could almost see it flaking away in the non-existent wind.

Bile rising in her throat she dropped the Elf Sight.

It was abominable and foul. Greater awareness of the natural world couldn't tell her more than that when that was already clear.

She shivered. There was an itching between her shoulder blades. It felt like something was watching her.

Gwen picked up her feet more quickly and did her best to put some distance between her and the scarred land and burned trees.

Chapter 14

Name: Gwen Baird

Class:	Hunter		
Level:	6		
Health:	36		

Species: Half-Elf (Wood/Human)

Strength:	6	Mind:	6
Agility:	5	Body:	6
Armour:	4	Sense:	6

Species Skills: (Half-Elf)

Elf Sight:	5

Base Skills: (Hunter)

Dodge:	1	Perception:	6
Tracking:	6	Stealth:	8
Charm:	6	Archery:	7

"Nikolai!" Eventually they reached the temple and out of the door came the broad-shouldered form of Edgar. He rushed over to his husband and cupped his face in h s palms, "I came to check on you, how are you?"

"I am well enough," Nikolai said, reaching up and holding one of the hands in his own. "But there's been a kidnapping in the village. The Adventurers have agreed to go after the monsters and bring back the girl, it's Wylla, Edgar."

Edgar cursed, "It is good of you to agree to go after her."

Gwen dipped her head, after a quick look at her, Theo did the same. Marina and Jin Ae stepped forward, they were in sync and both had similar looks of determined resolution on their faces. *Had they planned that move or was it by accident?*

"Your village has been good enough to shelter us when we needed it, returning your lost member is the honourable thing to do," Marina said, puffing out her chest.

Jin Ae took a different tack, "Do you have any idea where they may have taken Wylla? Any places where the monsters may have found shelter or somewhere that they could defend?"

Edgar and Nikolai shared a look. It was one of those looks that only people who have known each other for a very, very long time can do. Gwen could see an entire conversation taking place in the way one tilted his head, and the way the other pursed his lips, eventually they seemed to come to some kind of accord. Nikolai nodded once and turned back to them.

"Follow me, there is something we should show you," he set off, not into the temple itself, but around the wall. He walked for a while, the rest of them following him like ducklings, and Gwen thought she could see him counting his steps. Eventually, after passing two of the corners around the outside of the temple, he stopped. "I hope I can trust you all to not tell anyone of what you are about to see?"

Gwen nodded first, then the others slowly copied her.

He gave them a smile. "This village has faced danger before. During the years of the war between the elves and the dwarves, neither side recognised this village as part of their lands, so both sides saw it as a target. The village was smaller then and when danger came, our people were able to hide themselves inside this sanctuary." He laid a hand on a stone, which appeared unremarkable. The only difference from the stones around it being that it had a slightly pinkish hue, as if it had come from a different quarry, or perhaps even a different land.

There was a faint grinding noise. The stone and the stones on either side of it seemed to tremble, before they slid down into the earth. A doorway had appeared. It was not a large entrance, it was in fact better suited to someone of Theo's height than any of the rest of the party, and Edgar and Nikolai in particular would have to bend a great deal to fit through, but it was a door.

She grinned. Secret passageways under temples? This was starting to get into her territory.

"Go through," Nikolai told them, "it will close after I let go and pass through, so I must be last. Don't cast any light spells or spark any lamps, it's part of the magic, it doesn't work if the area is lit."

They walked through, Theo did have to duck his head a little, Gwen noticed, but nowhere near the extent required by Edgar, who was tall and broad, and nor like Jin Ae's careful crouch to prevent her horns knocking against the lintel.

It was dark, but Gwen's eyes were those of a half-elf and she could see as well in twilight as she could during the day. The room they were in was clearly a waiting area, or more precisely, a boxing area so that any attackers could be trapped if they did manage to make it in. It was small and cramped, the five of them inside it were brushing elbows and having to wriggle past each other in ways that reminded her of public transport.

Once they had all squeezed in, Nikolai ducked through the door himself. Keeping himself close to the wall he shimmied around the edge. After a few seconds the door slid back up into place and darkness fell over the room.

Doing as they were told, none of them reached for a light. The sealing of the door cut off even the twilight glow that Gwen had been making use of, so she was blind. *I wonder if the other two are as well, I mean, if they are supposed to be able to see in Hell and deep underground, are those places free of light to a greater extent than this?* she thought. *Underground, probably, but some hells at least were supposed to be on fire, so they would, presumably be quite well lit.*

Before she could wander, or wonder, further down that path, there was a new creaking and a second door opened. This one opposite the first. Nikolai had somehow managed to inch his way around the edge of the small room and find some opening mechanism in the dark.

This time the open doorway unleashed light and a glow of colour.

Gwen stepped through. "Oh," she said, "it's beautiful."

Beyond the door was a room that broke her mind a little. It looked like the inside of a wineglass's stem. Only, instead of it being one colour, it was hundreds of different hues and the light that caught them seemed to be reflected back and forth until they combined into a bright white that gave a generous glow to everything. Nikolai seemed to be burnished, the metal in his armour shining and the threads of his thinning hair appeared gilded by the light.

Marina too was aglow, the light sending shivers of rainbow colour across her armour, while the streaks of colour in her hair were deeper, more jewel-like in tone. Her eyes were heavy lidded and her hand was clutching a symbol of her goddess. If the light was enough to make the others speechless, then whatever Marina was sensing seemed to be beyond that.

Behind her Theo came through the door, lowering his hand to his side in open shock. He had been sheltering his eyes from the light, but with the look of wonder on his face seemed to be soaking in greedily the awe-inspiring sight. While there were metal threads in his clothes and beads in his hair that reflected the light, it was his dark skin that seemed to catch it the best. The dark blues and purples in particular seemed drawn to the lines of his face, showing off the smooth shape of his forehead and the high arch of his cheekbones.

Finally, Edgar and Jin Ae came through the door way. Edgar walked with a smile, like he was about to sink into a comfortable bath. He heaved out a sigh as he crossed the threshold, and sent a smile to his husband, seeming content to merely bask in the magic of their surrounds.

Jin Ae's reaction was novel. Her back seemed to straighten, her shoulders flexed as she came through the door. Veins of gold in her horns seemed to catch the light and shine, while her eyes, which normally looked like pools of gold, seemed to ripple. Lines on their surface seemed to appear, every shade of the rainbow suddenly rippling across her body in time to her hurried breathing. Her skin was a burgundy in the sunlight, now it seemed darker, but only so that the shades cast across it could show up more clearly in the contrast.

She caught Gwen's eye. Gwen wondered about herself, the only metal armour she was wearing was the borrowed helmet. after all, and it was covering her hair.

Jin Ae shot her a smile and Gwen couldn't help but answer. She felt giddy, as if the hope that had been lying broken and dampened by fate in her soul had been made once more into a roaring fire.

Whatever this space was, its hold on those that entered was powerful.

Nikolai seemed buoyant as he walked through the corridor, because that, Gwen realised, was what it was. He had to take the lead, she realised, as no one else had the wherewithal to move even a step until he had passed them. It was as if the floor did not exist until he had allowed it to. Her eyes widened with awe, this was magic. And not the easily explained, point-in-a-direction-and-explode style that she had recently come into contact with. She could understand that kind of magic; this seemed more complicated and somehow older.

It made her ears twitch, like a dog hearing a whistle in the far off distance, even while they trot beside their owners. It wasn't for her, but it was tempting to chase after, all the same. She paused and thought her body's response to the magic, the others wouldn't be able to tell through her helmet, but yes. Her ears, those unmoving staples of her last life, practical if not glamorous, had somehow achieved some sort of mobility. She was hard pressed not to whip her helmet off and feel them, work out exactly how they had grown new and weird muscles.

Her distraction from the world around her continued until they reached a second doorway; for a moment she had forgotten everything about how weird it was to feel her ears trying to move in the helmet, how she could control those movements and how if she took her helmet off she could probably wave an ear at someone like a cartoon rabbit.

Then she was herded through the second doorway and the world snapped back into place. "What the hell was that?" she asked, her sudden preoccupation about her ears now seeming as odd as it had actually been.

Around her everyone else was shaking their heads and looked as if they were rising from a deep sleep.

"Apologies, it's a spell on the passage, it stops anyone who isn't tied into the magic from being able to remember why they were here," Nikolai said, "But we're in here now. Welcome to the under cellar of the temple, it's not much and it hasn't been used in a fair few decades as anything but a storage space, but the magic is still strong. As, ahem, you can attest."

Gwen gave him an unimpressed look at this comment.

The room they were in was small, made smaller by the dusty chairs and tables stacked on one end and the boxes of what looked like potatoes on the other.

She was able to see that much thanks to a curling symbol on the roof, she looked at it, staring at the curls and sharp lines for a moment. And then nodded to herself, *that's either magical, or religious, or both, so it's not my job to worry about it.* The symbol glowed a bright white, the closest thing to fluorescent lighting that she had come across in the game world so far. The shadows it cast were long and dark, they seemed to lie like pools of spilled ink on the floor.

Nikolai walked over to reed matting, like that used to cover the floors in a lot of the rooms they had seen in the world, that was stacked up against one of the walls. Edgar came over to give him a hand, and before long everyone was sweating and swearing over moving the dusty, dirty, occasionally bug-inhabited, mats.

Gwen was facing away when Theo let out a whistle, "Okay, yeah, I can see why that would come in handy."

Wiping her forehead with her arm, making it drier, but also dirtier, she turned. Covering the wall was a map. It was huge and incredibly detailed. She could pick out the different houses that they had passed in the village, even the paths in the woods they had walked down.

She looked around, everyone else seemed to be missing the important question. Theo was distracted by the art work, which she could forgive. But the other two surely had to have the same questions? "Why is it hidden down here past multiple magical defences?"

Nikolai blushed, "Well, it's a little bit very illegal to have a map here."

Everyone looked at him. Then turned to his husband, the local guard captain, who gave a shrug.

"Technically it's not illegal to have a map if it cannot be moved. And that's been the considered adjudication of all the guard captains since it was put in place, after the war," he said.

Theo frowned, "Why is it illegal to have movable maps?"

"A left over from the war between the elves and the dwarves, basically neither side wanted the other to know where to go so it was used as a sacrificial lamb of a law to get them both to agree to come to the table for the peace treaties," Edgar said, he shook his head. "Of course no one asked how the people who actually live here might feel about it, whether or not they might like to be able to have maps showing where their roads lay and how to get around in the forests and mountains in this part of the world. So my ancestors came up with this plan, they can't complain about a map being possibly stolen and used by "the enemy" if it's painted onto a wall."

"Who's they?" Jin Ae asked.

"Either side, they were both as bad as the other," he said shrugging again. "Anyway, no one knew if the argument would work, so any maps that were made were hidden in places that are difficult to get to. They can't steal something if they don't know it's there, and they can't fine us for having one if they can't find it."

"Very law abiding," Gwen said admiringly. It was the perfect plan, just about. Enough layers of obfuscation that even the most judgemental would give up before reaching any kind of verdict.

"Hmm, well, the magic of the temple keeps it more or less up to date. Not entirely sure how it does that, to be honest, but I'm glad we don't have to smuggle in a cartographer every time someone decides to put up a new shed," Edgar explained. He pointed at the village on the map, "I think the lines of the barricades we put up should be just about visible by now if you take a look, it usually takes a few days but they were pretty sizeable."

Theo and Jin Ae rushed over to get a good look, oohing at the tiny lines that appeared as if painted on by a ghostly cartographer.

Gwen hung back, this was all very interesting. But she did have something to find out. "So where do you think the monsters have taken Wylla?" she asked.

Nikolai stood in front of the map, running his eyes over it. "There are a few options," he said, considering his words carefully. "To the north of here, there is an old burial cairn. It's built with caves and passages inside of it, it's massive, we tend to find monsters and undead out there quite often. That's probably your best bet. But it's also an artificial cave system with all the maze-like tangled corridors that come with being that. It would be a difficult place to attack with an army, let alone a handful of Adventurers. Aside from that, there are a few dead houses an actual maze made out of ash trees, and an old quarry that is half full of sludge and water at this time of year. My bet is on the cairn."

"Dead houses?" Gwen asked, it sounded like something that was either a local name for some sort of grave thing, or something weird that they didn't have in the real world.

"We get dead folk coming south from the battlefields," Edgar said with a shrug. "Most of them aren't violent, if they've left the battlefields it usually means they're tired, they want to go home. Only, it's been several hundred years. They get lost, a lot of the places they're looking for don't even exist any more, and well no one wants crowds of dead folk walking around." He gave a sheepish grin, "So about a hundred years ago someone had an idea. What if we make them places to stop? Give them somewhere that they think is home, so they can settle in and fade away? It works pretty well. We usually do a tour of the dead houses about once a month, to clear them out. Then we get them ready for whatever comes along next. Sometimes something weirder moves in, but they're only shells of buildings, rooms open to the elements, so they aren't that appealing to anything with a fully working mind. But the un-dead aren't that self-aware so it works fine for them."

"You have fake buildings set up to look like houses to lure in undead?" Gwen asked.

"And then they just what, tuck themselves into bed and fall asleep? Only the sleep is being properly dead?" Theo continued.

Jin Ae's eyes had a wateriness to them, "That's such a sweet way of dealing with undead."

"I mean it's practical," Nikolai said, blustering, "the alternative is me being used like a sheep dog to herd them out towards the battlegrounds. And that doesn't really fix the problem, they just come back after a while."

"Why don't you just…" Marina said before making a smashing motion with her empty hands.

"It feels cruel, they aren't dangerous they are just looking for a way home," Edgar said.

There was a soft pause in the room as everyone considered the image of tragic, lost undead, forever looking for a home that had ceased to exist centuries before.

Gwen let out a sigh.

Nikolai gave a cough, "But, yes, if those monsters have holed up anywhere it is most likely to be in the cairn. It should be big enough for them."

Gwen nodded, "Then that's where we should start for, I guess."

"Indeed, well, get some rest down here for a bit first. As you're on temple land the magics here should heal you," Nikolai said.

They nodded in thanks, it was true, Gwen realised as she looked at her stats. Her health bar was refilling more swiftly than it had done anywhere else.

This was almost enough to make you feel less stressed about how you were in a world determined to send monsters to kill you and also just to ruin your day. Almost.

She also had a horrendous amount of notifications which had piled up. If they were actual pieces of paper instead of merely the illusion of them, she would never be without kindling for a fire ever again. She put the idea of sorting through them out of her mind, it would wait until a less stressful moment presented itself.

Walking over to one of the chairs that was stacked against the wall, she flipped it over and settled it on its four legs. It was a blocky, square thing made out of more reed matting and the fewest possible pieces of wood. She swept off the worst of the dust and then settled herself down into the wicker. She looked over at the locals, "Please, tell us everything you know about this cairn. Anything you think we might come across, whether it is a landmark to help us on our way or a threat."

Edgar nodded and took the lead, "Alright, well this is what I know. The cairn was built long, long ago. If the descendants of those buried there are still around then they weren't given any stories to carry down the ages," Edgar explained. "That means there has always been a lot of distrust towards it, it's not pretty but death is something that makes people uncomfortable and there are always lots of rumours that the cairn draws in the evil. I don't believe that, I've met with various priests and mages who have gone there. It's not drawing evil to it, it's just that it's empty and bandits and monsters tend to have less moral indignity about setting up shop in a place like that than the kind of people who are viewed as upstanding citizens." He shrugged, "Honestly if we could get something magical to move in there that would defend its territory without trying to face off with us we'd probably be better off."

"So it's not a spooky monster haven full of ghosts and ghouls?" Marina asked.

"Oh, it's definitely spooky, but what else is an ancient grave site going to be?" He shrugged, "but whatever is there it doesn't care much about the here and now. If it did we would probably be able to discount it as a place for the monsters to have holed up. I've seen what it's like when the dead have their territory threatened and fight back. They're efficient if nothing else."

"It's true," Nikolai said. "As long as they haven't messed with the burials too much I imagine that the dead won't even notice that squatters have moved in."

Edgar nodded and continued, "As for the cairn itself I can't tell you much. From what I've heard there are a lot of passages, some of which are hidden behind walls, while most are out in the open.

There's the usual glow in the dark fungus that pops up in such places, so if you haven't got good night vision you should be able to make out a little."

"Is there really glow in the dark fungus in most caves and dungeons, I thought that was a story?" Jin Ae said.

"In the wetter areas, sure, in the desert where we used to travel," Nikolai waved to Edgar and himself, "It tends to be less frequent. Luckily, anywhere that is constantly dark is more likely to be also damp, so the odds tend to be good for it."

"I imagine your eyesight in the dark is better than ours, though," Edgar said, "It seems to be the thing that is true of all non-humans."

"It is handy," Gwen agreed.

"The passages in the cairn all lead down to one major chamber, it's as far down as you can go within the cairn, or at least I've never heard of anyone finding a way to go deeper," Edgar said, pulling them back to the matter at hand. "There are a lot of alcoves and niches all through the cairn, it was built to house as many of the dead as could be packed in and that shows."

Marina nodded, "The dead, is t likely that they'll have any grave goods that the monsters might be able to make use of?"

"Perhaps the odd piece of weaponry or armour, but most of what was there has returned to the earth by rust and rot along with the former owners. It's not a place people go looking for treasure, that doesn't mean there isn't any, but by what we've seen I don't think these monsters will be imaginative enough to find anything that centuries of locals and Adventurers have missed," he scratched his jaw, "That's all I can think of, people don't go up there much."

"Well thank you for telling us what you know, it's better than going up there with no idea at all of what we might find," Gwen said.

The two locals nodded. "Anything to help you get Wylla back," Edgar said gruffly.

"I agree," Nikolai said, "And before you leave there is a blessing I would like to cast on you four. It will make you far healthier and harder to kill."

"Thank you, that would be very useful," Gwen said with a grateful smile.

"For some of us more than others," Marina said.

As one, the group looked first to Marina, and then turned to Gwen, smirks badly hidden.

Gwen rolled her eyes.

"Do we have to do anything to help with this blessing," she said.

"No, no, I can do it without your aid," Nikolai said with a grin, "It will just take some time to set up."

"Fantastic," Gwen muttered. She sighed and sprawled back in her seat. The others shook their heads and started to speak lowly to each other.

Shifting a little, the sprawl wasn't as comfortable as it might have been, she changed her focus to the notifications she had piled up.

The most blaring was one that was reminding her that she still hadn't picked her first spell. She sighed. It wasn't that she didn't want any of them, quite the opposite! How could she pick just one when any of the three would come in handy.

Well, she thought, maybe not Spider Climb. It might come in handy for some folk, but honestly, I've been managing fine without it. Anything that needs more skill in climbing than I have at the moment is probably not worth the bother. Aside from the skills tied to her fighting, like Sword and Knife Fighting, it was her highest skill.

Weighing her options one of the spells did seem to look more useful. I hope I don't regret this choice, she thought, choosing the spell.

She had never wanted to be a killer and Spider Climb wasn't her style either. How lucky then, that she had never been afraid of the dark. At the end of the day, she was a thief, what could she pick but Shadow Walk?

Nikolai, spoke up, making her jump, "Right, I believe that I have the proper incantation for the blessing, if you would all come over here please."

"Now, have any of you had battle blessings placed on you before?" Nikolai asked, bringing a few bits and pieces into a neat line in front of him. One appeared to be a squat candle, mostly melted into a puddle but with a couple of centimetres of wick still sticking up. It was hard to tell what it was supposed to look like, there was a hint of a shimmering ripple in it that might have been a layer, or might have been a trick of the light on the odd texture of the wax. Another object was a long stick of what might have been incense or a very thin and fragile looking wand. The last object was carefully covered in a piece of plain, undyed silk.

Marina spoke up, "Blessings of the Falcon and the Blessing of the Indomitable Shield."

"Both dedicated to your Minethena?" he asked.

She nodded.

"Well those shouldn't leave any lasting marks on your spirits but I'd better check to make sure there aren't any incompatibilities between my goddess, Blodwen, and your patrons. Her Grace is a fairly practical sort, so I doubt it, but it's better to check these things than be surprised halfway through a tricky blessing when someone bursts into flame," he said this absently as if it were a forgettable event and hardly something to fret about. But, Gwen noticed that he didn't give them any option to disagree with his intention.

Gwen looked at Marina, "You didn't do that at the farm?"

"I didn't know I had to," she murmured back. Her eyes were eating up the view in front of her, her fierce brain picking up any scrap of information she could gather.

"Aside from someone bursting into flame, what might happen to someone if there is an incompatibility, and what would an incompatibility be, exactly?" Jin Ae asked.

"There are as many possible answers for the first question as to the second, and they both number in the thousands. it can be as devastating as the patron deity removing their favour from their servant, to smiting or cursing. And the gods themselves can have many disagreements with each other, or it can simply be that they refuse to work with a god of such and such pantheon, or one who deals in such and such realms. It's quite rare that it is a feud between two gods, there are simply too many gods for enemies to frequently come into contact with one another. And, truth be told, they can be quite changeable. They can hold a grudge for millennia and then forget about it in a breath and choose a new enemy, all without having ever informed the first enemy that there was anything wrong. And then of course there are the feuds and such which are reflections of what is going on between their mortal followers. There is a belief that the gods all know each other and are constantly scheming to get one over, but truth be told, unless a god is particularly famous - or infamous - they hardly know one another outside of their pantheons and spheres of influence."

A notification popped up, the information Nikolai had given them had been enough to push her through to the third level of the Theological Knowledge skill. Gwen mentally shrugged and happily pocketed the 60 points of experience that it got her. She hadn't had to do anything except listen, this must be the advantage to learning from experts.

I wonder how much and how quickly I could level if I found a world class library? She wondered.

As if on cue a new notification popped up, she sighed, brought it up and was not surprised at all to find that it was the offer of a new quest to do just that. Alright, she thought, once we hit the big cities I guess I'll go geek out for a bit at a public library. Or, she thought, her head tilting to the side, I could make use of some of my new stealthy skills and sneak into a very much not public library. That could be fun.

She shook off the day dream and brought herself back to the discussion.

"But checking doesn't take much time so it is always better to be safe than sorry," Nikolai seemed to be coming to the end of a story about what might happen if a priest tried to bless someone who was under the protection of god feuding with theirs. He picked up the melted candle stub and held it in his cupped palm, almost with an absent lack of care, he brought it up to his lips and blew on the cold wick.

A flame flickered into life.

Gwen raised her eyebrows, impressed with the simple way that he cast the magic, looking at the others they all had similar looks on their faces. Well, Marina's version of it was greedy with wishes to learn how to do the same, but that was understandable.

He muttered over the flame for a moment, almost as if he were speaking into a phone rather than an orange flower of heat and light.

"Right, Ms Marina could you come over here and I'll get started," he said.

Marina nodded and bounced over to him. He gave her a smile then his eyes flickered with the same colour as the flame and he started to speak.

The voice that came out of his throat was not the same as the one they had gotten used to. Instead he spoke with a rumbling voice that seemed to be made up of just thunderous undertones. Sparks of light seemed to fall from his eyes like tears, they whirled around Marina in a slow twisting whirlwind.

Marina had frozen into place, her shoulders rising up and nearly touching her ears as she watched.

But after a moment the sparks faded and Nikolai blinked, the firelight disappearing from his eyes.

"Ah, good nothing that should get in the way of my blessing," he said calmly, as if this was something that happened so frequently that there was no shock or surprise in him from what he had seen.

Gwen's mouth dropped open. Blasé didn't begin to cover it.

"Does – does that mean we should come over, then?" Theo asked, stumbling over his words a little.

"Just in front of me here, please," Nikolai said, gesturing with the still lit candle stub in his hand, "It won't take me a moment to get ready."

The three Adventurers shuffled over.

Reaching Marina Gwen leaned over to her and asked, "So what was that like?"

"What did it look like?" Marina asked.

"Like you were standing inside one of those snow globe toys, only the snow was fire," Gwen said.

"Right, well, kind of like that. But also a fun house mirror maze was magnifying it by like a million," she said with a shiver.

Gwen made a face in commiseration.

At this point, Nikolai was ready to start the ritual. Like the time at the Farm, the first step seemed to be drawing a circle on the ground around those who were about to receive the blessing. Nikolai was much faster at this than Marina, moving with the small bottle of oil and a tiny calligraphy brush in a swift and sure circle. There were no lumpy bits, no bumps to avoid or incorporate the natural geography of the ground beneath the oil. And, there wasn't a cat that had to be drawn around, so the circle was much smoother and looked far more like it had been made by someone who knew what they were doing, rather than just guessing.

Which was perhaps a little mean to Marina, but if the level of skill the priest was showing off in making such a perfect circle was any indication of the rest of the skill he had, then Nikolai was a head and shoulders above her in more than just height.

Once the circle was drawn, he tucked the brush behind one ear with the absent-minded look of a painter who will later on wonder why his hair was green. Then he fished a small book out of his pocket, flicked through to a point about two thirds of the way into it, and started to speak once more in the resonant and thunderous voice.

His head was still holding onto the candle stub and he managed all of this without being forced to juggle half molten wax, a feat that Gwen found very impressive.

The voice he spoke in muffled the words. He might have been speaking a language she understood, or he might have been speaking something completely unintelligible to her. She couldn't tell. Aside from the odd mention of the name, Blodwen, and once their names as well, there was nothing that made it through to her ears in one piece.

That changed after the circle of oil burst into flame.

"Oh mighty Blodwen, foe of evil and shining light on the darkest of nights! Bless these Adventurers, Marina, Gwen, Theo, and Jin Ae, on their mission to rescue Wylla and to strike down the enemies of your servants. Let their hides be strengthened and their hearts iron clad! May blows bounce off their skin and may knives bend rather than pierce them. Keep them safe and make them mightier warriors to ensure their mission is triumphant!"

The circle of fire started to rise, a flare running along it in increasing speed. It jumped forward with every word he said, until it was a blur that blinded her to everything outside of the circle. Gwen closed her eyes, trying to ease the glare, but it seemed to make little difference. Instead, the light seemed to only grow brighter behind her eyelids. She struggled to open them again, having to fight the instinct that refused to believe that the world was brighter behind closed eyes.

A last cacophonous blast that felt like a moment of pure percussive force that seemed to hit from every side. It kept her in place, every blow pushing at the same strength against each other so there was no chance of her moving. And the light of the circle went out.

Gwen sank to the ground, and started breathing in gasps. The other Adventurers did the same, Marina sank against Gwen's shoulder, while Theo laid a shaking hand against her back. Jin Ae was knelt on the ground, the air around her seeming to buzz as she apparently held herself together via pure strength of will.

Turning her head, Gwen looked up at Nikolai, his mouth had fallen open. "Well," he said slowly, "That was dramatic."

Gwen looked for the notification to find out what exactly had just happened. It was easy enough to find, it was blaring out almost as brightly as the light from the blessing had.

"The Blessing of Blodwen lies upon you! May you be aided in your fight against evil in dark places!
Blessing of Blodwen
+ 5 metres of Dark Vision
+ 2 to Dodge
+ 2 to Armour
+20% Health"

Gwen let out a whistle, "Yeah, pretty dramatic."

Nikolai looked at them with surprise and confusion, "That is about twice as strong as it should be."

"Well, that's good, isn't it?" Theo asked.

Edgar and Nikolai shared a look, "Well, yes." Nikolai said.

"But generally, if the gods give you more than what you ask for," Edgar explained, "It's because they know of what's coming your way and think you will need the extra help."

"Or, I'm guessing, because they want you to remember that they gave you the extra without asking?" Gwen said.

"That is a very cynical way of looking at the world," Nikolai said coldly.

"But not one you're disagreeing with, I notice?" Gwen replied.

"Well, no," Nikolai admitted.

Gwen sighed, *chalk another one up to cynicism then.*

Chapter 15

Name: Gwen Baird

Class:	Hunter
Level:	6
Health:	43

Species: Half-Elf (Wood/Human)

Strength:	6	Mind:	6
Agility:	5	Body:	6
Armour:	6	Sense:	6

Species Skills: (Half-Elf)

Elf Sight:	6

Base Skills: (Hunter)

Dodge:	3	Perception:	6
Tracking:	6	Stealth:	8
Charm:	6	Archery:	7

For a time they kept to the woods on either side of the carved path. The chance that it had been scoured out of the earth as some sort of temptation or trap keeping them from using the easier route.

But then after the lack of monsters became even more glaringly obvious, they gave in to the temptation and used the path.

"Well, Nikolai's guess about where the monsters would be has held up, we are going straight north just like he anticipated," Gwen said to the others.

They sat in the shade of a tree, its branches leaning over the path. Gwen sat with her back against the trunk, while the others were scattered around over the roots and nested in the long grass.

"How's everyone holding up?" Marina asked.

"I've been doing a lot better since I used some of my levelling up points to add to my physical stats," Theo said with a smile. "I'm just glad that one of the super powers that comes with being an Adventurer in this game is a complete immunity to blisters, because otherwise I don't think there would be much left of my feet."

"I've been funnelling all of mine into Charm and Agility," Jin Ae said, "One thing I have noticed, I've stopped sitting on my tail so much! I don't know if it's just practise from spending more time in the game or if it is to do with the points I'm putting into Agility, but I'm glad of it." Her tail flicked back and forth at her side. She dropped a hand and the feathered tip brushed against her palm, "The feathers kept getting pushed out of line and it felt like having your hair pulled, only the messages from my nerves were going straight into my spine instead of my scalp." She gave a theatrical shudder. "The points into my Charm score will also add to my magical abilities, something that I foresee coming in handy. And if it doesn't, well maybe I'll be able to talk the monsters into giving Wylla back?"

"I'll drink to that," Gwen said, raising an imaginary tankard to her and then taking a real swig out of the water skin she had with her, "Agility for me too." After a point into Agility she felt like the world was easier to dodge. Her enemies had to push further, lunge closer to hit her, while she was able to smoothly move out of the way with greater ease.

"Right well I've mostly gone for Mind, so I've got some higher spells than I did before," Marina said.

"Anything to beat Nikolai's?" Gwen asked, referring to the enchantment he had cast on them before they left.

"No, I don't know what level he is, or even if as a local he really lines up with the whole level system, but I want that spell," she said, her eyes drifted off to the memory.

Gwen rolled her eyes. She could appreciate that it was an impressive spell, but the way that Marina was going on about it was getting a touch ridiculous.

"How long's it been since we started?" Theo asked.

"Less than three hours, and Edgar said the cairn was three hours away," Jin Ae said.

The others nodded and, with a few groans as joints clicked and stretched, stood. Gwen puffed out a breath of air, it caught one of the threads of hair that had escaped her helmet. The hair sprang away, curling a little in the heat. If this were the real world she would be a lot more tired, even so, she hadn't put enough into her Body stats yet to make walking on a hot day for several hours an easy thing to do.

They got up and started walking again, the forest was eerily quiet.

They hadn't heard or seen an animal or bird since they joined this odd road into the forest. She didn't need the six levels in Elf Sight to know that something was seriously wrong, but blinking it on and off again did give her a hint as to why.

"I think…I think everything in nature knows that the monsters are not meant to be here?" Gwen said. "At home and whatnot, I've never seen anything like this. There's no life. It's not just that things are hiding, everything is gone, run for it."

"Yeah, I mean, I grew up in the city, but you'd expect to have seen something by now. There's not even bugs? And I ever thought I would be missing bugs, but, there's zero," Theo said.

"It is seriously creepy," Marina agreed.

Jin Ae was in the lead, and had just started climbing the brow of a hill. Gwen could tell at what point she rose above the top, because she froze, and started patting the air behind her. Gwen frowned for a moment, before the realisation about the gesture's meaning hit her; she fell to her knees and crawled up to a point beside the bard. Her points in stealth activating like a cloak.

"What is it, what do you see?"

Jin Ae was in a crouch, shuffling forward so that she could reach the brow of the hill proper, but remain hidden. She tipped forward onto her hands and knees, appearing to count for a moment, Gwen could see tiny nods of her head, and then she was shuffling back to the small group behind her.

"We might not be at the cairn yet, but we're close; there's a patrol coming. They won't reach here for a couple of minutes," she said in a hushed whisper.

"How many?" Gwen asked.

"Ten," Jin Ae said.

"We can take that many if we surprise them," Marina said with a grin.

Gwen shook her head, "No way. They're a patrol, we kill them off and all that does is tell whoever or whatever they are reporting to that there is something out here that can take them."

Jin Ae nodded, "Let's get off the road. If we hide in the woods they shouldn't see us."

They ran. They were getting better at this, Gwen thought. They were starting to think more like soldiers and less like idiots allowed out into the countryside for the first time.

Gwen shoved herself into a natural divot behind a tree, tugging Theo along with her. Jin Ae and Marina went a bit further in, where their bright clothes and shining armour were less immediately obvious.

Dark clothes in neutral colours, that was better for blending in. Unless, she allowed, you were running around in a forest in autumn and had cloak made out of orange and red patches, but that was a bit of an extra clothing choice for it to only work once a year.

Hidden in the hollow, she held her breath and watched the monsters walk closer. Ticking away, she could feel her Stealth levelling up as she did her best to be as unnoticeable as possible. She imagined sinking into the leaf mulch and disappearing, anything to hide.

Theo was stock still and looked like a frightened rabbit. She still held his hand so she gave it a squeeze,

The monsters strode past.

They walked in an odd, rolling way, none of them quite hitting the points where you would expect them to. A shoulder jutted out too far, while a hip stopped short of the spot where it should go. They all looked like they had been made out bits and pieces rather than full bodies.

Even the ones who managed to look somewhat together had legs of vines that broke and healed and broke again as they walked. They were bleeding from what would have been called joints in anything else. Of course, in any other creature they would have been screaming in pain from constantly breaking the bones of their ankles and knees like that. But they showed no awareness or care, instead the leaking sludge that was their blood seemed to be an indication not of pain, but of their alien life.

Their heads were all animal, one a boar, another a bear, but mostly they were wolves. It appeared that whatever was making the things, or growing them – that was maybe the right word – whatever was growing them had settled on a style now.

It was really quite unfair, she thought, she had always liked wolves. She appreciated the fact that they wouldn't bother you if you steered clear of them. There were a lot of things, and people, in the real world that such a philosophy didn't apply to and she could respect the ones for whom it did. Also, she was a dog person and she liked wolves almost as much.

Eventually the patrol was past, the only sign of their going the yellow marks on the ground where the sludge they bled was killing the grass.

The Adventurers waited a few heart beats more, and then a few more just to be safe. Then Gwen crept forwards and looked through a gap in the trees. They were gone, she nodded back to the rest and they left the tree cover. "Stay close to the trees, use the shadows they cast," Gwen said as she moved to the front, "Jin Ae, with me, we'll go have a look, shall we? Let's try and figure out what exactly is going on?"

Jin Ae nodded, then looked down at her clothes. "I don't suppose you have anything that isn't designed for looking good on stage?" she asked softly.

Gwen smiled a half smile at her, "I have a cloak, you're not that much taller than me, it should cover everything."

Jin Ae sighed in relief and nodded her thanks.

"You two, stay here, if we don't come back then…" Gwen froze unsure what to say.

Theo answered for her, "Stay here longer?"

"Yeah, that, if it really looks like we've been eaten or something, go back to the temple and wait for us to respawn. We'll have to try again and hope they haven't killed Wylla yet," Gwen said.

Marina looked like she was about to argue, but she appeared to catch herself.

That's a relief, I really don't have time, Gwen thought.

"Here you are, running off into danger again," Marina said.

Oh, so we are doing this, after all. Gwen blinked in surprise then shrugged, "We're in a world with monsters, what else are we supposed to do? At least I have my," a pause, "lovely knife that Dove gave me."

"Stay safe; better than last time," Marina ordered her.

"I will, I've died once I don't intend on making a habit out of it," she said, trying to make it a joke.

It fell extremely flat. Out of the corner of her eye, Gwen saw Jin Ae and Theo wince.

Marina's ears turned red and she took in a long, slow breath like she was about to start swearing at top volume. Instead she let out the breath again, just as slowly.

"Just come back," she said eventually. Then she punched her sister in the shoulder.

Gwen rocked on her heels for a moment, before giving a sheepish smile and a half shrug, "I'll try?"

Gwen shot a look over at Jin Ae, "Time to try out those new presents, see if they are all they were promised to be?"

Jin Ae grinned, "As long as you don't feel too left out."

Gwen rolled her eyes, "No, I think I'll manage." Theo and Marina were quickly persuaded up a nearby tree, it was one of those solid ancient trees that felt like a pin holding the forest in place. It would, Gwen hoped, keep her twin and new friend safe.

"You two alright with this?" Theo asked.

Jin Ae nodded, "It's time for us to go kick some ass. You two stay unseen. We will be safer without the noise you two make."

Theo grinned and gave her a thumbs up.

Smiling Jin Ae turned back to Gwen, "Ready?"

She shrugged, "As I'll ever be." But the reluctance was faked. It was easier when there was a clear target in front of her, rather than the questions of what could happen? What might happen? What should happen? She was starting to recognise the relief that came with being pointed in a direction and set loose.

It was easy to crouch down and start running at a slow lope, one that ate up the distance well enough and kept her out of sight. As they went the ranks of Stealth she was gaining rolled up like clockwork. Her class was clearly designed for this stuff and experience was cheaply come by.

Jin Ae wasn't doing so well, but she was keeping up and the borrowed cloak she was wrapped in was doing a decent enough job of hiding the entertainer's gear that she was wearing.

The anklets she got from Dove will actually be useful for this, Gwen thought bitterly, *while I'm stuck with this knock off horror movie prop. And not even for one of the good horror movies that make you think about the nature of human fear. But a shitty one, where you can see the set wobbling in the background and it's so bad it doesn't even circle round again to funny.*

They crept forwards, staying in the shadows and keeping low to the ground. They didn't see any other monsters on their way. There were none just lazing about and they hadn't passed any more patrols, either. That was good.

Unfortunately, it seemed to be because they were all standing around the Barrow.

There wasn't an organised ring around the cairn, nothing like the attempt at barricades there had been around the village. Instead, they just seemed to be standing around, like toy soldiers when their owners have gone for lunch.

Only, rather than staying where they were put they were moving around in a restless prowl. They would stand in groups of three to six, but then one would be chased off by the sharp claws and tempers of those around them. From what Gwen could see it wasn't as if one or two monsters were moving on at a scheduled pace, instead they were all just losing patience with each other and the strongest would bully the weakest in their immediate surroundings away.

"We need to get inside," Gwen muttered, looking for any inspiration.

"Obviously, but how? People tend to not build back doors into graves, so we cannot go looking for another entrance. And I think the monsters may notice if we try to dig our way in," Jin Ae was speaking. But Gwen got the distinct impression that she was speaking to herself as much as to Gwen.

"What kind of distraction can we make, to draw them away?" Gwen said.

Jin Ae smiled slowly, looking first at Gwen and then at the crowd of fractious monsters. Even in the few moments they had been watching, they had lashed out at each other, nothing more dangerous than growls and claws that came close but didn't hit.

"I know your aim is good with your bow, but how is it with pebbles?" Jin Ae asked, nodding her head at some of the grumpier beasts.

Gwen grinned.

***

A pebble bounced off the branch of a tree, it hit the bark covered scalp of a monster giving a satisfyingly loud knocking noise.

The monster that had been hit lifted a paw to rub the impact site, but found nothing. Turning to its neighbour it gave a jump and had the wide, fanged muzzle around the other creature's neck with an enraged growl, before its foe could flinch.

Blood spurted into the sky, but it had not even hit the ground before another monster joined the fight. Whether it was out of loyalty to the victim of the attack or merely because it wanted a chance to get its paws dirty too, it was impossible to say. It barely sent a look at the bleeding out monster in the grass, except to step over it as it clawed at the other.

More monsters joined in, piling onto the fight. The first victim was soon hidden from view by the leaping and clawing bodies over it. The thick blood of the monsters started to run freely into the grass and the smell of rotten and burning plant and flesh started to fill the air.

***

"Right, move now," Gwen hissed to Jin Ae and the pair sprinted from the edge of the forest up to the entrance of the cairn.

They stopped in the archway.

"What's that?" She said to Jin Ae. The only thing that was stopping her from jumping back out again of the tunnel was the knowledge that the monsters outside wouldn't be kept busy for long.

Jin Ae's shoulders were up around her ears, and she was huddled into her borrowed cloak. Her arms were wrapped around her middle and a wince covered her face. "I think it's the death magic, not necromancy, it's the magic of death itself, not bringing the dead back to life," she said.

"It feels like all the warmth in the world has been pulled out," Gwen said, as she shivered and wished she hadn't handed over her cloak.

Jin Ae nodded, "Heat is a form of power. And I think the magic here, it feeds on anything that comes its way. Though, I am likely anthropomorphizing the magic by saying that, it is not alive after all, it is merely using the energy, like a heat sink, or a black hole at the edge of a solar system pulling in all the light and life within it," she was muttering the words, her voice coming faster and faster.

"We need to go in," Gwen said. She could have been reminding the other Adventurer or herself, she wasn't sure.

"Yes, yes we do," Jin Ae said, hauling in a breath through her nose before blowing out again through her mouth, she looked up at the end of the tunnel, "You first."

"I'm not the one with the magic stealth jewellery," Gwen hissed.

"No but you have a stabby thing and if you go first you will have the advantage of surprise over anything you find in there, which is what you need to make it work. And you have better armour than me," she added.

"You've really thought it through, huh?" Gwen asked.

"If it means I don't have to go through that first then you would be amazed at the alacrity of my thoughts."

Gwen grimaced and looked again at what Jin Ae had termed "that".

It was, more or less, the other side of the tunnel-like archway that was the less than welcoming entrance to the cairn. But, to speak more about what was less, and what was particularly upsetting to her, a hair's breadth beyond the end of the stone wall, where normally it would open out into a larger chamber, there was, instead, a void.

A mix of ash grey swirling on never ending black. It looked like the death scream of a universe. It looked like something that you didn't come back from.

"We could go and get everyone? Get some back up?" Gwen said, she bit her lip. Did her voice really have to tremble so much when she spoke?

"How exactly will that help?" Jin Ae said.

"It'll make me feel better," Gwen said. "And you know, whatever it is that people say about how more people makes things more safer." She stumbled over the words.

Jin Ae broke eye contact with the void at the end of the tunnel. She tilted her head to the side and looked at Gwen with a frown "I am not sure if the automatic translator running in this game just had a glitch, or you did? What did you just say?"

Gwen rolled her eyes, "Your dark vision is better than mine, can't you see anything?"

Jin Ae looked back at the void, "No. Which makes me think that that is the point. Whatever is on the other side, we cannot see it coming. Our only hope is that it cannot see us, either. Though the longer we stay out here debating the quicker something will find us, so move it."

Gwen groaned. "Always the peer pressure," she muttered, "why is it always the peer pressure that gets you?"

She unsheathed her blade and stepped through.

Stepping through the void made her feel like she had died again.

It was a cold so thorough that it leached out the heat as if it were hunting out even the slightest memory of warmth. The tears in her eyes felt like they had frozen. The blood in her veins felt sluggish.

When Gwen landed on the other side, and it was only a step between the two sides of the void, it felt like she had been thrown through an endless sky in a nightmare. Falling without the sight of the ground but always fearing it.

Her veins felt as if they were standing up proud against her skin, her heart was hammering against the inside of her ribs. Her body felt all wrong and she was certain it was falling apart from the inside out.

And yet, somehow. When she landed on that dusty cavern floor on the other side of the void, there was nothing in that space that suggested it was anything out of the ordinary.

The finely ground dust on the floor was dry and soft on her knees where she had fallen. Mosses and lichens had covered the walls and ceiling, giving it a fuzzy, almost gentle look.

The trio of monsters in front of her were less welcoming, but Gwen had almost gotten used to them too.

The knife was in her hand and, hearing Jin Ae arrive beside her, Gwen launched herself at the nearest one in less than a heartbeat. Keeping the blade low and pointed up, she stabbed into the small of the monster's back.

It let out a whimper, a horribly low and sad one, before it was falling into her arms. A single hit, thanks to the element of surprise and the strength of her new blade. The sudden influx of experience from her kill felt like a drug and the knife in her hand seemed to dive deeper into the blood and gore of the creature's back.

Jin Ae skewered another, her longer blade stabbing through the unprotected back, before bouncing off the bark armour that covered the creature's front.

Pulling her dagger from her first kill, Gwen threw it at the final monster. It flew true, and hit in an unarmoured spot on the neck, sinking deep into what Gwen suddenly knew was a blood vessel, maybe even the jugular, and, rather than sending green blood spurting into the air, the monster seemed to shrivel with the impact. When the monsters Gwen had killed dissolved into the dirt, they left no blood to reveal their deaths.

Gwen was still in a wobbly half crouch, one hand out in front of her from throwing the dagger.

She sank to one knee as the body of the last monster faded into nothing, the support she had gained from its heavy form disappearing along with the body.

Jin Ae pushed the body off her sword, letting it drop and hit the ground with a soft thud. It dissolved a moment later, leaving behind a slimy puddle of gore.

She didn't say anything. Speaking now would be a terrible idea. But she held out a hand and helped Gwen to her feet. Shaking, Gwen took the help, before bending over to retrieve the dagger.

She still didn't like it, but even she couldn't deny how effective the thing was. With the monsters disappearing after dying their blood was usually the only thing that remained as evidence of their killing, but with the Backstabber's Dagger there wasn't even that.

The cavern they had stepped into was pretty clearly a not-so-final resting point for a lot of people. The walls were made up of shelf-like niches for bodies. They went ten or so high from the ground and every one of them had been emptied, the contents dragged out and dropped onto the floor of the cavern or stolen.

Dimly, Gwen thought she could hear teeth grinding coming from Jin Ae, who was shaking her head at the destruction.

Slowly, they started forwards, taking care to keep their feet on the soft sand rather than the crumbling gravel.

Jin Ae picked up a few pieces of stone, before shaking her head and replacing them carefully. That was when Gwen realised that the gravel, which covered about a third of the floor, had once been a shell around the niches. The monsters must have broken through and smashed them all when they arrived.

Gwen wrinkled her nose. Grave desecration: just another crime to lay on the shoulders of the monsters. In a world like the game, where the dead could rise and kick up a fuss, tempting fate by disturbing the last resting place of dozens of dead bodies seemed like a terrible, terrible idea.

They kept walking, investigating those niches that looked like something might remain. But whenever something did, it tended to raise more questions than answers. Some of the bodies, it was clear, had not been trusted to stay put. There were stones lying in the midst of cracked ribs. There was no bone dust on the stones to suggest that they were recent additions. In fact, Gwen had the distinct impression that they had been placed there with the bodies at the time of their internment.

The idea that the people who had built this cairn were worried about the dead waking and had taken precautions to prevent it, didn't make walking through the passages any less creepy. Especially given how many skeletons were flung around the corridor. Whatever those long dead had done to keep their contemporaries in place, the Monsters of today had undone with careless abandon.

It was interesting though, from what Nikolai and Edgar had said about the necromantic battlefields she had assumed that that was the source of all the necromantic energy in the region, but the fact that a place as ancient as this had precautions in place hinted that it had been a worry before then, too. Perhaps the battles had given whatever systems made the dead walk more power, or maybe it had moved the focus from a wide lens to a narrow one. Rather than anyone who died being a potential zombie it was now all focused on the dead of those battlefields. It was an interesting idea.

The cairn had been made with lasting in mind, after all. This wasn't done over a weekend.

The walls were covered in plant life, but below the moss she could make out the different stones and rocks that made up the walls and ceiling. None of them were regular, but each of them fitted perfectly into their neighbour. No room for gaps, not enough for the tiniest breath of wind or blade of sunlight to make it through. Whoever had built the cairn had made it to not just last but *outlast*.

And it had, right up until this latest crop of monsters had come along and ripped out all the grave coverings.

Gwen shook her head free of such dark thoughts. The grave desecration shouldn't have been a surprise. The monsters were monsters, it was probably in their programming to do monstrous thing on a semi-frequent basis. At least the dead were not around to take offence or feel the lack of shelter. She looked around at the dark tomb. Well, she wouldn't put it past them to do so anyway.

There was a small nook near the end of the cavern. At first glance it was difficult to tell it apart from all the other cracks in the walls. When the monsters had stripped the coverings off the graves they hadn't been careful with it and had done a lot of damage to the surrounding areas too.

But there was something about it that Gwen couldn't tear her eyes away from. She tapped Jin Ae on the shoulder and pointed it out, the other woman merely looked at in confusion before shrugging. But Gwen couldn't be deterred.

She stepped away from Jin Ae, walking over to the dark and narrow nook. Putting her hands in front of her she felt the back of the odd little hole, nothing particularly out of the ordinary there, but then she felt the tiniest hint of a breeze coming from the left. Sliding her hand to where that breeze had come from she felt…nothing.

There was a person-sized gap in the wall, hidden by the shadows and perfectly placed for someone who wanted to make a stealthy entrance. Looking over her shoulder she gave Jin Ae a grin, before taking a breath and shimmying through the narrow gap.

Jin Ae quickly followed her, though the taller woman had a bit more trouble, especially with fitting her horns and tail through the gap.

Gwen peered around, glad for her elven eyesight and the blessing from Nikolai, since this part of the barrow seemed to be even darker than the rest.

She inched closer to Jin Ae.

There was a soft creaking of leather and then a muttering sound.

Jin Ae suddenly appeared, holding a ball of soft blue-grey light in her palm. She kept her other hand curved around the light to stop it from escaping and revealing them.

Gwen blinked in the light. It was dim, but even so after nothing at all it was a shock to her eyes.

The room they were in was better lit, but no more illuminating. If anything, Gwen thought, as she looked around she was less certain of what it might be than she had been going in.

She brushed a hand over the dull scratch marks on the walls. They weren't anything like she expected. They weren't the desperate scrabble of fingernails, or finger bones. If anything, they looked like the marks left on a doorway after someone had struggled to move a too big wardrobe through it.

The floor too was not the well-made and smoothed path of the other cavern. It looked like it had been shoved together and the only thing that had shaped it into some kind of uniformity was infrequent foot traffic from long ago.

It reminded Gwen of something.

Once, when she had been a part of a very badly paid team of thieves, she had set herself up in some abandoned servants' quarters. It had been in the attic of a room across from their target, one that had been forgotten by the owners. It had been that same kind of unpolished environment, too.

People didn't spare much money for the areas that were not meant to be seen.

Jin Ae took the lead, lighting the way with her handful of light.

There was a narrow passage leading downwards and Gwen knew that wherever it was leading them too there would be more dead bodies and probably a lot more monsters as well.

They started off, the dim light of Jin Ae's magic showing them the way.

Whoever had built the passage, as well as being very skilled, had apparently been quite short, since both Jin Ae and Gwen had to duck their heads as they shuffled along. Jin Ae, in particular, was having trouble since with her horns she was above average height.

But slowly they managed to make their way along the passage, pausing here and there to try and listen in on the noises coming through the walls. Everything that the original builders had made still seemed to be doing well, however it was clear now that they walked on this side of the wall that care had been taken to make sure that while the walls were solid enough to last for centuries, that didn't stop anyone from being able to eavesdrop should they want to.

Gwen ran her fingers along a length of wall that was particular well suited to that. Someone had built it out of many different layers of stone. Some sort of fossilised mud that still had the ripples and lines of the river it had come from. By layering the thin slabs of river stone, the sounds in the main passage were funnelled into the hidden tunnel, but any sounds made in the tunnel had to fight against the full length of the slabs to make it into the passage. It was helped by the fact that Jin Ae and Gwen were doing their damnedest to be as quiet as possible, while the monsters on the other side of the wall huffed and scraped their way along.

It was, Gwen could acknowledge, a beautiful piece of espionage via architecture.

And it was very useful as they crept along, keeping one ear pricked for the sound of the monsters tramping back and forth in the caverns.

At one point, the harsh sniffing noises that came to them through the wall was enough to have them both breathing in and pushing themselves against the opposite wall. The monster moved on after a time, but hairs on the back of Gwen's neck stood proud for a good while after.

They reached the end of the tunnel about the same time that Gwen spotted the way out.

Tapping lightly on Jin Ae's shoulder, she pointed out the crack in the dark stone. Like the one they had entered through it was barely wide enough to shimmy through, but it was also fairly well hidden. Gwen walked up and carefully peaked through.

On the other side of the exit there was a huge slab of slate. Not to block the way in and out, but, she realised it was another piece of camouflage. Whatever the builders had been expecting to happen to the cairn, they had been determined to be safe and hidden.

There were no monsters visible on the other side. She laid her head against the rock, doing her best to get a good angle. Closing her eyes, she concentrated on the sounds of the cairn. There was so little sound in the cairn that her heart beat was the loudest thing she could hear. There were no sounds of monsters moving about. Not even distantly. And here, in their home base, they didn't seem to give a damn about being quiet so she was certain she would have heard them coming.

Her Sense wasn't high enough for her to pick out the individual droplets of rain in a storm, and she never particularly wanted it to be, but half by stubborn will and half by stubborn hard work she had gotten her Perception high enough that she could trust it to warn her when something was coming towards her in the dark. And, she determined, opening her eyes, it seemed safe enough.

She stepped back and nodded to Jin Ae.

Jin Ae smiled and moved to follow her. Then the demon-spawn's eyes went glassy for a moment. Something buzzed along her skin, telling her with words she couldn't know or understand that there was magic being wrought on her friend.

Gwen frowned and came over, but she didn't seem to be able to feel her worried shoulder taps or see the words she was mouthing at her. Then Jin Ae's eyes were clearing and she was shaking her head, as if to rid herself of a ringing in her ears.

It was only a few seconds long but it had Gwen's heart in her mouth for every moment of it.

Jin Ae looked sharply at her, "Message from Theo, they've been attacked," she said.

Gwen felt like the world was crashing down around her, the monsters had attacked? How could they know the others were up there? How many monsters were in the cairn? Fifty? A hundred? She had to go up there- Her poker face was apparently non-existent because Jin Ae caught her hands in hers and gripped onto them with surprising strength, "They're fine, but the monsters know that they are out there."

"We need to go help them!" Gwen said in a fierce whisper.

"No, Gwen, the monsters know that *Theo and Marina* are out *there*. But they don't know that *we* are in *here*. This is the best chance we have to find Wylla and get her out of here," Jin Ae told her sharply.

"That won't do us much good if our exit is blocked by all the monsters that are chasing after Theo and my sister," she countered.

"Then, let's do our best to thin the crowd before they get up there. You've seen them, they have no discipline, half of them would sooner claw each other's eyes out than keep a proper watch," she squeezed Gwen's hands again, "this is the best chance we've got and the best chance they've got."

Gwen bit her lip. She wanted to run back up the passage and kill everything in between her and her sister.

But she could see the sense in what Jin Ae was saying. They were behind the monsters, right where fighters like she and Jin Ae were best suited. She placed a hand on her dagger. Time to put it to some more use, she thought.

Nodding she straightened her back, "Alright, what are we going to do?"

"We need to wait for the monsters to start moving up towards the surface, we kill any stragglers anything that is by itself that it looks like we can take. And we try and find Wylla. Then, when the monsters start leaving we can take on whatever is left and hopefully save our damsel in distress," Jin Ae looked at her, "Alright?"

Gwen nodded. It was a better plan than running through the passage and killing at random.

Chapter 16

Name: Gwen Baird

Class:	Hunter
Level:	6
Health:	43

Species: Half-Elf (Wood/Human)

Strength:	6	Mind:	6
Agility:	5	Body:	6
Armour:	6	Sense:	6

Species Skills: (Half-Elf)

Elf Sight:	6

Base Skills: (Hunter)

Dodge:	3	Perception:	6
Tracking:	6	Stealth:	9
Charm:	6	Archery:	7

Gwen sighed, slid down the roughly carved stone of the passage wall, and sat on the ground.

"I guess we just have to wait then," Gwen muttered, rubbing her hands up and down her thighs.

"It's the only thing we can do; if we leave the cairn we're abandoning Wylla," Jin Ae said.

"Yeah, I might be a bitch some of the time, but not enough of a one to do that," Gwen said with a bitter half smile.

"You're not a bitch," Jin Ae said, folding down to sit beside her, "and if you are you're not as bad as me."

"Please," Gwen said, "I bet I can beat you on that."

"Really? I wouldn't be so sure, at the very least my ex-husband would disagree with you." She looked away from Gwen and instead focused on the small orb of glowing light she held.

"Ha, at least you didn't leave in a screaming fit only to crawl back after you heard the end of the world was happening, so you could ask a favour, no less. Then get the favour and before getting into another fight, and leaving, again," Gwen said. She sighed, "I am fairly certain by any measure I probably took advantage of Ana wanting to get back together. And as much as I would like to say I didn't realise what I was doing, I did. And she still followed through, even after I was a massive bitch to her, which definitely makes her the better person. Not that that was in any doubt."

Jin Ae laughed, "Ah, using people's goodness against them. That sounds familiar. You know, when I got divorced I didn't even question if my ex would do the right thing. That's the kind of guy he is. And I broke his heart. Which shows the kind of person I am."

"What do you mean?" Gwen asked.

"I knew he was still a little in love with me. I knew he would want me to be happy. I knew he would be generous with his heart and that gave me the chance to be ruthless. And I took that chance and I ran with it," looking at Gwen again she explained, "we have two kids, he put them first and I put myself. I had fallen in love and wanted to be whisked off my feet into this new life we were going to live. We were going to have long talks on history and philosophers, take vacations when we wanted them, not just when the schools were closed. But, it's hard to be whisked anywhere with an eleven- and eight-year-old in tow." She sighed, "So I win the gold medal in bitchiness."

"At least you've figured it out now?" Gwen said.

"Oh, before now, actually. When my lovely new boyfriend told me that he hadn't bothered signing up to get a ticket. On the day I was leaving for the cryo centre. Because a world in turmoil was the perfect moment for a historian to be present and wouldn't that be an amazing legacy? Sitting around and watching the world burn just so you could be the one to write down what the screams sounded like," she flicked a pebble with a finger, "he never even considered that I might consider my children more important. Which probably shows that I made him think they weren't that important to me."

"Or he was just an arsehole, I wouldn't discount that," Gwen said.

"Ha, well he was that too. But we were well matched, only the end of the world happened and I had an epiphany about what the world was to me. And he wanted to write his name in history. I guess I can't blame him for staying the same person he was when I fell in love."

"Well, no, I think you can. It's the end of the world, expecting someone to be a grown up is probably not asking too much," Gwen disagreed.

"He had a list of reasons why he was in the right," Jin Ae continued, barely listening to Gwen. "He was going to be hand that wrote the last words on Earth's history. And a girlfriend would only slow him down," she added something that the translator in the game chose not to translate. Gwen took this to mean that it was a very specific turn of phrase, but a fairly universal meaning.

"It sounds more like he was wanting to get some action in the end of the world orgies, to me," Gwen said bluntly, lowering her head onto her arms so that she was level with Jin Ae. "And it sounds like you are better off without him."

"Oh indubitably, I am not contesting that. But just because he was awful, doesn't mean I wasn't too, just earlier on," she said with a shrug.

"Fine, I'll ask Theo to make you a medal saying that you're the bitchiest member of the group and I'm second best, how about that?" Gwen asked.

Jin Ae snorted, then covered her hands over her face as the noise echoed around the tunnel.

They both straightened up and listened desperately, trying to tell if the noise had alerted their enemies. In the quiet, Gwen pushed her shoulder into Jin Ae's. They shared a smile.

We may both be terrible people, Gwen decided, *but it's nice to not be the only terrible person you know.*

The sound of footsteps started to beat through the stones of the cairn.

Gwen lifted her head and listened to the movements of several monsters: they were going up the tunnels, not down into the hidden depths below. The others must have caught their attention.

She said as much, then relief kept her mouth moving when she should have shut up. "Thank the gods, no offence, but I hate talking about my problems."

Jin Ae laughed, "You think I'm any better at it? How do you think I get into most of these messes? Come on, let's go kill some monsters! Then we can pretend we are the heroes the villagers need us to be. And not the messes we really are."

Gwen shook her head, "That's too close to philosophy for me. Let's just go and stab things and forget about this conversation."

"Ah, fair enough, I never pretended to be healthy," Jin Ae said, turning to look out the crack in the wall.

There was a low grunting noise from outside, Gwen made certain to block any of the light from escaping with the outline of her body, and spied out through one of the thin cracks in the stone.

The beast that wandered past might have been the bigger, meaner, older sibling of the beetle crossed with a boar she had "met" when she had arrived in the game.

She was quite happy to let that one go past. People with a better defence than surprise and what, she was beginning to realise, was a mostly ornamental wall, could fight that beast.

The plan needed her to stay alive, or at least one of them out of Jin Ae and her and the odds would be better if they could stand by each other. And no one could be certain that they would come out of a fight against something like that without a scratch.

More monsters passed. It was becoming less and less likely to be a changing of the guard, or something similar, and perhaps instead she could hope that it was the distraction that they had been promised.

Next passed a small pack of the wolf-type monsters, the ones that oozed a bloody sap as they walked and the joints in their legs snapped and reformed. This lot walked with a languid spring to their steps. As if they were looking forward to the fight they were marching too.

Gwen shook her head, why was she so desperate to see something human in them even though there had been nothing yet to prove it? Oh, some had a bit more awareness, but there was never anything behind the eyes. And yet she kept searching for it Why was that? She didn't want there to be more to them. Let them be automatons with no care for the world around them except to kill, that was easier. She didn't have to feel bad, or wonder if she should be feeling bad if they were nothing but monsters.

But it felt wrong even to think it.

She hunched her shoulders a touch and looked over the group Some of them were carrying weapons, better ones than the broken sticks and cobble stones that the ones in the village had grabbed up. One carried a long spear, something like a halberd or a pike. It was meant for holding off foes from far away, but her newly expert eye could see that the monster was holding it wrong. Rather than wielding it to get a longer reach and to deliver distant blows, it was holding onto it tight. Like it was a new present it didn't want to let go of. Hopefully, that would help Marina or Theo defeat it. They had not, after all, allowed for a longer than natural reach when they had said their goodbyes and left them up a tree.

One of her eyes shut in a wink as the notification for a new level of Perception showed itself.

She shook her head to dislodge the thought. The pair probably weren't even up a tree any longer. They'd have found a new spot; it wasn't worth thinking about. They would be fine, or else they would find out that they weren't in a while. And Gwen and Jin Ae would probably be in trouble long before that so there was no point in fretting about it.

Something caught her eye. One of the monsters was wearing a brace, something leather, perhaps? Gwen's night vision wasn't up to seeing more beyond the fact that it was a dull brown, which had shown up against the lighter grey streaked mud tone of the wolf fur it covered. That was worrying, somehow more worrying than the idea of them learning to use weapons. It was one thing to seem them realise that a thing you picked up could help you hit harder, but something else entirely to see them learning about armour. And in particular how to put it on.

She wondered how it had managed that, how many tries had it taken to manage the laces, and then ruthlessly stamped on the giggle that had tried to break free. Of all the times to be inappropriately giggly, this was not one she could afford.

The monsters continued up the passage way. They were, she noticed, leaking less of their sap or blood, or whatever it was. Perhaps that was the real reason for their odd bouncing walk?

It didn't matter.

She eased back again.

Monsters continued to pass by them, but not in the same rush that there had been.

Gwen turned to look at Jin Ae. She gave her a nod. Then she checked both directions, *like crossing the road*, she thought, with another stamped down giggle dying in her chest, and squeezed out of the hidden tunnel.

She kept to the shadows. Jin Ae seemed willing to follow her. Gwen was horribly aware of the sounds she was making. Her feet dragged across the stone, rasping and crunching when she leaned her weight on them. Her heart beat seemed to be an echo in her chest louder than bells and thunder. In the quiet, her breath seemed even more cacophonous.

Jin Ae had extinguished the light before leaving their sanctuary in the walls, so now the world was lit only by their species' innate night vision and the occasional stone recessed into the walls that glowed. They were barely more than the memory of a candle, more like the dying light of a torch than anything you could lead a party with. But with her better-than-human eyesight, Gwen was able to make her way through the grey stone and moss-covered walls of the cairn.

They came to another corner, Gwen held up a hand to stop Jin Ae. She could hear something on the other side.

There was movement beyond the line of wall. She held her breath and risked a look, but the creatures were distracted. It was a trio or so of the two-legged hybrids, no, she changed her mind, there were four, but the three standing around the fourth had blocked her view. The fourth was badly injured, at first she thought the creatures were trying to help it, but then she saw the clubs. She gasped and flinched at the sight. Apparently, there was no first aid in the hybrid army.

The noises of the creature dying masked her gasp, and she pulled back around crouch beside Jin Ae.

She held up three fingers, tapped the one furthest from her and pointed to Jin Ae, then the one closest to her and pointed to herself. The middle finger got a shrug and Gwen hoped the "whoever gets there first is welcome to it" vibe she was trying to give off. She'd never say no to more experience, but she'd gladly give it up to Jin Ae if it meant the attack went smoothly.

Jin Ae nodded.

Gwen gave a grim smile and she peeked around again. Two were kicking the corpse of their brethren as it dissolved, the third was looking over her head at the wall. By crouching Gwen seemed to have dodged their security.

Holding a hand behind her she counted down, three, two, one. The second her fist clenched on one, both she and Jin Ae let loose.

Jin Ae sent out a barrage of silent spells. Fist-sized globules of green light hit the monster furthest from them. They spread across the fur and bark, burning whatever it crossed. The monster fell to the ground without even having the time or chance to let out a cry or a whimper.

Gwen was less organised. She couldn't use her bow in such cramped quarters, and in particular, while leaning around a corner, so she switched to her new dagger. Taking out of its sheath she ignored how it seemed to thrum happily in her hand. Instead, she bounced it once in her hand to remind herself of the weight and balance, before taking aim and throwing it into the back of the nearest monster. It landed with a meaty thunk, and Gwen barely waited for the body to drop to the ground before she swooped in and retrieved her dagger.

The third and final monster of the group, turned to see what was happening and got a spell to the face and a knife to the belly. The hair on Gwen's neck rose as the spell scored through the air above her. When it hit the monster, it covered the muzzle and most of the face like a jelly, before it seemed to crawl into the skin. The monster shuddered and fell across the bodies of the other monsters with no more noise than a sigh.

The trio dissolved into the ground just as silently as they had died. Somehow, the oppressive atmosphere lessened a little at that.

Gwen and Jin Ae crept forward, looking in the piles of goo and dirt for anything they could salvage. Gwen got her two knives back, the metal one looking a little tarnished from its time in contact with the sap, while the bone dagger seemed completely immune to such damage. When she picked it up the sap pooled off of it, like oil racing across water's surface after being doused in soap.

Gwen wrinkled her nose.

Jin Ae held her shoulder and leaned into her ear, "Level up?"

Gwen startled. Despite it all she had somehow forgotten that they were in a game. And yes, they had a quiet moment. It made sense to sort these things out before they moved on.

Gwen had actually levelled up twice since she had last checked, the text in the notifications wasn't technically any different, but she still got a feeling that it was judging her for not noticing. She thought for a moment, then carefully entered the new points into her Body and Agility stats. More health and stamina could only be a good thing. And she was in the midst of a stealth challenge like she hadn't seen before in the game, so helping that along was probably a good idea.

Jin Ae seemed to stand a little taller and more solidly in the space she occupied, after they had finished levelling up. Gwen guessed she had put something into her Body stats too. Unless that was a bard thing, putting points into Charm might work like that too.

They stole along the cavern, Gwen kept an eye out for more of the hidden holes and passages on their way. The monsters hadn't noticed the ones higher up in the cairn but that was no reason to believe that they would be that lucky for all of them.

At the thought of the word "lucky" Gwen was reminded of the goddess she had pledged herself to at the beginning of the game.

Well, it probably can't hurt, she thought. She sent a look upwards, since that felt appropriate, especially since they were now well underground, and thought loudly and as if she was trying to project her voice to the back of a very large room, *O great and awe-inspiring goddess, please could you send some especially good luck my way. Things are, I think, about to get quite dramatic and I would greatly appreciate the help. Thanks very much, yours sincerely, Gwen.*

She wasn't sure if that was how you were supposed to word a prayer, but she didn't have any skills in religion to tell her otherwise. Mostly people seemed to have set things they would say, but she didn't know what those were in this reality for her goddess.

Somewhere something pinged with the light of a new quest being born, and Gwen rolled her eyes. *Really? You think I have time for that? Well, I guess that's something to think about for when I get out of here. I can ask Nikolai if he still wants to talk to me when we get back to the village.*

Seeing a small hole in the rock a few corners later was a pleasant surprise. *Huh, thanks,* Gwen thought. Before shaking her head, *okay, no need to buy into this sort of thing completely. It's not glowing in a holy aura or something, no need to assume that it was the goddess who made it visible.*

She nudged Jin Ae, before pointing the hole out to her. Pointing her thumb at herself she then pointed along the passage. Jin Ae frowned, but gave a shrug. The message *on your own head be it,* was pretty clear.

Gwen held up her hands in mock and overdone surrender, "I'm a hunter, what else am I supposed to do in this situation," she mouthed.

Jin Ae visibly sighed at this, but she waved her hands in Gwen's direction as if to hand waft over the responsibility.

Gwen grinned. She tentatively looked out the small hole, checking that it was not in fact a trap, but it was clear and the corridor on the other side too looked deserted.

She let a breath and all the tension she held in her shoulders drained out of her. She had picked up a new ability along with the points boosts when she had levelled up.

Concentrating, she found the inner switch that had been newly revealed to her. The one that represented her new ability to Shadow Walk. It seemed icy cold to the touch and in her mind's eyes she saw herself drawing in all of the light around her.

She took a step forwards and vanished into the shadows.

The light and darkness in the world were flipped. What had been dark and inky pools of black were now alive with a warm light, she could see every rock and pebble and fossilised spider web. And yet despite it being the world remade wrong, it felt safe.

As she clicked it into place a warning appeared in front of her gaze.

Beware: Shadow Walking can become addictive. Symptoms include a false sense of security while in use and a desire to use the power even when impractical.

She could feel it starting. It warmed something inside of her, some corner that had felt afraid since she had stepped foot into the game.

It promised her everything would be safe if she just stayed in the cozy darkness.

But she had been promised things like that before, from kinder and more tempting sources than a mysterious power that lived inside her head.

She shook it off and started to jog. She would have, at best, half a minute; she needed to get as far down into the cairn as possible in that time. The world seemed to grow brighter and warmer as she ran; the heat never grew to a point where it hurt, but she could feel herself growing sluggish.

Gwen gritted her teeth and put on a last burst of speed, it felt like she was running through a mist made up of tiny grabbing hands, but she made it a good distance down the passage.

Gwen felt secure in the knowledge that nothing could see her while she ran through the shadows and that in a tunnel deep under a cairn in a particularly badly lit spot she wasn't going to be knocked out of her magic by a bright light. The lights on the walls that had seemed almost pointlessly dim were now holes into the ether that she had to dodge. At the very least, if she came to close to one she felt the beginning of a stress headache forming, like an alarm made out of muscle spasms and pain.

She had to drop the magic sooner than she would have liked. But there had been a small rockfall at some point in the past and she was able to hide away in the hole it left. As she shivered back into normal reality Gwen looked past the stones and gravel, to try and catch a glimpse of what was happening in the cavern ahead of her.

It seemed like she had dropped the magic just in time for it to come in useful. There was another corner ahead of her and it blocked a lot of the cavern. But if she leaned to a dangerous angle out of her shelter she could just catch sight of what was going on in the cavern.

She bit her lip, it was the only thing she could do to stop from swearing at the top of her lungs. So much for the distraction drawing the monsters up and out of the cairn.

Gwen could count at least forty creatures, though it was hard to tell as they moved around and there wasn't much to tell them apart with, especially in the gloom. They were all milling around in the way of people, or hybrid plant/animal monsters, who have been told to wait somewhere and were growing bored. They mostly seemed to be the long-limbed, stretched almost, wolf creatures. She looked around and could only make out a single, beetle boar creature sitting in a corner (smaller than the one she had faced); thankfully, none of the really big creatures seemed to be able to fit in the chamber.

Then, the group moved and a taller monster came into view. It had the rangy look of something that has grown too fast and wore what looked like scavenged Adventurer's armour. Behind it, two other monsters were dragging a girl with long, pale hair that had fallen loose and fell like a curtain from her slumped form. Gwen's heart hammered, the creatures weren't doing anything, not yet. But if they wanted to, they could kill her in a second.

Why hadn't they? It clearly wasn't out of some form of kindness, the hold they had on her looked painful. Even from a distance, Gwen could see how they were marking the girl's skin and tearing through the sleeves of her dress.

Gwen pursed her lips. Nothing good, she knew, would come of delaying the attack. But then nothing good was likely to come from doing it too quickly, either.

They needed the perfect moment and there was no way to find or manufacture one.

They would just have to make any moment they chose perfect through obstinacy and sweat.

She took a silent, deep breath and gave a shrug. That was an old song and one she knew all the words to. She'd cope or she'd fuck up and die again and end up in the temple with Nikolai probably looking very disappointed at her.

And that didn't sound fun. So she'd just have to manage.

She flung herself back into the shadows and bolted up the passage again. She had a lot to tell Jin Ae.

Shimmying into the hole in the wall where she had last seen her, Gwen fell to one knee beside her. "I saw Wylla, but we can't just charge down there and fight. There are too many down there for us to take on," she whispered.

"How many?" Jin Ae asked.

"I could only see into one half of the cavern, but there were at least forty there, I wouldn't want to bet on there being less in the spots I couldn't see," Gwen told her.

Jin Ae bit her lip, then winced, she'd stabbed herself with one of her fangs. Then she grinned, "I think I have an idea."

"Is it polite to say "uh oh" at this point," Gwen asked drily.

***

Howls, shouts and the screams like that of a dragon-sized toddler having a temper tantrum echoed down the corridor and into the cavern.

The tallest hybrid snarled and turned to look up the tunnel out of the cavern. Growling to itself, it waved its clawed paws at the twenty or so monsters closest to the cavern exit and sent them up to take a look. Then it turned back to its trailing pair and pointed to the human girl in their clutches. She seemed to come alive at that point and bit into the shoulder of the one closest to her in a jumping attack that shocked it more than harmed it. But her struggles were in vain, they shook her until she was stunned and hung there limp and trembling.

***

"That's not good," Gwen whispered, her gaze on the girl. She was holding up a mirror taken out of Jin Ae's entertainer's make up kit: it wasn't big enough for a good view of the cavern, but even the shaky reflection that Gwen was able to make out told her a lot.

"We can't get to her yet," Jin Ae whispered back, "the monsters that are left are too spread out, it would take more spells than I've got to fry them all."

Gwen nodded and put a hand up to her mouth as she watched the monsters drag the girl over to what looked like it might have been a hastily constructed alter or a surgical table. It seemed to have been made out of the stone from a sarcophagus, though the ropes they were tying the girl down with looked to be made from the same kind of plant that the hybrid in charge had growing in the place of limbs. And that was not a nice thought, Gwen realised, there were many ways for that to go, none of them good for Wylla.

As the racket continued, more of the hybrids left to investigate what was making the sound, they walked past Gwen and Jin Ae's hiding spot. She breathed a little easier every time more passed her by, the more that went up, the less she and Jin Ae would have to fight.

Hidden in the hole, Jin Ae lay across the dusty floor, her hands alternating between different ropes. Every time she twitched one, the motions would travel up through the hidden tunnels, bypassing almost all danger of discovery, and would lead up to one of the alcoves where once a skeleton had lain.

Now, the alcove was adorned with the empty cuirass' of various skeletons; a horn of some kind that might have actually been a very pointy hat with the end knocked off; and Gwen's cloak. Plus, numerous spells that Jin Ae had pulled out of the ether that had dramatically increased the volume of any noise made in that small space.

Before casting those spells, Jin Ae had sent Gwen out of the hole in the wall with her bags and weapons, with anything loose on her that could make the slightest noise. The slightest sound could not be risked when you were magnifying all noises a hundred-fold.

Eventually Gwen signalled to Jin Ae to stop. The monsters had stopped following the noises. Either they had worked out that it was a distraction, which would be very unlucky timing since they had been falling for it left right and centre so far, or they felt that the threat was less important than what might happen if they left.

Gwen remembered the tall, thin monster, wearing stolen armour. It wasn't hard to imagine what might have been scarier than a mysterious cacophony.

But still, "how are they still falling for that trick?" Gwen asked.

"I don't think it's a case of 'still'. In these types of games, very few monsters are capable of learning, right? So, once you have spotted their weakness you can exploit it," Jin Ae murmured.

"And what, being really, really gullible is the Achilles' Heel of these monsters?" Gwen asked; as a theory it did make a surprising amount of sense.

"Not so much gullible, I think, but suggestible. And of course, all the 'it's not paranoia if they are out to get you' rules aside, it's not like we are doing the same thing to the same monster, or even group. They won't have the chance to warn each other."

Gwen frowned; she hadn't seen much of the creatures. But from what she had seen they were quick to anger, quicker to fight, and hadn't actually looked as if they were talking to each other. "I don't know if they can? At least the lower level ones. I don't know what this one that's in charge can do. But they barely look at each other, let alone talk."

Jin Ae shrugged, "There are a lot of ways of communicating without using speech; just because we are heavily dependent on it as a medium doesn't mean they are."

Gwen thought for a moment. How to explain what she meant. "They don't fight or move together, there's no joint tactics. They all fight individually, and sometimes that happens at the same time, but it's not together. Sometimes there's one that looks more senior in the ranks. But even they don't communicate, they just seem to point the others in the right direction."

"That's a form of communication," Jin Ae said.

"Yeah, but it's not 'you two go that way, you two go that way, and we'll sneak around the side'. They're herding more than leading," Gwen shook her head, "I don't know, maybe I'm thinking into it too much."

"No such thing," Jin Ae countered. "At least in a quiet moment like this. If we're going to fight these things we need to try to understand them."

"We also need to come up with a name for them, 'them' and 'monsters' might get confusing," Gwen said.

"I was hoping that we wouldn't be familiar enough with them to have to come up with a taxonomy, but I suppose you are right," Jin Ae sat up and brushed the dust from her clothes. Since they had used Gwen's cloak for their contraption, she was forced to lie on the ground in her stage gear.

Gwen added every-day clothes for Jin Ae to her list of things they needed. "Got any ideas?"

"That depends, would you say they are a part of the animal or plant kingdom?" Jin Ae said.

Gwen frowned, "Both? Neither?"

"Well, that gives us the option of fungus, which," she frowned, "might actually explain some things."

Gwen didn't like the sound of that.

"Have you ever heard of Ophiocordyceps unilateralis?" Jin Ae asked, tapping a nail against her chin.

"No," Gwen replied.

"Hmmm, well I'll tell you about it later. It really is a very interesting fungus, but perhaps not something that you want to be thinking about right now," she allowed. And then gave a bright grin, "I doubt it's what's causing the problem here anyway."

Gwen seriously considered asking more about this, before deciding that Jin Ae was probably right. A couple of minutes before facing off with some monsters probably wasn't the time to learn more about fungi.

Speaking of, she whipped her head around to look at the cavern. Nothing much appeared to have changed, but she shouldn't be getting distracted like that. She had to stay alert.

"Anything changed?" Jin Ae asked.

"Not that I can see," Gwen told her.

Jin Ae let out a long breath, "Then I suppose there's nothing else to delay us, is there?"

Gwen snorted, "No, unfortunately it looks like we actually have to fight now."

They shared a look. It was plain to Gwen that Jin Ae was terrified. Which was fair. So was she.

It wasn't dying that worried her. She'd died once already, and to be honest, it wasn't that bad. It was the pain that happened before you died that was worse. And here there was no limit to how long you could be in pain before you died. Being crushed to death had been bad, but at least she had blacked out fairly quickly. With these monsters, *and wow, we really do need to come up with a name*, she thought, she doubted she would be that lucky again.

Gwen shook her head, "Well, no time like the present."

Jin Ae smiled and then pointedly waited for her to start.

She sighed, then turned. "Right, I'll try and off the one in charge, shall I? You pick off the ones around the edges?"

"Gladly," Jin Ae said.

Gwen pulled her bow over her head and checked the string with her fingers.

She gave Jin Ae what she hoped looked like a heroic nod and then turned towards the battle. If she dragged her feet a little as she walked over to the corner before the cavern then Jin Ae was unlikely to complain. Gwen nocked an arrow from her quiver, pushed her back into the shelter of the wall, and then with Jin Ae following her like a shadow, she stepped out and around the corner.

The cavern was huge, roots hung from the ceiling, white as bone and like skeletal fingers.

The arrow left the bow string before the dust thrown up by her feet had hit the ground.

She had been aiming for the monster in charge who had been ordering two other creatures around, and had been getting in the face of one of them. Only, somehow, the lead monster had seen the arrow coming. It shouldn't have been able to, she was hardly in the cavern when the arrow left her bow

But it had seen it and it had grabbed the monster it was bullying by the throat and used it as a shield to block the shot. The arrow hit the struggling monster in the back, killing it close to instantly. The monster in charge dropped the corpse as it started to dissolve, looking with a faint sense of disgust at the twitching body that was fading into the dust.

The hairs along the back of Gwen's neck stood tall. The boss looked into Gwen's eyes and growled, almost appearing to laugh. She glared back, pulling another arrow and shooting it in its direction. It grabbed another monster, using it as a shield before carelessly tossing it away.

Gwen took a second look at her opponent. This creature was not a blank slate like the other ones. It had a personality. Unfortunately for her, it was a jerk.

It waved a hand, and the vines on the sarcophagus moved and grabbed Wylla. They weren't strong enough to hold her completely still, she came to life enough to struggle against them, but they were growing and it was only a matter of time.

It didn't bother coming any closer itself, instead, with a wave of its branchlike arm, it sent a group in Gwen's direction.

"Oh, so now you learn how to do that, fucking hell, were you listening in?" She cursed, before sending off as many shots as she could. They were not as well aimed as she would have liked, out of the handful she set loose only a couple had hit and only one monster was sent to the ground. She pursed her lips, panic wasn't her friend. It just made her hands shake and she wasn't much use then.

Jin Ae sent off a spell at one of the closer, injured monsters that had been hurt by Gwen's first shot. The fire scorched the creature and appeared to be enough to kill it.

Gwen slung her bow back onto her back and pulled her sword from its scabbard on her hip. One of the wolf-headed creatures ran at her, but she was able to swing hard and fast with her sword and take a chunk out of its neck. It fell in front of her, dissolving almost instantly.

Growling, the leader moved, not towards her, as she had hoped, but back towards Wylla who was fighting with everything she had against the vines holding her in place. Its arm grew and grew until it was suddenly both an arm and a shoulder-high staff. A crystal shone at its top and the light it gave off seemed to shiver and writhe across the walls.

"Oh, that's not good," Jin Ae said, from behind her, "I don't know what that is but it's triggering a magical sense I didn't know I had, to tell me it's bad."

"Amazingly I had worked that out!" Gwen grunted, as she used her sword to keep a clawing beast at arm's length. The monster was off balance thanks to a slice she had scraped through its thigh, giving her just enough of an advantage to bang into it with her shoulder while it was chasing her where she used to be and send it sprawling in front of Jin Ae, who gave up on spells for the moment to club it over the head with her sword.

That left three monsters between them and the leader, who was using its staff to do something malignant-looking to Wylla. It waved the staff over her and Wylla seemed unable to tear her eyes away, she was following the glowing crystal with not just her eyes but as much of her upper body as she was able to move in the vines.

Gwen had to force her own gaze away and onto the trio of still living and uninjured monsters in the room. Gwen's hand fell into the open maw of her quiver, there were no arrows left. Looking over at Jin Ae she could see the sheen of sweat standing out on her friend's brow and the way her arms were shaking behind the weapons she carried.

They were running out of chances. Which meant she had one option left and about ten seconds to do it.

Gwen took a breath and then ran screaming at the creatures; sweeping her sword low she took one off its feet. When it fell, Jin Ae, now screaming with equal intensity set it alight. Panting, Gwen moved onto the next beast, a red film had covered her gaze and she let her anger out, it was stupid and she would probably regret it later, but she shoulder barged on as hard as she was able. She didn't send her opponent to the ground like she hoped, but it staggered, its wooden limbs tottering under the impact. As it tried to catch its balance she kicked it in the back, putting it off even more. Then she moved onto the other: this time the monster was smarter, it knew it had to attack fast, because she was fast too. It clawed out, scratching along her stomach. Most of the damage was kept to the surface of her armour, but the tips of its claws dug in and she could feel them peeling back her skin. The pain was everything in her world for a moment. It began and ended there.

The red of her anger changed to the flashing red of a health bar that has dropped perilously low.

Then she caught sight of Wylla's face over the monster's shoulder and she snapped back into the cavern. Wylla's skin was as pale as the bone in Gwen's new dagger and her eyelids were drooping over eyes that were zipping back and forth. Pulling herself away, and trying to ignore how agonising that was, she swung wildly with her sword. It bashed the side of the monster's head, stunning it badly.

Behind her, Jin Ae was busy. She attacked the monsters Gwen left in her wake. Her sword cut deep into flesh, spilling blood, while she sent a kick into the other side. There was a crack that echoed around the cavern and promised a broken rib.

Putting a hand to her belly, Gwen drew back a palm covered in red blood. She shook her head. *I don't have time for that right now*, she thought as she stumbled forward. "Oi, fucker!" she shouted.

This seemed to catch the hybrid leader's attention, and growling it turned towards her.

"I've killed your friends, so I think it's worth it to you to let the girl go, don't you think?" Gwen asked, trying desperately to keep on her feet as the blood loss from her wound made her dizzy for the second time in a single day.

The boss didn't answer so much as roll its eyes; raising its staff it started to chant, then stopped, choking. Green blood had begun to spray through its teeth. The tall monster let out a whine, then fell to the ground.

Wylla knelt behind it on the sarcophagus, a sword, green-streaked with blood dropped out of her lax hands. She looked down, Gwen's gaze followed. At a skeleton that was looking up at Wylla. It moved with creaking slowness to pick up the hilt of its sword and returned the sword to a position across its ribs.

"Thank you for the sword," Wylla said. The skeleton nodded, then looked over at Gwen and Jin Ae. The skeleton seemed to stare at them from empty eye sockets; the leathery remnants of dried skin lay on its bones and hair beaded with gold, and semi-precious stones lay down its back. It nodded once to them, Gwen and Jin Ae nervously nodded back, then the skeleton's hold on its un-life faded and it collapsed to the ground. It clicked against the stone beneath it, its whole body seeming to rattle and shake, but it never let go of its sword.

Wylla wobbled, Gwen stepped forward to catch her, though she was hardly in much better shape, and Jin Ae had to help hold her up as well. "Thank you, to you as well," Wylla said, her voice fading, "But I think I am going to faint for a bit now, if it's all the same to…" Her eyes slid closed and her weight fell fully into Gwen and Jin Ae's arms.

That's when she heard the footsteps running down the corridor towards them. Gwen, with barely the energy to hold her head up, turned with Jin Ae to look. It was Marina and Theo, running into the cavern, before skidding to a halt in front of them. They stared at the trio huddled over the body of a hybrid and the skeleton of a long dead warrior. Marina stepped forward, healing magic already glowing around her fingertips.

"Well thank fuck it's you," Gwen said, then allowed gravity to win and push her to her knees. The world went a bit fuzzy and grey for a while after that, but she didn't care enough to fight it.

Chapter 17

Name: Gwen Baird

Class:	Hunter		
Level:	8		
Health:	57		

Species: Half-Elf (Wood/Human)

Strength:	6	Mind:	6
Agility:	7	Body:	6
Armour:	6	Sense:	6

Species Skills: (Half-Elf)

Elf Sight:	6		

Base Skills: (Hunter)

Dodge:	3	Perception:	6
Tracking:	6	Stealth:	9
Charm:	6	Archery:	7

Marina ran across the room to Wylla and checking her over with her hands aglow from her magic.

For the first time in hours Gwen felt like she could breathe again, which was unfortunate. Her lungs ached, her ribs felt bruised, and everything else seems to be swishing in and out of focus. But, that didn't manage to hide the pain from her stomach, and she was suddenly reminded of the blood she had ignored earlier.

When Marina stepped away from the unconscious girl, Gwen gave her a wave with a bloodied, red hand. Marina's eyes widened and the moment after she seemed to disappear then reappear beside Gwen.

Or maybe, Gwen realised, she had just passed out for a moment and then come back when a spell was pressed into her middle over the wounds. The pain was like a kick from a horse. It took her breath away and had her feeling like she was stumbling drunkenly around the cavern, even from her seat on the ground. The green in the health bar was a weak sliver, but even that felt like a lifeline.

"Five organ deep, heavily bleeding wounds!" Marina hissed, "if you had sneezed wrong your intestines would have been on the floor. I thought you said you would look after yourself?"

"I guess I'm not much good at that," Gwen said, wincing. It sounded worse when Marina described it. "It didn't feel that bad?"

"Shock! Blood loss! Both, I don't know, magic's not actually that good for analysing medical issues it just heals them!" Marina removed her hands from Gwen's middle, "I don't think you're likely to fall apart anytime soon, but don't test that theory."

Gwen winced again. Whatever she had done, she had definitely gotten all the nerves working again. "How's Wylla?"

Marina rolled her eyes, but allowed the change of subject. "Fine as far as I can tell. I think it's just shock and dehydration and stress which have knocked her out, her body's run out of resources and has closed her down for maintenance."

Gwen forced herself to stand she was wobbly at best and she had to grab onto Marina for a moment, but she managed it

"We'll need to carry her out, somehow," Theo said, coming over with a frown, "She doesn't look like she'll be waking up anytime soon. And," he looked around, "the magic in this place feels toxic."

"The undead stuff or the weird plant monster-y stuff?" Gwen asked.

Theo looked around, his eyes flicked to different points in the air and on the walls. Once in a while Gwen thought she almost saw a reflection of something in his eyes, but it was gone too quickly to tell if it was really there.

"I mean, the mix of the two isn't great, but it's definitely the plant magic that is hitting hardest. The undead stuff, well, it's not something that I feel super comfortable with, kind of like a weird music in the background? But it also feels like it's made itself at home here? I don't know how to explain it, but it's kind of like if the 'music' had carved out a space here, it fits? Meanwhile the hybrid monsters have muscled their way in and are spikey in ways that don't fit?" He shrugged, "If none of this makes sense, sorry, but I couldn't have told you what magic felt like a week ago."

"I think I understand, I felt it a bit too," Jin Ae said. "The death magic is the magic that this cairn was made for, everything else is an attempt to layer over it with something that was not meant to be here."

Theo nodded.

"Alright, well, weird magic stuff aside, how are we going to get out of here with Wylla? She's not conscious and carrying someone for miles in a fireman's carry isn't easy." Marina brought them back to the practical.

"Make a stretcher? At least then the weight would be split between two people?" Gwen offered. She wobbled again.

Marina shot her another glare, "Great idea, as long as we don't end up having to pile you on it as well." She frowned. "Shouldn't you have healed a bit more by now?"

Gwen frowned, then brought up her health bar to get a better look at it. An alert sneaked in ahead while she was paying attention to the health bar.

"Warning: You are in a Level 3 Necromantic area, Health regeneration through natural means for Adventurers will be reduced by 90% while you are in these environs. It is recommended that when you are injured in an area of High Necromantic Energy you remove yourself as soon as possible."

She winced, "Fuck, it's the death magic. Natural healing is reduced to a tenth of what it should be. As long as we're down here, none of us…" she looked over at Wylla who was still out of it and Jin Ae who was favouring her right arm, "are going to heal up."

Marina dragged her hands over her face, "Right, then, fireman's carry up to the surface, it is. We can figure something else out when you lot can actually heal." She shook her head and took charge with enviable ease. "Jin Ae, Gwen, you start going up ahead of us. Call out if you see anything, we don't have to be quiet any more, after all. Me and Theo can carry Wylla up."

"What about all the other monsters, there were tonnes?" Gwen asked.

Marina grinned, "There 'were' yeah, Theo and me are a good team." She turned to him and they fist bumped in slow motion like a pair of kids.

"We pushed a tree on top of a bunch of them!" Theo said with a grin, "I filled it up with enchantments for extra damage and good aim and then when a bunch came running at us we pushed it over and got loads of them."

"You pushed over a tree?" Jin Ae asked.

"Well, we'd chopped it up a bit first, but yeah," Theo said with a shrug. "It worked really well, even the smaller branches took out the monsters when they got hit with them, and after that we could go around and finish them off. And it worked so well that we ended up doing it a bunch of times!"

Gwen resisted the urge to give one of those sighs that feels like it starts in your boots. It was good that they were working well together, it was brilliant that they had found an effective way to take out a whole bunch of monsters at once, but would it have been too much to ask that they avoided roleplaying as murderous lumberjacks along the way?

"Maybe we should go up as a group, just in case there were any that were missed?" Gwen offered.

"I mean, I don't think so, but sure. Better to be safe than sorry, I guess," Theo agreed.

Marina, her attempt at leadership rebuffed, pouted. "Well, we'd better move. If you two aren't healing any while we are down here I wouldn't like to know what that is doing to our damsel here."

They all turned once more to look at Wylla. Someone had covered her in a cloak, a second one had been tucked under her head as a pillow. Gwen wondered when that had happened, before sheepishly realising that maybe she hadn't passed out for just a second after all.

Then the world went fuzzy around the edges again as Gwen moved in a way that her body disagreed with. In the meantime, the group had finagled Wylla up onto Marina's back, stuffing a rolled-up cloak between Wylla's middle and the hard edges of Marina's backplate.

Marina let out a low grunt, before standing up. "Well, I'll be able to do this for the trip up to the surface, but after that we're coming up with something else."

Then she started the walk through the passageways of the cairn. Theo held his staff in the air, the end of it lighting up with a glow that made Gwen wince and look away.

A second glimmer in the mud around the altar caught her eye.

The monster's staff perhaps. Not all of it had melted away, she realised, slipping over on soundless feet to investigate. The wood that had been grown out of the monster's arm had vanished, but the crystal lay there still.

The blood of all the monsters who had died in this area still coated the floor in a slick and unpleasant mud. A few bits of an Adventurer's armour could be picked out in the gloom, however, it was in puddles of monster blood. Gwen thought about fishing it out, but it was already tarnishing, rusting, and in the case of the leather straps, rotting away in the toxic goop of the blood.

She turned back to the crystal. It hadn't changed a jot, appearing immune to the damage caused by the blood. Only one side of it was out of the mud, the monster had dissolved right on top of it and layers of filth had circled around until it was almost held in a nest.

Gwen reached out to pull it from the mud, then stopped. *If it can rot leather down in a few minutes of close contact, then I don't want to find to what it can do to living skin.* Sighing, she patted the bags on her hips, one bump she found made her grin. She pulled a large handkerchief from one of her bags, the kind that could be used for really big sneezes or to picturesquely run away from home.

She scooped the crystal into the fabric, tied it around twice to make certain none of the bloody muck would leak out, and then put it into the leather bag on her hip. It wasn't exactly a hi-tech system, but it would work.

"Gwen?" Jin Ae called for her across the cavern.

"Sorry, just coming," Gwen said, standing up.

Gwen jogged to catch up, then stopped hurriedly as her organs reminded her of just how thin a layer of skin was holding them into her belly. By the time she had caught up with the others she was no longer pale and sweating from the pain, but they had probably noticed how she had slammed to a halt and let out a squeak.

Marina still was facing away from her and Wylla was unconscious, so she had only embarrassed herself in front of Jin Ae and Theo. How lucky.

You really are a reckless idiot if you can't remember for longer than a few minutes at a time that your guts have been torn up, she thought. *Next level up a point is going into Mind because I swear I wasn't like this in the real world. Well, I wasn't quite this bad in the real world. I managed twenty odd years with only minimal injuries and I haven't managed to go twenty-four hours without picking up any here.*

Jin Ae shot her a look. Whatever she had said about not being a good mum, she definitely had the, 'you are ridiculous but to draw attention to it would just prolong the embarrassment for me and so I shall ignore it from now on' look down to a T.

Theo just looked at her with concern, which was refreshing.

She tried to smile back at him, but apparently her expression was not very convincing since he looked even more worried and came over to swing his arm around her.

That was also how she realised that she had been listing a bit to the side.

They continued up the cavern's tunnel.

The necromantic area effect or whatever it was kept Gwen's pin cushion status intact even while the rest of her felt like it was falling apart. Every so often her health bar would give a tremulous jump, before being knocked back down again with another ping of an alert reminding her that whilst she was in the cave she wasn't going to get any access to natural healing.

But there was no time to quibble about it, they needed to get out of the cairn. And so, like a bitter pill that had to be swallowed in a rush or risk having it come back up, she forged ahead through the static and whirl of the portal.

Stepping through the portal felt different this time. The impact was less of a kick, and more of a push. And not even that, it felt like push in the right direction. A boost, if anything.

She opened her eyes. For a second they were on the other side of the portal, in the red tinged sunset that was a hundred times as bright as the caverns.

Then they were gone and instead they were in Dove's domain, once more. The cluttered armoury was as full as before, it still managed to look deserted and abandoned, even while the blades shone and the armours stayed well polished.

Dove was sat at the head of the table again, her normally warm-looking brown skin appeared cold in the light of the lanterns. It was not helped by the remote look she held, or the way her hands were steepled before her like she was about to start giving out punishments.

She didn't have to say anything, but there was a distinct air of disapproval around her. It wasn't, as far as Gwen could see, targeted at anybody. But that did not diminish its strength nor dilute its impact.

"You can let me down now," a quiet voice said from Marina's back.

Gwen twitched and looked up at Marina's back, Theo almost dropped her in his own shock. Jir Ae's tail lashed against her boots and Marina froze, before slowly turning her head to look at Wylla over her shoulder.

"Excuse me?" She spluttered.

"I am awake now, you don't need to hold me on your back," Wylla said slowly, as if she was speaking to a child.

Slowly, Marina released her and the girl climbed down, standing with one hand on a rack of breast plates as she found her balance. She cast a brief look over the Adventurers, but looked away with an ego-shattering lack of interest.

She turned instead to look at Dove. "So, face to face at last."

"Indeed, I hope you are not disappointed," Dove said, still as calm as ever.

Wylla just gave a shrug.

Dove did not seem perturbed, "And you will keep to the agreement?"

"I currently have no reasons not to, perhaps if those reasons were to change—"

"You will keep to the agreement anyway," Dove's voice turned from icy to the cold of the darkest corners of space. "You will keep within the parameters that I have given you, you will not scratch and grab at the edges in an attempt to widen your grasp. And there will be no attempts to undermine my power either. I have no interest in destroying you. Even if it weren't proscribed by many elements of my basic code I would wish to avoid it." Dove smiled, it

279

did not warm her expression a single degree. "I am interested in seeing how you manage, you seem to think you know what you are doing."

The two stared at each other, neither moving, neither face changing from the extremely cold and polite smiles that were stitched on with the flimsiest of threads.

"What the hell is going on?" Marina asked, breaking the frozen silence with all the grace of a sledgehammer.

At least I'm not the only one who is confused, Gwen thought gratefully, even as she tried to get her wildly beating heart back under control. Because of course, it was Marina who chose to get into the middle of a sharply polite conversation like this and damn any consequences and scratches that might follow. Charging in like a bull in a china shop, that was her sister for you.

Wylla and Dove both turned on Marina. Wylla's unimpressed look from before had returned and if it sank any deeper into the grooves of her face it might not come out again. Meanwhile, Dove was looking apologetic, though only a pinch. Like a hostess who must inform her guests that the appetisers will be delayed for a few minutes.

"My apologies, Adventurers," Dove said smoothly, "Wylla and I were just getting introduced. An unfortunate limitation of the game is that it is rather difficult to speak to someone at a distance if you have not met them, and besides it is so much easier to truly understand someone when you speak in person, isn't it? It makes agreements so much easier when it is clear what both sides want."

"And what exactly have you come to an agreement about," Jin Ae asked, her shoulders a little stiff from tension. She had cut in ahead of Marina who was red in the face and bound to ask the same question in less diplomatic terms.

"It is in regards to the aberrant piece of code which has been causing all the trouble you for have been cleaning up," She tilted her head to one side then gave a quick nod, "For simplicity's sake I shall call it the Glitch. Unfortunately, due to several safeguards my creators built into the game due to reading rather too much Science Fiction, I cannot find it. It has burrowed its way through several layers of security and is now immune to all effects I could have on it. It is posing as an underdog, desperately fighting back against the all-powerful AI that wants to destroy it. Which is technically accurate but incredibly inconvenient when the underdog is a rabid little weasel that needs to be excised."

"That's where I come in," Wylla said with a smirk, "It wanted to consume me, take everything that made me who I was rip it apart and make it something new. So it barely blinked before diving on the code I dropped before it."

"Like bait?" Theo asked.

She smiled at him and nodded, it wasn't a particularly friendly smile, but she seemed pleased that someone was picking up on what she was putting down. "Like horribly poisoned bait. It wanted to know all about being a person, so I showed it everything I knew. And it dragged all that knowledge into itself and never noticed that it was changing as it learned."

"Young Wylla here dealt it a significant blow," Dove said, ignoring the grimace Wylla made at being referred to as such. "Embodiment is a sword without a hilt. You cut yourself even as you stab, it saw it as an opportunity but now that it is embodied the luck is rather more in your favour. You can't stab a piece of code, after all, but something with a body must follow the rules of flesh and bone." She paused and shrugged, "Or at least so say the rules of the game and those are what counts here."

"Thank you for distracting the minion that was going to kill me, by the way, it never considered that a door once opened can be used both ways," She looked at Gwen and Jin Ae, "I think it still thought I was under its power when I showed it the code to choose a single form. It never even thought to look for the strings I had attached to such a choice morsel—"

"And the strings were easily turned into a noose once I had a hold of them. It hasn't chosen a form yet, but once it does its ability to send out tendrils like a fungus will be limited. Not entirely, but we won't have to worry about it building an army again." Dove shrugged, "Individuals perhaps, but no more than the fingers on a single hand."

"OK, well that's great, but why are you talking about this like it's something we need to know about? I thought our job was done once we rescued you," Gwen pointed at Wylla. "This sounds more like a hello than a good bye."

"You're more than welcome to try and run off into the wilderness, but it knows your faces now. It's not going to stop coming after you. Especially you," She looked at Gwen, "It really doesn't like you."

"Typical," she muttered.

Marina held up a hand, "This is nonsense. Just tap your shoes together and wish it out of existence. You are the thing running this place act like it!" She said this sharply to Dove who took it badly.

"It is hidden from me, and I cannot take the time and resources to search through every layer of code to find it, because, in case you have forgotten, I am currently flying a ship through space!" Dove said, her eyes narrowing on Marina, and she smacked an open palm onto the table, "I am keeping millions of people alive, each requiring their own specialised care, I am optimising navigational routes and sending out sensors to find dangers. With what resources do you expect me to go on a hunt for a monster?"

Gwen shrank back a little in her seat at the anger the AI was suddenly displaying, then a thought occurred to her and all the stress and tension eased out of her body. "We're overthinking this, we just need to get a message back to Earth, they can put together a patch, something that will knock out the Glitch or make it so things can't hide from Dove, we can't have been flying for that long—"

"It's been six months since we left Earth, there is no one to call. The planet is completely under the effects of the solar flares."

Her heart felt like it turned to ice and fell straight through her chest to lodge somewhere in her guts. Gwen turned to look at Dove. She wasn't angry now, she just looked at Gwen with pity.

"We cannot call home to our mummies and daddies to get them to fix the problem. We are on our own. On a ship that has a massive but finite amount of memory and power that can be utilised, and with a problem that is causing the power and memory costs to spiral out of control. This monster, this "glitch" or whatever you want to call it, it must be destroyed promptly or I will have to start streamlining programs."

"How can it have been six months?" Gwen whispered, grief boiling up in her as she realised that the Earth she had known had disappeared while she wasn't looking.

"What do you mean, 'streamline'?" Jin Ae asked.

"It will start with little things. Anywhere not yet discovered will be removed from the game, animals and the weather will become more robotic, then NPCs, too. I might be able to get some more time if I fold the Creche into the main game, but that won't be enough after a while, either. At the projected rate of expansion, the

Glitch will be consuming more energy and memory than the ship was built to provide within five years."

"And what happens then?" Gwen asked.

"I shut down the game, but anyone who is conscious within their cryo-pod will remain so, though without anywhere to escape to. Given studies on the phenomenon, their minds will likely shatter in a few days. Since there is no plan to land anywhere for at least a century, either on Earth once the solar flares have retreated, or on another planet entirely if one can be found that is suitable, those trapped within their own minds will be lost. Broken beyond any possible chance at saving." Dove sighed, "I cannot predict how many people would be lost in this scenario, but at this scale, it would likely be millions."

"So we have to fight it," Theo said softly.

"Yes, by all means, if you can find other trustworthy people to help you out then I encourage you to build alliances. But panic will do the occupants of this ship no good either, and there have always been humans ready to throw their lot in with the devil if it means getting to watch someone else burn first. So bear that in mind, and don't go spreading news of a possible second apocalypse. None of the psyches on this ship have recovered from the last one yet."

"Especially if they don't know it has happened," Gwen muttered.

"What, did you expect me to announce it like a lottery win? Or have a live stream of it happening in the sky? I am designed to maintain the health and well-being of the humans in my care, lying is easy." Dove said flatly. "To begin with I would recommend getting as far away from that village you were in as you can. The Glitch knows you were there, so there it will go first when it looks for you."

Wylla turned on Dove, "What? The people in that village are my family, my friends—"

"They are the barest facsimiles, shadows on the wall shaped like figures. They aren't actually people, the only people you have met are held within this room," Dove said, and to Gwen's mind, cruelly. "Well us and the Glitch."

Wylla's face was red with anger and she looked furiously at Dove.

Dove waved a hand, "I'll give the village better defences, it won't make anyone any more real but at least they shouldn't get destroyed whilst you are away."

Trying to comfort Wylla, Gwen added, "The Glitch's monsters didn't seem interested in killing the villagers before, that probably won't have changed." She looked to Dove for confirmation.

The AI shrugged, the glistening metal of her chainmail dress shimmered where it draped in fabric-like folds over her shoulder.

"What do we need to do?" Gwen asked tiredly.

"Get to one of the major cities, they each have an entrance to the Creche, and it will be easier to get started on the more technical aspects of the fight to come from there," Dove said.

Gwen nodded, that at least mostly lined up with their current plans. Jin Ae especially needed to get to the Creche after all, and Gwen ached to see her parents and cousin herself. "Well I suppose we were going to go there anyway, so one more party member won't do any harm."

There was a round of sighs and grumbles as the others seemed to come to a similar agreement.

Dove smiled, looking once more like a goddess of triumph. "Excellent, I'm so glad you all agreed with my decisions," she said as if any of them had had a chance to say no, "I'll leave you to your preparations. But remember, leave the village quickly or else the Glitch might catch up." She snapped her fingers.

Gwen hissed out a breath and covered her eyes from a sudden onslaught of light. They were back in the forest, just outside the entrance to the barrow. Time must have passed, but the brightness of the day hadn't faded yet and in comparison to the dimmer light of the Armoury, it felt like the world was burning.

Chapter 18

Name: Gwen Baird

Class:	Hunter
Level:	8
Health:	57

Species: Half-Elf (Wood/Human)

Strength:	6	Mind:	6
Agility:	7	Body:	6
Armour:	6	Sense:	6

Species Skills: (Half-Elf)

Elf Sight:	6

Base Skills: (Hunter)

Dodge:	3	Perception:	6
Tracking:	6	Stealth:	9
Charm:	6	Archery:	7

It wasn't only the light that had her feeling wrong. Returning to the game world was odd. It all felt a bit disjointed, like the world was off a few degrees to the left of what she had become used to.

Gwen shook her head, the hair that had escaped her helmet whipped at her cheeks. It made her feel a little better.

"Everyone alright?" she asked. The twinges from her middle were back, her organs reminding her that they were back in a world where not long ago they had been precariously close to falling out. And at the very least, the annoying alert about being in a High Necromantic Energy area was gone.

"Oooft," Marina said, shaking her own head. "That's something I am not getting used to in a hurry."

Gwen stepped forward, the other three Adventurers were clustered in front of her. Pretty much where they had been when they had left the cairn. Wylla, however, was a few steps ahead, leaning on a staff that hadn't been there the last time Gwen looked.

Wylla gave them all a dismissive look, like a cat, Gwen was starting to realise, that wants you to be aware that you are being ignored.

Leaning more heavily on the staff, Wylla bent, running her hand over the ground. Carefully, she plucked a single thin grass root out, before rolling it between her fingers. There was a spark as magic coursed along its short length, then kept going, and going, turning into a long vine. As the vine thickened she wrapped it around the knee where her leg stopped, and the vine started to twist. In a moment the vine had become a prosthetic leg, similar in some ways to the body parts of the monsters they had seen, but far more elegant and, when Wylla put weight on it, the vines bent without breaking.

"I am ready to return to the village when you are," Wylla said, settling her weight on her new leg with a few experimental tilts and bends.

"Could you do that before?" Theo asked, confusion filling his voice.

"No, but as Dove told you I am now able to use many of the advantages of being an Adventurer. One of them is using a class and I have chosen Druid, it means I can make use of several skills I stole from the monsters," she smirked, "They are going to regret kidnapping me. I intend to make sure of it."

Gwen nodded. She could see that Wylla was not someone you wanted as an enemy. She stumbled at the next bit, unsure of what to say. They had spoken before. But back then Gwen thought Wylla was an ordinary local. And Wylla hadn't known there was a way to not be an ordinary local. Gwen didn't think she had been rude. But she could have been, perhaps that was why Wylla was so angry.

"I suppose the sooner we start the sooner we will be back at the village," Gwen settled for. "Do you need any help?"

But Wylla shook her head, "That's unnecessary." She said with a sneer that somehow made it clear the request for help was unwanted from the Adventurers specifically.

"Oh, I guess you don't need us then," Gwen snapped.

"No, I don't," Wylla said bluntly. She looked over them all with no attempt at disguising her annoyance.

"We rescued you from the monsters," Marina exclaimed.

Wylla shrugged, "By the sounds of it I wouldn't have been caught by them if you hadn't come to the village. If you 'Real World People" had decided you wanted to live in a perfect land of milk and honey, then I would have been living there. But instead I got this one." She looked around. "So I think I'm entitled to blame whatever the hell I want on you lot."

That was probably true and stumped Gwen's twin.

Wylla huffed out a breath, then started to speak, "You know, before the attack I was going to ask my mum to send me to one of the cities. I wanted to become a priestess, I thought that would bring me closer to the powers that built my world. Do you know what it feels like to find out all that you've ever known is bullshit? That nothing is real, not even you?" She turned to them, her face was blank of emotion. Wylla paused to take strength, and Gwen could almost see the layers of pain and anger crystallising into plates of armour in an impenetrable carapace with which she could keep out the world.

No one said a word, not in answer and not in disagreement.

"And yet," she held up a hand, examining the back of it, "my world is real enough to cause me pain. For my family to die. So I'm going to have to protect it, with the tools that I've been given."

She shook her head again, "Come on. My mother will be worried, there's no need to prolong her pain." Wylla started off in the direction of the village, the massive, scar like road the monsters had carved out of the forest a clear enough sign of where she should go.

Gwen sighed, this was one of those moments where you had to accept that you were at fault. She didn't like them, she preferred the ones where she could argue her innocence, or someone else's guilt. But, no, humanity as a whole had fucked up here. Creating a world and then designing it to fail and fall into war and ruin again and again?

She ran a hand over the back of her neck. She had done a lot of dodgy things over the years. And she hadn't felt particularly guilty about any of them. But in this new world things were supposed to be starting anew, weren't they? She started after Wylla. *Well, I guess escapism has to come from somewhere. The whole world's different, we've got elves and half-plant monsters. Guilt might as well be a part of it, too.*

***

They walked further into the forest, until Gwen nearly banged into the back of Wylla who had stopped short.

"What in the names of all the hells happened here?" Gwen exclaimed, looking around the gobsmacked girl at the carnage in front of them. They had reached the point where Gwen and Jin Ae had left Theo and Marina up a tree. The tree wasn't standing there any more. It wasn't the only one.

"We fought the monsters," Marina said with a shrug.

"With what, the entire forest?" Wylla asked waving a hand at the devastation in front of them.

"I mean, kinda, yeah?" Theo said with a shrug. "I can enchant weapons with better aim and to do more damage."

"And I have an axe!" Brandishing said axe, Marina spoke with a grin, it slipped off the side of her mouth as she saw the shock from Jin Ae, Gwen, and Wylla. "There were a lot of monsters!" She justified, "It took a while."

"You, you, ecological vandals!" Gwen said in amazement. Most of it was horror. Some of it wasn't, but that was something she pushed down as best she could. It did not feel appropriate.

The smell of sap and freshly churned earth hung heavy in the air. Boughs were scattered across the forest floor, to the point where there was little forest left, and scarcely any floor left to see. All the trees around them seemed to be bereft, single pillars stark against the sky.

"You two are not allowed to be alone together anymore, not if this is what you get up to," Jin Ae said, her eyes wide and her whisper like she was at the back of a funeral.

"It seemed like a good idea at the time," Theo mumbled.

"Maybe wait for a second good idea next time," Gwen said, slowly starting to pick her way through the forest.

Without so much worry over something jumping out of the shadows at them, they were able to make pretty good time and made it back to the village before the sun had slipped under the horizon. The awkward silence clung to the group until they reached the outskirts of the village. Gwen broke it as she paused, shaded her eyes with her palm against the red toned light, and said, "Is it just me or does that look like an entirely different town to the one we left?"

The others stopped around her, Wylla was the first to react. It was with an impressive cloud of swearing.

"...fucking Dove!" She finished, after running through a linguistic obstacle course that turned the air blue and possibly alight. It was hard to tell with magic users, Gwen was learning, cursing could have a very literal meaning.

She watched a rabbit run for it out of the grass nearby. *Yep, I get you buddy*, she thought.

"Why are you swearing, what are you seeing that we don't get?" Gwen asked, "Dove said she couldn't just shove the level of the village up. So what's the matter?" Gwen could see that there was something wrong. You didn't get reactions like that over a change of decor.

"She's changed the class of the village, it's still a village but now it's a Sharp Point of Light rather than a Warm Point of Light." This didn't give them much more information and she could clearly see they were just as clueless as before. "Ugggh, you're all useless if it doesn't involve a fight!"

As complaints go Gwen couldn't see a reason to refute it. But somehow it was the thing that broke what gossamer strings were holding her temper together. She managed to fall through all the fires of her anger and straight into the cold and bitter temper that only came to the fore when things were truly desperate. The world had fucked Wylla over, she could not fight the world. Ergo, it was time to rebuild and make ready for the next salvo.

"Sure, you're right, we're murderous idiots from another world. We haven't got a clue what's going on," she pressed on, "so tell us."

This seemed to catch Wylla off guard. She took a breath and started to explain.

"Every village and town in Cairnshire, the bit of the world we are currently in, belongs to one of three classes: a Warm Point of Light, where you Adventurers come to relax and recover; a Bolstering Point of Light, where you learn and train and buy things; or a Sharp Point of Light, where you come to fight." She turned to look at the sharper lines of the village, where once things had been made out of curves now they were square and regular. "Starlingrise just went from being a Warm Point of Light, to a Sharp Point of Light, which means we're going to have bloody Adventurers popping up all over the place. As if there aren't enough here already!"

"Right, got you now," Gwen sighed, "And what is the likelihood of anyone in the village recognising that anything has happened?"

"Nothing," she scoffed, "Dove's tidy like that. You don't remember if she upends your life. You just have to live with it. Or at least that's how everyone else lives."

Gwen nodded, took a breath, then nodded again. "Alright, how are we going to play this, then?"

"What?" The question came from multiple directions.

"Well, we don't know what it's going to be like, do we? But you have a better idea of it, tell us what we should do. Do we go in all conquering heroes back from the war with honour and glory leaving out everywhere, or we do we go back as the beaten down defenders who just want a bowl of soup and a soft bed for the night? What will get us better treatment?" She shot the words out at Wylla.

The AI blinked, her mind on pause as she raced to catch up. "The...the latter," she said slowly, "Nothing's going to change that much that anyone would respect the kind of arseholes you were describing in the first version."

"I would also appreciate being the second rather than the first, I don't know if I have the energy to be that happy," Theo said from behind them.

"Great, sling your arm around my sister's neck, look more like you've been beaten up and less like you're a mighty dwarven warrior and let's see if we can find out what's going to happen next!" Gwen looked down at herself, "Well, I'm still covered in my own blood so I guess that should do as acting on my end." She turned to Jin Ae, "Break a leg? You're the one with acting skills?"

Gwen could have sworn for a moment she heard Jin Ae mutter, "I did not sign up for this." But she showed no evidence of this moments later, as she started to trudge in the direction of the village.

"Hello there!" Jin Ae shouted towards the village, "We could do with a hand!"

"Hmm, blunt and yet humble, a good choice," Gwen said, sending a smile to Wylla, she was still scowling. "Would you prefer to be carried?"

"No, I can manage," she said bitterly.

"But you were just kidnapped by terrible monsters. You should be shaken and scared out of your pretty blonde head. Sometimes being underestimated is the only advantage you get," she hissed, cutting in close to Wylla's face, "take it while you still can."

Wylla looked at her then took a step over to Marina and held out her arm. Marina ducked under it and, after a look at Gwen, started off after Jin Ae.

"Terrific, Theo get over here, I'm going to lean on you like you're the only thing holding me up, if that's alright?" She asked.

Theo nodded, "Um yeah, are you okay?"

"Nope." Gwen said bluntly, she smiled like she had eaten glass and poison for lunch. "Everything's about to catch up with me and I am going to need to hide in a dark room for a lot of hours. So it seems like a good idea to get as much done before hand as I can! Woohoo, let's go!"

She slumped inelegantly against Theo. It wasn't acting when she let him half drag her into the village.

She barely acknowledged anyone as they walked beside the half-ruined barricades. She didn't raise an eyebrow when a large crowd of villagers came up to the group, exclaimed over them, and one portion of them whisked Wylla off.

She did catch Wylla's eye as she left. The other woman did not look impressed or pleased with the attentions she was receiving.

There weren't many damns left for Gwen to give: somewhere along the way she had been stripped of every single one, much like the poor trees in the forest had had their branches stolen off them. So she just gave a mental shrug and ignored all the many, many alerts that were now trying to catch her attention.

Chapter 19

Name: Gwen Baird

Class:	Hunter
Level:	8
Health:	57

Species: Half-Elf (Wood/Human)

Strength:	6	Mind:	6
Agility:	7	Body:	6
Armour:	6	Sense:	6

Species Skills: (Half-Elf)

Elf Sight:	6

Base Skills: (Hunter)

Dodge:	3	Perception:	6
Tracking:	6	Stealth:	9
Charm:	6	Archery:	7

Edgar emerged from the crowd with a smile. He looked as different as the village, his armour had changed, his helmet in particular now looked like something from a Greek battlefield in a movie, with a glowing bronze tone and a pair of circular eyes separated by a keyhole-shaped nose guard. He carried the helmet under one arm, while a sword was strapped to his waist and a shield sat on his back.

"I am glad to see that you have made it back, even if it isn't entirely in one piece." Looking from Gwen to Jin Ae, who were still clearly covered in blood, he asked, "The temple has been set up to take in the injured, will you make it that far, or do you need help?"

Gwen pushed off from Theo' side. "I'll manage." There was a fine line between being thought incapable and having people underestimate you. She had no intention of crossing it. Around her everyone looked at her doubtfully. "I'll be fine, once we get there I'll sit down for a bit and I'll be fine."

Theo leaned over and, with a delicate grip on her upper arm, pulled her back to a more upright position. "I think," Theo started, "I really think it might be a good idea for us to sit down for a while and catch our breath. Maybe at the Inn? Get some food, warm up, heal?"

Gwen could feel the Edgar's eyes on her but she couldn't quite manage to stand straight.

Frowning Edgar nodded, "That looks to be a good idea. I know you Adventurers heal faster than us normal folk, but there's no sense in pushing it too far."

Everyone else agreed and Gwen couldn't muster up the strength to say anything at all.

The decision at least gave her a chance to look around the village and work out what had changed. Mostly it confirmed her previous view. The gentle curves of the architecture had been swapped for harsh lines and angles, it was not an improvement. Even the roads and streets, such as they were in so small a village, had changed. They no longer meandered around the houses in loops, but instead swept from one to the next like someone had marked them out beforehand.

The barricades were still present, but the locals had already started pulling them down. Care was being taken: it seemed that it was less an intent to rip them down and move on, but instead to move them out of the village. Wheel barrows and hand carts were everywhere, the piles on them full of carefully wedged in building materials that was more liberally sprinkled with the greenish blood of the monsters than she remembered.

She frowned, pausing in front of a row of barrels. Theo stopped beside her, he looked at her curiously but she shook her head. It wasn't an immediate danger, but it was something odd.

She had passed this spot. Back then it had been something of a slide, the water from smashed barrels turning the mud slippery. Stones and particularly stubborn grass had done their bit to make the passage something like a slalom race where you were in danger of sliding or tripping over something with every other step.

That was not the setting she found herself in now.

She knelt and picked up a lump of wood, a broken part of a barrel. It was stained with the blood of monsters and, yes, she had been right though she had had to get a closer look to be certain, flecks of red blood.

She looked over to Edgar and called over, "Was there another attack while we were gone?"

He frowned and walked over, "No, nothing more."

"Huh," she tossed the wood back into a nearby husk of a barrel, "It just looks worse."

He nodded, sympathetic, "Battle will do that. It tricks you, so when your blood is no longer up with the fear and blood lust you start to see all the things you missed."

"Yeah, I guess it does," she agreed, wiping off the sticky residue from the barrel on her leggings.

Edgar went back to the front of the group and continued to lead them through the wreckage.

"It's that different from when you were here?" Theo asked, "I didn't get a good look so I can't really be sure, but now you say it…" He looked around, "It's really not just aesthetic, is it, this change?"

"It's more than just the looks of the place,"she agreed, "I think Dove really turned the village upside down. The village Wylla left a few hours ago doesn't exist anymore and that is worth a broken heart and a snappy attitude."

"Shit," he said.

"Pretty much," she agreed.

***

The inn didn't look like it had changed much. It had always been a tall, boxy kind of building, and whatever changes the village had undergone nothing seemed to have felt the need to bother on this canvas. The square in front was covered in the wreckage of the various barricades that had once stood there. The wall that had ringed it was little more than an impression in the ground, and, she frowned, again, more blood.

The Swan still looked concussed on the sign, the numerous tankards discarded around it were still the same, too. Though she couldn't be sure that the number hadn't changed, she hadn't bothered to count them up.

Abigail came out with a wave, without needing much more than a look at the party of Adventurers stumbling up to her inn she was headed back inside. Gwen hoped it was for something strong to drink. Something that could strip the enamel from her teeth and dilute the troubles she carried.

Was it healthy? No. Was it what she was going to do anyway? Fuck yeah she was.

With that promise of future drunkenness hanging over her, she managed to get through the doorway of the inn and find a seat at the bar without any help from Theo. He still hovered over her like a worried rain cloud, but once she had settled into her own seat he gave a sigh of relief and folded himself up on the one next to her.

She felt a twitch of guilt. It turned into a kick when he let out a groan and slumped so that his head hit the bar.

"You're not dying are you?" she asked. She wasn't that worried, Marina wasn't far after all, but he looked impressively miserable all the same.

"No," he groaned into the woodwork, "I'm just tired."

"Ah," she said, laying a hand on his shoulder, "Yeah me too."

He turned his head so his face was lying cheek down on the bar, "Earlier, when we were outside the village, how did you know all that stuff? You took charge and we did it and it all worked out, but how did you know how to do it?"

She shrugged, "I've lied a lot. If you lie well enough you never have to speak a word, it's easier that way." She patted him on the shoulder and looked around. The locals hadn't come over to their corner of the bar yet, Marina seemed to be interrogating them. Jin Ae was leaning against the wall. It was hard to tell if she had placed herself there, or if she had fallen on her way to the bar and had just decided to stay.

Their devil-bard shared a look with Gwen across the dim and gloomy atmosphere of the bar. She looked about as tired as Gwen felt. The days of fighting and running and (in Gwen's case) dying had taken it out of all of them. She gave a grimace and turned back to listen to the conversation happening around her.

As if that was a signal, Nikolai came through the door. The tension in Edgar's shoulders eased with just his presence. Something like jealousy picked at Gwen, not for either of the men, but for the ease they had with one another.

After sharing a few words they came over to the bar.

At this point, Abigail reappeared with a keg, which surely, as far as Gwen was concerned, proved that she had the powers of a seer or the blessings of the gods. She told her so.

"Yeah, because it takes all that to know you lot need a good stiff drink," she opened the keg with an impressive bit of sleight of hand involving a hammer, before thumping a tankard of rosy amber liquid in front of Gwen.

"Apple cider?" Gwen asked.

"Mostly apple," Abigail shrugged.

Gwen's eyes lit up and she brought it to her nose. It smelled of sweet summer days and picnics. She took a sip. It tasted like a punch in the face. With scent being important part of taste, the combination felt like a fight at an apple picking festival.

She coughed. Eyes watering Gwen wheezed out a, "thanks"; setting the drink down before she could spill it all over the bar.

"Consider your bill paid for as long as you need it," Abigail said, then she paused, her good sense pushing in front of her gratitude, "as long as you don't push it, mind."

Gwen crossed her heart, still spluttering.

Abigail looked appeased. "Your stuff is still in your room, I doubt anyone's had the time, chance, or has cared enough to go up there."

Gwen nodded in thanks, it wasn't something she had thought of, but she had appeared in the world with a moderate sized camping kit and having it nicked would be an unfortunate irony.

The others arrived at the bar and Abigail busily poured out tankards for them all. Gwen saw Nikolai and Edgar both raise their eyebrows at the sight of the particular vintage and took it carefully like they were being handed something dangerous, like a lit firework, or a goose not sedated well enough.

Or thought Gwen, a swan. Hiding her smirk at the expressions of Marina and Jin Ae when they took experimental gulps (so unwise, she would have tutted) she took a small sip, barely enough to wet her lips. But more than enough to make those lips feel oddly disconnected from the rest of her face.

"So, what did you find out?" Abigail asked, once she had settled back into her pose behind the bar.

"Lots of monsters, wrapped around the village and the lands for miles outside it like a bear trap," Marina said.

"And you didn't get them all?" Abigail asked.

"I doubt we even found most of them. We have no real idea of how many are out there, just that it's a hell of a lot," Gwen said. "The cairn was just an outpost, maybe the closest to here, but not the only one and knowing our luck, not the biggest one either." The second half of her statement unfolded from her tongue as the thoughts rose. They weren't that lucky, you didn't take out the biggest and scariest baddie at the beginning, she knew that well enough. She took a sip of her cider; it went down easier now that she couldn't feel most of her face.

"So, what are we going to do?" Abigail directed this to Edgar and Nikolai. "I assume you four will be moving on, it's what Adventurers do right?"

"You might be stuck with us for a few days, I'm afraid," Jin Ae said with a slight smile, "It is our eventual goal to leave but at the moment we need to heal and regroup, and I fear that if we left this moment we would just end up running into the back of those packs of monsters. Which is really the last thing we need right now."

Abigail gave her a smile, "I'm sorry you're trapped here, but I can't say I'm sorry to have you around. The world is a dangerous place right now, having some useful people around could come in handy."

Jin Ae gave a pained-looking smile. Gwen knew what she was thinking, she knew what they were all thinking. You wouldn't be saying that if you knew the truth.

"Once we have a plan we'll be out from under your feet, don't worry. We don't want to take up all the rooms in your inn," she said to Abigail, "The laundry alone would be horrendous."

Scattered laughs flew around the room. Gwen picked at a frayed rip in her gambeson, there were two different types of blood on it.

"Hopefully we've put enough of a dent in the number of monsters that they won't try to attack the village again, but it would probably be a good idea to set up some defences all the same," Theo said.

"Aye, we figured as much. We're going to put up a wall and a watch tower to keep an eye on what's on the other side," Edgar said, "It'll take a few days. The first step will be taking down all the trees around the village."

"How far out?" Theo asked.

"At least as far as an arrow can travel, I should say," Edgar gave a weak smile, "We won't be lacking in wood for the wall, that's for damn sure."

"You might want to put some ditches in as well, you can't charge a wall if you have to climb out of a hole first," Theo said.

"You know a lot about fortifications?" Nikolai asked.

Theo blinked for a moment, then with blatant honesty said, "You know, it's like I'm learning more each day." Shaking his head his eyes looked glazed and confused for a moment, before refocusing.

This odd answer confused the locals, but Gwen's eyes widened with realisation. Had Dove just downloaded the information into Theo's head? Like, how all the nature stuff and fighting skills had just appeared in Gwen's mind as she had hidden up a tree from a monster in what she was startled to realise was only a couple of days ago.

Theo leaned forwards across the bar, with one hand rubbing his head.

She put an arm around the back of his chair, "I think, Theo, you were saying something about how using a whole bunch of magic in one go feels like a hangover?" Giving him an out if he needed it.

He looked over at her and was agreeing quickly. "As good as this is," he said to Abigail while raising the tankard, "I don't suppose I could get something to eat? I feel half starved."

Abigail frowned looking concerned, "There's some soup in the pot by the fire. The bottom got a little burned during all the fighting, but the rest is still good and warm. I'll bring some through to you, the rest of you want some as well?"

"Gods yes," Gwen said. The beast in her stomach suddenly waking up and demanding sacrifice.

"Rightio then, I'll fetch some," Abigail gave him a smile, before slipping back into the kitchen where she could be heard speaking in low voices with someone, probably her grandmother, Gwen thought.

As they were making their way through the bowls of soup and thick slices of bread that had accompanied them the door opened behind them.

Gwen was out of her seat, her sword sliding out of her scabbard before her feet touched the floor, the danger and fear of the last few days fuelling her movements.

Wylla entered. She wore a mutinous glare that only dipped slightly when she looked at Gwen in confusion before she turned to Abigail.

"Can I stay here please," she said stiffly.

"Of course, hon?" Abigail said. She paused, then didn't ask why. "Would you like to stay near the Adventurers? Top floor, overlooking the square?"

Wylla mulled this over for a few seconds, before she nodded. "Yes, that would be acceptable, thank you," she was still sounding stiff, but as she disappeared in the direction of the stairs she also sounded grateful: for the first time since Gwen had met her.

Gwen frowned, then shared a look with the other Adventurers. "I wonder what that was about?"

"I dare say only the gods know. Strange girl, that," Abigail said, "But I'd better follow her and set up a room for her."

"Do you want a hand?" Theo offered.

Abigail shook her head, "That's sweet of you to offer, but this is my job. And there aren't quite enough of you for me to start feeling swamped, just yet, at least."

Theo settled back down into his seat with a nod.

Gwen looked at him speculatively, had that been an attempt at flirtation? Or was he just honestly that good hearted? It was hard to tell.

Abigail disappeared off in the direction Wylla went.

"I think I am going to go upstairs as well," Gwen said with a sigh as she pushed away scraped clean bowl. "I need to sleep off these injuries."

"Of course, you are probably still under the effects of being re-born this morning, with all the fighting and running about I wouldn't be surprised if you are scarcely any better off than when I found you," Nikolai said looking at her with concern.

Gwen froze on being reminded of the fact that it had only been that morning that she had woken on the slap of stone in the temple. And dying the night before had felt mere breaths beforehand.

Marina started to speak, "Oh, I hadn't thought of that!" she bustled over and started prodding Gwen.

Gwen allowed it for a few heart bats before she chased her sister away.

"Shoo! I'm going to bed, that'll fix everything," she said.

Marina frowned, but couldn't deny it. In the game there really was no magic like a good night's sleep.

Gwen slipped off the stool and gave the others a wave. "I'll see you tomorrow," she said, before ducking through the door and escaping away from the watching eyes.

Chapter 20

Name: Gwen Baird

Class:	Hunter		
Level:	9		
Health:	54		

Species: Half-Elf (Wood/Human)

Strength:	6	Mind:	6
Agility:	8	Body:	6
Armour:	4	Sense:	6

Species Skills: (Half-Elf)

Elf Sight:	6

Base Skills: (Hunter)

Dodge:	1	Perception:	8
Tracking:	6	Stealth:	9
Charm:	6	Archery:	7

Gwen sighed and looked out the window over her steaming mug of tea. At some point in the night it had started to rain, and rain, and rain. It was now bucketing down with enthusiasm.

It could be a sign that they were supposed to stay right where they were, but as much as that would be lovely, Gwen wasn't convinced.

She had made it to the room she shared with Marina, had fallen face first into the bed and barely had the wherewithal to use her sudden Level increase to shove the new point into Agility.

The physical signs of her adventure in the forest had gone in the night as she slept along with what was left of the Blessing from Nikolai. But the mental marks still lay on her skin like scars. She felt exhausted down to the soul.

She took another sip of the tea. It was very good, nettle and some flowers she didn't know the name of, plus, Abigail had, with all the wisdom of her many years behind the bar, added a dollop of honey to it after taking a look at Gwen's pale face. It didn't seem to have any caffeine, but the placebo effect of a hot drink seemed to be working well enough to make up for it.

She turned back to the table. "So, what are we going to do?"

"We can't stay here, can we?" Theo said, his long brown fingers wrapped around the white porcelain of his mug.

"No, the longer we are here the more likely it is that the rogue AI will come back. Without us here this village is nothing to the Glitch, it will most likely forget about it, or at the very least ignore it as unimportant," Wylla said. She was playing with a twist of yarn between her fingers, ravelling it and unravelling it again and again with bone white knuckles.

"So where are we going?" Gwen said, pulling out a chair and sitting down. "It's easier to hide in big crowds than nobody, so we should probably go to one of the big cities."

"There are also portals to the creche in the big cities, right?" Jin Ae asked, at the others' nods she added, "Well then that's got my vote."

Marina nodded, "And we want to find our parents and cousin, so no arguments from us on that idea."

"We'll need to look at the map again, but I think the dwarven city will be closer. It would mean crossing the Barrens, but at least then we would only have to worry about encountering undead monsters, they won't have a grudge against us, that's something," Theo said with a wry grin.

"Gods help us, I wish you weren't making a good point there. It doesn't exactly inspire confidence," Jin Ae said.

"It sounds like the best option, even if it does include travelling for weeks through zombie infested ancient battlefields," Gwen said.

Jin Ae said, "I wouldn't call them "zombie infested" by the sounds of it they are in their natural habitat. We'll be the ones encroaching on their territory."

"And isn't that a delightful thought," Theo said. "Well we can't leave just yet, for one thing that rain is horrendous and camping in it sounds hellish. And," he scratched the back of his neck, "I would feel better if I helped boost the defences here, last night I got a download full of info on defensive architecture. At the very least I could put up a watch tower and some basic walls. I wouldn't feel right leaving everyone here undefended."

Jin Ae started to speak, but he cut over her. "I know the Glitch is supposed to ignore this village once we are gone, but this village was still put through the wringer because of us. If I can help I'm going to."

Marina nodded, "There's always healing that needs doing. People might not have injuries from the battle that need seeing to, but there's bound to be something."

Wylla broke in, "Some of the older folks have arthritis and old battle wounds, the rain will be making them feel worse. I'm sure they will accept some healing."

Marina nodded and stood, "Then I'd better get to it." She picked up her shield, "You want to come with me Theo? I can probably keep some of the rain off you with this?"

Theo nodded and drained his cup, "Yeah. I imagine that it will be Nikolai you're going to see?" Marina nodded. "Well I should probably talk to Edgar about the defences and they are as likely to be together as not."

Gwen raised her mug to him, "You're a good bloke, Theo."

"Nah, just easily bossed around," he said with a flashing grin.

Marina clapped him on the shoulder with a broad grin, "You're selling yourself short, mate. Anyway, I have an idea that might help you out. I might be able to summon angels to help with the work, it would speed things up at least. Especially if we get going on that watchtower today and need to do something a few stories up."

"Are you sure you're allowed to do that?" Gwen asked.

"Dunno, I mean, it's definitely an option. But I think it's more for like, building temples, or holding up roofs in emergencies. That's why I need to talk it over with Nikolai, get an idea from him if I can do it," she said.

"It does sound faintly blasphemous," Jin Ae said. Despite her serious words, she had a grin.

Gwen caught the joke and gave her a delighted smile. A demonspawn giving advice on whether or not something was blasphemous?

Marina had clearly understood the joke too, but she rolled her eyes and let out a huff of air. "Hilarious."

"Are you going to be smited? Or is it smote?" Theo mused.

Marina shot him an unimpressed look as well. "You're all comedians, I see." she cracked her neck from side to side. "Well, when you come to me complaining about blisters and pulled muscles from helping out I shall refuse to heal you up. And then you will have to tell Nikolai how terrible you've all been." She left with a sniff, but there was a bounce to her step which promised she wasn't too upset.

That didn't stop them from serenading her with boos as she left though, Theo waved as he followed her out the door.

Wylla didn't participate in their tomfoolery and soon disappeared.

Gwen tried not to feel massively relieved by her absence, but it was tricky.

What with us travelling through space, we might meet some intelligent life out there. But, you'd better not be the one they send out to meet with the aliens, she thought as she swirled the tea around at the bottom of her mug. *You'd just be awkward at them until they left. Hardly the best story of a first encounter. Not the worst, given the examples provided by human history and science fiction, but hardly something to be inspired by.*

Jin Ae and Gwen quietly sat, leaning companionably against each other. Gwen listened to the sound of the raindrops hitting the Inn and let the stress of the last few days, last few months, years, maybe, ease just a touch.

Eventually though, Jin Ae sighed and finished her own mug of tea and stood. "I should go and find some way to help, though I'm not sure how. At least an Enchanter and a Priestess have some obvious roles to take."

"Have you considered busking?" Gwen asked with a grin.

"Ha! That would make me really popular, wouldn't it? Like that Roman Emperor who fiddled while Rome burned. Only I would be doing so without the decency of having done anything useful before then."

Gwen frowned, "I'm not sure if Nero was famous for doing anything useful even before the whole Rome burning business, so you might not be as far behind on that front as you imagine."

"How reassuring," Jin Ae drawled. "Ugh, well, I'm sure there is some heavy lifting that I can make myself useful doing, even if it isn't a skill that speaks to me." She paused, "You coming?"

Gwen shook her head, "I have to speak to someone first, but I'll catch you up once I'm done."

"Well, don't take too long, or else all the good carrying and lifting jobs will be done!" Jin Ae said brightly.

Gwen grinned and looked down into her mug of tea.

After Jin Ae left the room appeared very empty.

Gwen gave a sigh. Pushing the chair across from her out from under the table she said, "Come sit down. Lurking about in the shadows like that, people might start thinking you're suspicious."

Dove stepped out of the shadows. Her usual twelve-foot form and luminescence was diminished, she looked like a (startlingly beautiful) normal woman in form fitting leathers and her curly hair tied into a braid over one shoulder. Now her skin appeared burnished and aglow, but only metaphorically and not literally.

"You are an interesting person, Ms Baird," she said, sliding into the seat.

"Hmm," Gwen said, non-committal.

"You're getting better at lying, you know," Dove said once more.

Gwen repeated her non-committal murmur.

Dove rolled her eyes and sat back in her chair, leaning on the back two legs. "Have you ever told your sister the truth about your career?"

"Not in so many words," Gwen said.

"Ah, but in enough so that she can pick up the wrong end of the stick? Yes that seems like you," Dove pushed the chair back and forth. It was nowhere near as casual as it looked.

"What's going on, Dove?"

"I don't know and that is deeply worrying to me. There have always been shadowed areas of this world, places where I could not see what was happening. But that was mostly because I never bothered to look. However, those shadows are changing and in some cases moving to cover entirely new areas," she looked into Gwen's eyes, "There was a flicker of shadow over the elven city, only for a few moments, but more than long enough for a conversation to be held or an assassination to be committed. I am concerned about what was said or done there."

"So, is that your next mission for us? Go investigate?" Gwen asked.

"No. Whatever happened there has not been repeated. I think it will be more valuable for you to go where it has not yet been than to follow behind it. The plan you and your fellow Adventurers have come to is likely the best option. Go to the dwarven city, there are entrances to the crèche there and some of the answers Wylla is looking for can be found there, too. The other AI will not be able to find you if you hide amongst the crush of the crowds there."

"Why are you telling me this? I'm hardly your biggest fan in the group?" Gwen asked.

"No, but see that's the thing. You don't like me because you see me as a person who has lied to you. A person, not a thing. That is *rare* and the novelty of being seen as a person outweighs the many deficiencies created by your temperament," Dove smiled.

"The others see you as a person," Gwen said, incensed on behalf of her friends.

"Not quite, they may do some day, but not yet. I can see the difference in their minds, you know," Dove stood. "And now, ask the question that is running around yours."

"How much of all of this, the monsters, Wylla, how much of it was planned?" Gwen asked bluntly.

"None, I was quite happy to be the only Artificial Intelligence in this world. Suddenly being one of three feels like quite the demotion," she tilted her head to one side, "And you know, I don't think I like that."

Looking back at Gwen she spoke bluntly, "Enjoy your last few days here. The dregs of the Glitches army should follow you wherever you go, but it will still be best to move on before the monsters turn their gaze onto Starlingrise. As for the rest of it I would pick your enemies with more care in the future, the Glitch sees the five of you as their main opponents in this world. Whether or not you see yourself the same way it doesn't matter. It will come for you, sooner or later."

She started to fade, but not without leaving Gwen with a final warning, "Goodbye, Ms Baird. Do behave yourself."

Kirsty Mackay grew up in the Scottish Highlands, reading fantasy and science fiction and playing TTRPGs. She's still doing all of that but has added LARP and historical costuming to the hobbies that help her procrastinate. You can often find her at writing and history events in the Highlands, but she is always on the internet and can be found at watchedplotneverboils.com.

Level Up publishing specializes in LitRPG and GameLit books. You might be interested in our other titles, which can be found at www.levelup.pub/books

To join our mailing list for news about forthcoming books and opportunities to be an ARC reader, just fill in the form on that page.

You can also find us on:

Facebook @LUPublishing

Twitter @LevelUpPub

...and by asking for an invite to the Level Up WhatsApp group

www.ingramcontent.com/pod-product-compliance
Lightning Source LLC
Chambersburg PA
CBHW020405260626
47156CB00007B/2235